D0466118

LUCKY BONES

LUCKY BONES

Michael Wiley

This first world edition published 2020
in Great Britain and the USA by
SEVERN HOUSE PUBLISHERS LTD of
Eardley House, 4 Uxbridge Street, London W8 7SY.
Trade paperback edition first published
in Great Britain and the USA 2021 by
SEVERN HOUSE PUBLISHERS LTD.

British Library Cataloguing in Publication Data
A CIP catalogue record for this title is available from the British Library.

ISBN-13: 978-0-7278-8982-9 (cased)
ISBN-13: 978-1-78029-711-8 (trade paper)
ISBN-13: 978-1-4483-0432-5 (e-book)

All Severn House titles are printed on acid-free paper.

Severn House Publishers support the Forest Stewardship Council™ [FSC™],
the leading international forest certification organisation.
All our titles that are printed on FSC certified paper carry the FSC logo.

MIX
Paper from
responsible sources
FSC
www.fsc.org   FSC® C013056

Typeset by Palimpsest Book Production Ltd.,
Falkirk, Stirlingshire, Scotland.
Printed and bound in Great Britain by
TJ International, Padstow, Cornwall.

For those who put their foot in it

ONE

S am Kelson met Genevieve Bower at Big Pie Pizza on North Avenue. She had pale skin and bleach-blond hair and, for the meeting, wore a little blue sweater and red leggings. She ordered a Coke and a side of garlic knots and said, 'My boyfriend's stealing my Jimmy Choos.'

'Your *whos*?' Kelson's left eye twitched until he caressed his forehead.

'Jimmy Choos. Designer sneakers, pumps, sandals, wedges. A hundred pairs. Mine are fakes. He's stealing them.'

'Counterfeit shoes?'

'You'd never know. He also took two Rolexes.'

'Fake too?'

'Do I look like I'd buy real?'

He stared at her pale skin, her red leggings, her little blue sweater. 'You look like an old-time stripper named Carol Doda. I saw a TV show. They called her the Topless Tiger.'

She gave him a long gaze. 'Marty said you've got a problem keeping your mouth shut. Something about getting knocked in the head.' She'd gotten his name from Marty LeCoeur, a one-armed man Kelson knew through his friend DeMarcus Rodman.

'He's right,' Kelson said.

'I want the shoes back,' she said.

'So you're a crook and you want me to steal your counterfeits from another crook?'

'I'm a businesswoman.'

'You know, I used to be a cop.'

'Yeah, Marty said. You got fired.'

'No, I got shot.' He touched a scar over his left eyebrow to show where. 'On duty. Now I say things I shouldn't. Do things. The doctors call it disinhibition. Frontal lobe damage. I'm better now, mostly. I'm a good guy. I love everyone. The state lets me carry a gun. I pay my bills. My eleven-year-old daughter stays with me on nights when her mom doesn't have her. For Christ's sake, I've got two kittens. I'm dependable. But the department retired me on disability.'

The waitress brought the Coke and garlic knots, a Sprite for Kelson.

Genevieve Bower tore off half a knot and nibbled at it.

Kelson said, 'Point is, I think you want someone else for this job. I try to work on the right side of the law, and if I cross over I can't help talking about it. The disinhibition. That's bad for people like you.'

Chewing, she said, 'Marty says if you see a chick you like, you tell her. Strangers, friends, it doesn't matter. You can't help yourself.'

'It's happened. But less lately.'

She swallowed.

He watched her swallow.

Something about her lips and the way her food disappeared inside her, all snug in her little sweater, switched a switch in his head, and his synapses seemed to spark like loose wires. 'I should know better,' he said.

'Sorry?' She sipped from her Coke. Swallowed.

'What's his name?' he said.

'Whose? My boyfriend's?'

'Unless someone else has been stealing your fakes.'

She curled her upper lip. 'Jeremy Oliver. He's a DJ. Eighties music. If you want to shake your bootie to Journey blasting "Don't Stop Believin'" or Joan Jett belting "I Love Rock 'n' Roll", Jeremy's your guy.'

'Huh.' At the mention of Joan Jett, an impulse tickled Kelson. 'How long were you together?'

'Nine days. We met four weeks ago at a party at my cousin's. A whirlwind, you know? And then the wind died.'

'Nine days counts as a boyfriend?'

'It's five days longer than Marty.'

'You have a picture of him?'

She tapped her phone and showed Kelson a shot of an olive-skinned man with a shaved head. He was giving the camera a wicked smile full of gleaming white teeth. He looked in his early thirties.

'Handsome guy. Text that to me, OK? Any idea where I can find him?'

'That's the thing,' she said. 'He posts his club and party dates on his website, but I went to the last three and he was a no-show. Once he had a stand-in. The other times there were just a bunch of angry partiers and an empty DJ booth.' She wrote the website details and Jeremy Oliver's phone number and home address on a paper napkin and gave it to Kelson. 'No one's seen him in two weeks.'

Kelson read the napkin. 'JollyOllie.com?'

'I know, but the things he could do with his tongue.'

'Please don't tell me.' Kelson folded the napkin and slipped it into a pocket. 'How much are the shoes and watches worth?'

'The watches, maybe a hundred bucks. The shoes about sixty thousand.'

'For sneakers?'

'Designer sneakers. They start around five hundred a pair and go up. I want them back. If you get them, I have another job for you.'

'I'll ask around.'

As she wrote a check for a week's work, Kelson found himself humming Joan Jett's 'I Love Rock 'n' Roll.' She raised an eyebrow at him and said, 'Brain candy?'

He said, 'The first night I had sex with my ex, it was playing.'

'I'd rather not know,' she said.

'We went back to my apartment, turned on the radio, and Nancy did a striptease. I always hated the song, but now it gets me.'

'I see.'

'I mean, *really* gets me.'

Genevieve Bower got up. 'Let me know when you find Jeremy.'

'What about the rest of your garlic knots?'

'You eat them,' she said. 'Delicate tummy.'

When she reached to shake his hand, her sweater stretched tight over her all of her, and he said, 'Sorry about the Carol Doda thing.'

'Look,' she said, 'you're human. You don't need to apologize for that.'

'I like you,' he said.

'You only need to be sorry if you use your screwed-upness to hurt someone.'

'Screwed-upness?'

'Yeah, you seem to have a bad case of it.'

'Really, I just got shot in the head.'

She left then, and he sat at the table alone, dipping dough into marinara, listening to the conversations of other diners and talking out loud to himself about how crazy he was to let a woman's sexy swallowing of a garlic knot persuade him to take a job that sounded as if it would only aggravate him and, if he succeeded, force him to convey counterfeit goods.

The waitress refilled his Sprite and he complimented her on her hair and her neck and, because he couldn't help himself, her knees. After that, the manager kept an eye on him.

All would have been well if the conversation at the other tables hadn't experienced one of those lulls just as the ceiling speakers started playing a new song – Joan Jett's 'I Love Rock 'n' Roll.'

'Oh, no,' Kelson said out loud.

Oh, yes, his brain answered.

'Don't do it,' he said.

Do it till you're satisfied, his brain said.

Do it all night long.

Do the hoochie coochie.

Do the Watusi.

Kelson stood up at his table. His eye twitched. His arms twitched. His legs twitched. He fumbled with the zipper on his pants. He said, 'No, no, no.' His brain said *Yes, yes, yes.* He stripped off his pants and danced with his chair. Two months had passed since he'd done something like this, and his head buzzed with the pleasure of a long-denied joy.

'Freedom,' he said to the waitress.

As 'I Love Rock 'n' Roll' pumped from the ceiling speakers, he climbed on to his table and sang along. Then the table legs blew out, and he landed butt-naked in the deep-dish pie of a lady in a nearby booth.

'Ma'am,' he said, 'your pepperoni just poked me in the ass.'

The police arrived and shot him with a Taser. He shook on the floor to the bass beat until they jolted him a third time.

TWO

As the police booked him at the Harrison Street Station, Kelson chattered about being an ex-cop, about the undercover work he did on the narcotics squad, about his friends, acquaintances, and enemies still on the force, and about his kittens. Then he asked to talk to his old commander from the narcotics division, Darrin Malinowski. When the officers ignored that, he asked to talk to Dan Peters or Venus Johnson, homicide cops he knew from the biggest case he'd worked since going private. 'You wrecked a pizza,' said one of the cops. 'You ruined a lady's appetite. That don't count as homicide. Maybe sex crimes wants to talk to you. Maybe Miss Manners.'

'Call Sheila Prentiss at the Rehabilitation Institute. Dr P. She's my therapist – she'll explain my deal to you.'

'Not much to explain,' the cop said. 'Indecent exposure. Disorderly conduct. The lady whose pizza you sat on, she's threatening to sue Big Pie – and you.'

'My lawyer,' Kelson said. 'His name's Ed Davies. I want him here *now*.'

'For a guy that can't keep his pants up, you got a lot of needs,' the cop said.

Malinowski, Peters, and Johnson never came, and the police put Kelson in a cell where a guard checked on him every fifteen minutes.

'Suicide watch?' Kelson asked on the guard's fifth visit.

'Making sure you don't hurt yourself,' the guard said. 'If I was anything like you, I know *I'd* want to.'

'Not me,' Kelson said. 'I like life. Even when a punk shot off a piece of my left frontal lobe, I refused to die.'

'Glad to hear it,' the guard said.

'If anything, I'm too lively – from others' perspectives.'

'I see.'

* * *

In the evening, Kelson felt the start of one of the headaches he got since the shooting. When he asked the guard for a Percocet, the guard said, 'You know how many screwballs ask me screwball questions every day?'

So, with pain twisting into his skull, Kelson lay on his skinny mattress, gazing at the jail-cell ceiling. 'Has it come to this?' he asked. The ceiling said nothing. 'Ask a stupid question, get a stupid answer,' he said.

At ten, the guard came by and said, 'Nighty-night, screwball,' and a minute later the jail-block lights went out.

When Kelson slept, his first dream started well. He was in his apartment with his daughter Sue Ellen and the kittens she'd named Payday and Painter's Lane. Sue Ellen was teaching them to play dead – so Kelson clapped, and they leaped from their splayed backs and zipped in circles around the apartment. Sue Ellen burst into that laugh of hers that always sounded to Kelson like wonderful bells. But then Kelson turned his back – maybe he only blinked – and Sue Ellen transformed into the seventeen-year-old street dealer named Bicho who shot him in the head before he returned fire, killing the boy . . . or maybe Kelson shot first – that detail was lost to frontal lobe damage and the morgue – and the things Bicho was doing to the kittens no one should ever do to the living or the dead.

Kelson jerked awake, sweating, tears in his eyes. He said, 'What I would—' but then his misfiring synapses left him word-less. In the dark, he did the deep breathing exercises Dr P taught him, and after a while his heart stopped pounding wildly. He closed his eyes, but that only woke him more, so he went back to the breathing exercises.

The next day, Kelson sat in lockup until after two p.m., when Ed Davies bailed him out. When the police released him, Davies was waiting outside the jail with a box of Kelson's belongings. As Kelson threaded his belt through his pant loops, Davies said, 'I appreciate your business, but I'd be happy to miss you for a while.'

'Think you can get the charges dropped?'

'I'll talk to the lady – tell her about your heroic background, offer her a pizza gift card. She'll look as silly as you do if the news catches the story.'

'She wants to sue.'

'Sue a disabled ex-cop who took one in the line of duty? A man who still fights the good fight? A man who's come back against the odds?'

'A man who sat on her pizza.'

'Let her try.'

Kelson took a taxi back to Big Pie to pick up his car, a burnt-orange Dodge Challenger he'd bought with his disability settlement. It was the twenty-second of May and, like most Chicago days at the end of spring, chilly and gray.

Sitting in the back of the taxi, he checked the messages on his phone. He had one from his daughter Sue Ellen, three from Genevieve Bower, and one from DeMarcus Rodman.

Sue Ellen had called the previous evening from his apartment. She'd waited for two hours for him to take her to their weekly dinner at Taquería Uptown, and now she was bored . . . and now she was hungry . . . and now she was calling her mom – and, she said, 'Mom's going to be mad at you. Sorry.'

The *sorry* broke his heart. He swore at the phone loud enough to get a look from the driver, then dialed Sue Ellen's number. It was three o'clock, the end of the school day at Hayt Elementary, but his call went to voicemail. 'Tomorrow,' he said to the recording. 'Taquería Uptown tomorrow night. If your mom says it's OK. Extra guacamole. And *I'm* the one who's sorry.'

Then he listened to Genevieve Bower's messages.

She had first called an hour after Sue Ellen, while he was kicking back in his jail cell. 'Surprise,' she said. 'Jeremy just texted. He has the shoes and everything else. He wants fifteen thousand.' She asked Kelson to call back as soon as he got the message.

She'd called again five hours later, around two a.m. 'I talked to him,' she said. 'He can't get rid of the stuff. He says he'll burn it if I don't pay. He must've thought this would be easy.'

She'd called again in the morning. 'Dammit,' she said, 'I paid you to do a job.'

Kelson dialed her number.

She picked up. 'Where have you been?'

'After you left, I did a striptease at the restaurant. Then I spent

the evening flirting with a jail guard. I hung out in my cell today
till my lawyer bailed me out.'

For a moment Genevieve Bower went silent. 'OK, I get it.
None of my business. But I paid you and that *is* my business.
Jeremy's threatening to burn my stuff if I don't pay him by six
this evening and—'

'He won't. He thought he'd unload the things he stole from
you, and now that he can't, he's panicking,' Kelson said, and the
driver glanced at him in the rearview mirror. 'Let him panic. It'll
be good for him. He wants two things. He wants money, and he
wants out of this. The longer you wait, the more he wants out
and the less he cares about the money.'

'And then he burns the shoes.'

'Do you want to pay him?'

'I want to string him by the balls from a light post.'

'Did he give you a number where you can reach him?'

'Of course.'

'Don't call unless you're willing to pay. Let him call you
again, and when he does, don't pick up. Let him leave a
message. He thinks he has power over you. Let him know he
has nothing.'

'He has—'

'The shoes are worth nothing if no one will pay him for them.
Play this out for another twenty-four hours, and see what he
comes back with. Unless you want to give him fifteen thousand.'

'I want to give him a kick in the balls.'

'I'm picking up on the theme. When he calls, which he will,
let me know.'

'Are you going incommunicado again, or will I be able to
reach you?'

'I'll be around if I keep my pants on.'

'If this doesn't work, I'll hold you responsible.'

'You can sue me,' he said. 'But you'll need to get in line.'

He hung up and listened to the message from Rodman,
which his friend had left just forty minutes before Ed Davies
sprang him from lockup. 'We've got a problem,' Rodman said.
'They're threatening Marty.' Marty LeCoeur worked as a book-
keeper at Westside Aluminum, a tedious job that didn't keep him
from getting in deep trouble once or twice a year. Though Marty

was only five feet tall and was missing an arm, Rodman claimed he'd seen him take apart men three times his size.

'Huh,' Kelson said to the recording. Then he called Rodman and asked, 'Who's threatening him?'

'That's the thing,' Rodman said. 'Can you come over?'

When the cab reached Big Pie and Kelson paid the fare, the driver said, 'I wouldn't want to be you, buddy.'

THREE

Kelson drove to the southside neighborhood of Bronzeville, parked in an alley by the Ebenezer Baptist Church, climbed two flights of stairs, and knocked at DeMarcus Rodman's apartment. The door opened, and all six foot eight and two hundred seventy-five pounds of the man consumed Kelson in a hug that left no doubt in Kelson's mind that, if Rodman wished, he could break Kelson's ribs and squeeze them out through his nose. When Kelson told him so, Rodman gazed at him with his gentle eyes, set a little too close together on his gentle face, and said, 'Why would I want to do a thing like that?'

Then Rodman's girlfriend Cindi, wearing green nurse's scrubs, stepped in for a kiss on the cheek.

Marty sat on the living room couch between his girlfriend Janet and a skinny man in ripped jeans and a gray hoodie. On the wall behind them, portraits of Malcolm X, Cindi, and Martin Luther King, Jr, watched the room as if they'd seen it all before.

After Rodman poured coffee for everyone, Kelson turned to the one-armed man. 'Who's bothering you, Marty?'

'Buncha fucking idiots,' Marty said. 'No big deal. DeMarcus worries too much.'

'The owners of a place called G&G,' Rodman said. 'Out in Mundelein. They threatened him. They want some fancy accounting – Marty's specialty.'

'A thing I do for friends,' Marty said. 'Don't knock on my door if I don't know you. The fuck they think I am?'

'You said no?' Kelson said.

Marty had a high-pitched laugh. 'I said fuck no.'

'They took it hard?'

'They said I'm the only man for the job. They had another guy, but he's gone. They had a guy before him, but he's gone too. I said thanks just the same. They said everyone says yes. I said I'm saying no. They said you don't want to say no. I said what happens if I do? They said how much you like that one arm of yours?'

Janet stroked the arm as if she felt the insult. She was very large and had what friends and family called a skin condition.

'What did you say then?' Kelson asked.

'What d'you think I said? They hurt my fucking feelings. I told them, they cut off my arm, I stomp their fucking heads. But I don't mind telling you, these people scared me. I mean, who keeps a fucking hunting knife in a bank office?'

'G&G's a bank?'

'A holding company. G&G fucking Private Equity. Customers gotta buy in big. The website says G&G invests and manages. It doesn't say if you got cash you need to clean, G&G's got the machines. Or if you want to hide money from your ex-wife, they got the holes to hide it in. The IRS? Fuck the IRS – compared to G&G, the IRS is a baby.'

'Sounds like the kind of thing you do,' Kelson said. 'But no means no?'

'So they get out the hunting knife,' Marty said. 'Like twelve inches. I think it's a gag. Or maybe they got it in the office because the boss has a hobby. Fuck if I know. Then this guy – he's in fucking pinstripes and a tie, a red fucking tie – he holds the knife to my nose. I don't mind telling you, I still got trauma from my arm, and I was just a fucking kid. I'm sweating. So, like a jackass' – he glanced guiltily at the skinny man beside him – 'I tell them 'bout my nephew. I throw him to the fucking wolves. I ain't proud of it. But he knows numbers as good as I do.'

'Better,' the other man said. He had a bowl haircut and the start of a beard.

'A moment of weakness,' Marty said. 'He's tough as I am, but he has twenty years on me – and he's got both fucking hands. He's like *two* of me. I told them if they wanted a man for the job, they should talk to Neto.'

'I don't mind, Uncle Marty,' the nephew said. 'I need the work.'

'Not this work, you don't,' Marty said. 'Now they say, if Neto fucks up, they come after me – and him.'

Kelson turned to Rodman. 'What do you want to do about it?'

Rodman's voice was gentle and low. 'Nothing now. We wait and watch. Marty wants Neto to get in and out quick and clean. The last two G&G accountants – guys Marty knew – didn't work out, and Marty hasn't seen them since. Maybe they made their bundle and took off. Maybe not. So we keep Neto safe, and if the G&G people start rumbling, we let them know they should worry about Neto's friends too.'

Kelson asked Marty, 'Exactly what does G&G want done?'

'It's a fund distribution,' he said. 'Once a year – more often would ring alarms – they move money out of G&G and shift it around for the clients. Offshore accounts, shell companies, whatever they got. Next distribution is in two days. The accountant – Neto this time – is the firewall. He erases G&G from the money, which is how G&G and the customers both want it. Invisible money. Fucking deniability.'

'Why not take this to the cops or the feds?' Kelson said.

'Why not fuck your mom?' Marty said. 'One – I'd cut off my own arm before I'd snitch. Two – what would I tell them? The G&G people live in the daylight. They golf and go to church. Their kids play soccer. G&G owns a building in the middle of a fucking office park. That's why they find guys like me and Neto. We're buffers. Throwaways. Dirty gloves. If we go to the cops, the cops say, *Who the hell're you?* If we walk into the SEC or FDIC and tell stories about these rich boys, the feds kick us in the fucking asses. G&G looks clean.'

'Unless they're scrubbing blood out of their carpet after they cut you.'

'Sure, unless that, but I figure they buy good carpet cleaners.'

'You got any names?' Kelson asked.

'Yeah,' Marty said. 'The three I talked to at the meeting. Sylvia Crane, Harold Crane, and Chip Voudreaux.'

'How'd they even find you?'

'Lady I dated a coupla times before I met Janet told them about me. Her name's Genevieve.' He squeezed Janet's hand.

'Genevieve Bower?'

'Fuck *you* – you know her?'

'I'm doing a job – because *you* mentioned me to her. She hired me.'

'Careful around her,' Marty said. 'She's a crazy one.'

'So, how does it work with G&G?'

'The accounting's done offsite,' Marty said. 'No way to trace it back. Two days from now, they send Neto to a Holiday Inn or a DoubleTree or somewhere with public computers. They give him a password. He follows directions. Four or five hours, and he's done. The last transfer is ten grand into his own account – pay for a half day's work. They say it's easy. It ain't easy.'

'We don't do anything right now,' Rodman said. 'We're on standby. Maybe the thing goes smooth and Neto takes us to dinner at Gene and Georgetti. Or maybe it goes bad.'

Kelson asked Neto, 'Are you up to the job?'

'Yeah,' Neto said, 'I'm a genius.'

Marty said, 'When he was in high school, MIT wanted him. Caltech. Princeton.'

Kelson said, 'Why didn't you go?'

'Too busy,' Neto said.

Marty laughed. 'They found out about his criminal record. Fucking kid redirected funds from Banco Santander Río when he was fifteen. Had all of Argentina pissed off at him.'

Neto gave an *ah-shucks* grin.

Kelson eyed his shabby pants and hoodie. 'Looks like you invested your earnings badly.'

'FBI took the cars,' Neto said. 'The judge made me pay back the rest.'

'Fucking feds,' Marty said.

Neto smiled the way some men smile when they have nothing to lose. 'I've got expenses.'

Marty said, 'You do this job. You take your pay. You get out. If you go in deeper, you'll never come back up.'

'Right – you said.'

'I ever tell you wrong?'

Neto gave him a loving punch on the shoulder without an arm. 'Wasn't Banco Santander Río your idea?'

'I might've said I heard something about their electronic

security. I might've. I didn't say a hotshot fifteen-year-old should go climbing through the hole.'

Neto spoke to Kelson. 'I was always impressionable.'

'Well, impress *this*,' Marty said. 'We get you in, we get you out, and you never go back.'

At five that evening, Cindi left for a nightshift at Rush Medical. The others ordered Chinese from Little Wok. Kelson picked wood ear mushrooms from his moo shu pork. Rodman ate pounds and pounds of egg foo young and shrimp fried rice with the delicacy of someone picking at tea-party finger sandwiches. Marty spooned some of everything on to his plate and stirred it into a mash with a chopstick.

Neto ate nothing at all but stared at Kelson. 'Marty and DeMarcus say you're good,' he said, 'but I don't see nothing so special about you. What's so special about you?'

Kelson ate a dumpling and said, 'I don't think I'm so special.'

Marty laughed that high laugh. 'He's nothing you wouldn't see at Ripley's Believe It or Not. Between the two-headed cow and the fucking Chinaman who drilled a hole in his head to carry a candle.'

Neto wrinkled his eyebrows.

Kelson ate another bite and said, 'Is Neto your real name?'

'Nah,' Neto said. 'James. But when I was little I couldn't ever hold my excitement.'

'So you said "neat" or "neato"?'

'I said "fuckin' A". Marty taught me. But my mom and dad figured a nickname like that would get me in trouble.'

Kelson said, 'So, Neto?'

'So, Neto.'

'Me, I've always been Sam Kelson. In court, Samuel. Thing is, since I got shot in the head, I've got disinhibition, which means you can't shut me up and I'll tell you the truth even if I really, really want to lie. But I've also got autotopagnosia – I sometimes don't recognize myself. I look in a mirror and say, *Holy shit, who's he?* So, sure – I'm a two-headed cow.'

'So you're like Jason Bourne in those movies?'

'Yeah, I wish. That's dissociative fugue. He doesn't know who he is. Me? I know, sort of. But I don't always recognize myself – and I can't stop telling people about it. Did you know Jason Bourne is named after a real guy – Ansel Bourne – who also forgot who he was?'

'Nope, I didn't know that.'

'Neither did I, until Dr P told me.'

'Who's Dr P?'

'My therapist. She's putting the cracked egg back together.'

'Wow,' Neto said.

At eight that evening, Kelson drove to his building. He rode the elevator to his floor and went down the hall to his apartment. He fumbled his keys outside his door and dropped them on the hallway carpet. Then a sound came from inside. He reached for his belt – but he'd left his guns in his office. 'Dammit,' he said, and the lock tumbled. The knob turned and the door swung open.

An eleven-year-old girl stared at Kelson and said, 'Gotcha.' His daughter Sue Ellen.

FOUR

'What're you doing here?' Kelson said, and kissed her on the forehead. 'Why aren't you at your mom's?'

'I needed to feed the kittens. Mom said they locked you up again.' She held Payday in her arms. The kitten purred like a little engine. 'Someone needs to be responsible. Payday has a cough.' With her long black hair, Sue Ellen looked more like Kelson's ex, Nancy, than him.

'A cough?'

She squeezed the kitten to show him. Payday purred louder.

'Cat's don't cough,' Kelson said.

'I think Painter's Lane gave her a cold,' Sue Ellen said, and at its name the other kitten emerged from the kitchenette. 'Or she might be starving.'

Kelson lived in a bare-walled studio two miles from the house he once shared with Nancy and Sue Ellen. He went to the kitchenette and peeked in. Sue Ellen had filled two cereal bowls to the top with Friskies Surfin' & Turfin'.

'So you're running around the city after dark but you want me to feel guilty,' he said.

'Yep.'

'Grab your stuff,' Kelson said. 'I'm taking you back to your mom's.'

'What are you doing tonight?'

'Driving you to your mom's, thanks to you.'

'Thanks to the kittens I saved.'

As they drove to Nancy's house, she asked the question she asked almost every time they got into a car together. 'Can we play Stump Dad?' She'd invented the game when she realized Kelson's cross-wired brain made him answer every question she asked.

'No.'

His answer mattered little. 'Next time they put you in jail, can I visit you?'

'There won't be a next time,' he said. Then, 'I hope.' Then, 'Why would you want to do that?'

'Because Mom says I can't. But I want to see what it's like.'

'It smells.'

'If you could be any kind of fish, what would you be?'

'*Enough.*' Then, 'A tiger shark. And I'd eat anyone who asked annoying questions.'

After dropping off Sue Ellen – and explaining the ass-in-pizza, night-in-jail, and starving-kitten episodes to Nancy, stopping only when she closed the door in his face – Kelson turned back toward home but then decided, since the kittens had eaten, to go to his office.

His desktop was clean. A gray metal cabinet stood against the wall behind his desk chair, out of sight unless he turned to look at it. A plain light fixture stuck from the ceiling. The walls, like his apartment walls, were white and bare except for a framed eight-by-ten picture of Sue Ellen and another of Payday and Painter's Lane. The pictures also hung behind his desk chair. Ever since he took a bullet in the head, clutter gave him head-aches bad enough to knock him to the floor, which, in his office, he'd covered with gray all-weather carpet. Percocet helped – and some days he dropped six or eight blue tablets – but as an ex-narcotics cop he knew the dangers.

Now he checked his guns – the Springfield XD-S he kept in the bottom desk drawer and the KelTec he strapped under the desktop. He popped the magazine from each gun, checked that it was loaded, rolled it in his palm, and snapped it back into the pistol housing. As he checked the Springfield, he said, 'Mmmm,' as if the gun soothed him, and, catching himself in the feeling, added, 'that's just – odd.'

He put the guns away and took his laptop from the top drawer. When it booted up, he spent a half hour on the Genevieve Bower job. The JollyOllie.com website showed Jeremy Oliver's menu of DJ services. Oliver promised to 'bring out the boogie' at weddings, bar mitzvahs, corporate events, and birthday parties. He could do special effects like strobe lights, 'Dancing on a Cloud' dry ice, pin-spot lighting, and fireworks. He listed his hundred favorite Eighties party songs, leading with Bon Jovi's 'Livin' on a Prayer', Michael Jackson's 'Billie Jean', and Van Halen's 'Jump'. His JollyOllie blog included images of Eighties Camaros and Corvettes, Bruce Springsteen album covers, and girls with big hair. Kelson clicked one of the video links. A middle-aged man sporting a white tuxedo spun his date to 'Girls Just Want to Have Fun' under lighting suited for a high school prom. 'Ain't Joan Jett,' Kelson said when he froze the video. He clicked on the video of a corporate holiday party and watched office workers let loose as they did the Macarena.

He tried the business phone number from the contact page. A recorded voice – Latin accented and enthusiastic – identified itself as JollyOllie and promised a 'big party for your next big occasion' if you would leave your name and number. Kelson left his name and number, then dialed again, this time Oliver's private cell number, which Genevieve Bower had given him – knowing that if he reached Oliver he would have to phrase his conversation just right to avoid making the man ask the wrong questions. On the third ring, an unenthusiastic Latin voice answered, 'Yeah?'

'Jeremy Oliver?'

'Yeah?'

'I want the Jimmy Choos.'

'What?'

'Don't make me say "Jimmy Choos" again.'

'Who told you I've got Jimmy Choos?'

'See?' Kelson said. 'That's exactly what I didn't want to do. Genevieve Bower.'

The man's voice got sly. 'Tell her if she wants her stuff, I need cash.'

'I'll tell you what,' Kelson said. 'You give back the shoes, I won't drop a brick on you.'

'A brick?'

'His name's DeMarcus Rodman. Let's meet tomorrow – to talk in person.'

'I've got a better idea,' the man said. 'Why don't you fuck off?' He hung up.

'Progress,' Kelson said.

Before shutting his office for the night, he googled G&G Private Equity. The website told him nothing worth knowing. The site was done up in black, brown, and white. 'I smell mahogany,' Kelson told it. He googled Sylvia Crane, Harold Crane, and Chip Voudreaux, the people who Marty LeCoeur said had tried to hire him. He found only a single hit, for Chip Voudreaux, who appeared on a list of sponsors of a charity called Second Chances. 'Like ghosts,' Kelson said. 'Hard to stay that invisible. Pay someone to wipe the internet clean of them.'

FIVE

That night, Kelson slept hard and woke at dawn with Payday nestled against his mouth. He blew fur from his teeth and went into the bathroom to shave and shower. He fried bacon, laid two strips on a plate with scrambled eggs and toast for himself, and set a strip for each of the kittens on the floor. Payday attacked the meat, pouncing as if Kelson had bought her a pet gerbil. Then the kittens eyed each other, seemingly unsure whether they would fight. Then each bit into her bacon and disappeared with it under Kelson's bed. 'Huh,' Kelson said, and ate his breakfast.

The windows in Dr P's office at the Rehabilitation Institute faced an alley and, beyond the alley, a one-story utilities building topped with air-conditioning units, cooling pipes, and a bunch of brightly painted metal boxes of unclear purpose. Dr P was staring at the boxes when Kelson came in.

'I've been thinking about metaphors for you,' she said, without looking at him. 'All those machines – the fans and tubes, the shiny, noisy things that belong inside – you've got them on the outside. It's fascinating.'

Kelson looked out the window at the rooftop. 'And ugly.'

'No, only fascinating,' and she turned her eyes to him. 'How are the breathing exercises working?'

'Not so well at Big Pie Pizza. Fine afterward.'

'Were you drinking?'

'Only if Sprite counts.'

Dr P narrowed her eyes, as if that would help her see inside Kelson's head. 'Instead of asking for assistance, some people self-medicate.'

'I know,' Kelson said. 'Got any advice for keeping my mouth shut during a civil trial if the pizza woman sues?'

'Sure. Settle out of court. You live . . . a complicated life. Still, some people with disinhibition have it much worse. You're a lucky man.'

'Yeah,' he said. 'Bet for me next time you go to Arlington Park. Win, place, or show.'

After Dr P kicked him out, Kelson went back to his office, checked his guns as he'd checked them the previous night, and turned on his laptop.

He googled 'Jimmy Choo'. He brought up the website and scrolled through the women's sneakers, stopping at the Norways – black tennis shoes with strips of fur, like squirrel tails, pasted where the laces belonged. 'Cool,' he said, 'and creepy.' They sold for $875. As he scrolled through other styles, he said 'cool' again for the Malias – gray suede high-heel sandals with a go-go dancer fringe. $1,150. 'But *these*,' he said, clicking on a pair of studded and leather-strapped black boots called Bikers – $1,795 – 'I like.'

The site linked to 'A Style Lesson with Blanca Miró Scrimieri', a Spanish fashion expert with fashion model cheekbones and severe shoulders. 'For you, Blanca,' Kelson said to her picture, 'the Teslers' – high-heel boots with a rabbit-tail puff at the top. The Jimmy Choo 'Celebrity Sightings' included pictures of Emma Stone and Nicole Kidman. 'Whole worlds I didn't know about,' Kelson told Natalie Portman.

Then he closed the computer on Jimmy Choo, locked his office, and went down to the street. As he walked into the parking garage, the attendant wished him a good morning, and Kelson said, 'Keep your pants on.'

He drove to the address Genevieve Bower gave him for Jeremy Oliver – on North Hermitage, a mile and a half west of Wrigley Field.

Oliver rented rooms in a green single-story bungalow with a high attic. A dried flower wreath hung on the front door, and an empty flowerbox balanced on the porch railing. Kelson climbed the porch steps and stared in through a window at a living room furnished with a green-and-white striped rug, a set of raw pine bookshelves, a blue overstuffed armchair, and a matching sofa. A child's crayon drawing of an elephant hung over the fireplace mantel. 'Don't think so, JollyOllie,' Kelson said, and went down the steps. He walked around to the back of the house. A set of painted wooden stairs went up to a separate entrance to a dormered attic apartment.

Kelson went up and again peered through a window, this one facing into a little, dark kitchen. He knocked on the glass and waited. When no one came, he knocked again – and then harder on the wooden door. No one came. He moved close to the door and listened. Nothing.

He went back down the stairs to the backyard. A detached garage faced an alley behind the house. On the brown lawn between the alley and the house, someone had built a brick fire pit and surrounded it with a mix of wooden and plastic chairs. Years ago, while working a case as an undercover cop, Kelson had chased a crack dealer through a backyard like this. He'd caught the dealer when he tried to vault a fence separating the yard from the alley. 'The world gets bigger and bigger, and I get smaller and smaller,' Kelson said. 'Chasing a damned shoe thief.' He climbed the back stairs again and tried the doorknob.

It turned, and he pushed the door open.

'Bummer,' he said.

He stepped inside and patted a wall until he found a light switch. 'I'll get killed this way someday,' he said. The kitchen smelled like new paint, though the walls were grimy with cooking grease. The attic ceiling slanted from the low walls. He called into the apartment, 'Mr Oliver?'

Nothing.

'Jeremy Oliver?'

Still nothing.

Kelson moved around the kitchen. 'I know better than this,' he said. There was a scraped breakfast plate in the sink. In an open garbage can next to the stove, there were broken eggshells, a balled paper towel, and an orange juice carton.

Kelson called into the house again. 'JollyOllie?'

Nothing.

'Yeah, I wouldn't answer either,' Kelson said.

A hallway led toward the front of the house. As he walked up it, he poked his head into a bedroom. A shade covered a dormer window. A red velour bedspread was bunched at the bottom of a black-sheeted bed. A row of shirts, most of them black, hung inside an open closet door. The top drawer of a dark-wood dresser was open. A half pint of Hennessy – the cap off, the last of the cognac skimming the bottom of the bottle – stood on a night table. Kelson peered under the bed. No Jimmy Choos.

Kelson moved on to the bathroom – filthy enough to give him a niggling pain above his left eye and make the eye twitch. 'Compulsive risk taking,' he said. 'Ask Dr P.' He pulled back the shower curtain on an empty tub.

The hallway ended in a living room with a slanting ceiling, exposed ceiling beams, and a broad front window facing the street. In the middle of the room, a red throw rug, little bigger than a bathmat, covered a patch of floorboards. A large-screen TV and short shelves stood along one low wall. A black fabric couch stood against the other. A barefoot man in black jeans and a black silk shirt sat on the couch. Kelson recognized him from the picture Genevieve Bower showed him on her phone and the images on the JollyOllie website. But now the man's olive skin looked gray. His hand – limp – held a small black pistol. His head – hanging – had a spot of blood above the left eye, just where the headache had started to niggle Kelson in the bathroom, and a spray of blood on the cheek below the eye.

'Huh,' Kelson said, and, though he already knew, 'Mr Oliver?'

The man said nothing.

'That's what I thought,' Kelson said.

SIX

When homicide detective Dan Peters heard Kelson's voice on the line, he said, 'What now?'

'I respect you professionally,' Kelson said, 'but I dislike you personally.'

'Same here,' Peters said, 'but forget the professional part.'

'That makes you the perfect person to dump this on,' Kelson said. 'Got a pen? Jeremy Oliver – dead.' He recited Oliver's Hermitage Avenue address and added, 'Attic apartment, rear entrance. Single bullet in the left temple.'

He hung up before Peters could ask questions he didn't want to answer. When his phone rang a moment later, he silenced it. Then he stared at Oliver's dead face. 'The thing is – why?' Yesterday evening, Oliver had sounded anything but suicidal.

So Kelson searched the apartment, opening drawers and cabinets, lifting cushions, leafing through a pile of mail on the kitchen counter. He found nothing of interest. He went back to the living room and stared at Oliver some more. 'Sorry, buddy,' he said, and dug into the man's pockets, pulling out a wallet and a phone.

Oliver's wallet contained $103 in cash, a driver's license, a Visa card, and a Discover card. Kelson laid the license and credit cards side by side on the couch and snapped a picture of them with his own phone. Then he returned the cash and cards to the wallet and put it back in Oliver's pocket. Oliver's phone would take more work, and so Kelson removed the battery and put the components in his pocket.

He went out the back then and down the stairs. He walked around the house, checking for outside basement access. There was none. He walked to the detached garage and peered into the dark through the side door. The garage was empty except for two bicycles and, in a corner, gardening tools. He tried the knob. Locked.

Kelson drove to his office, pulled into the parking garage, and wedged the Challenger into a spot. He stared at the concrete wall in front of him as he'd stared at Oliver's dead body, and he repeated himself. 'The thing is – why?' Then he dialed Genevieve Bower's number. After it rang four times and bumped to voicemail, he left a one-word message. 'Why?' He hung up, stared at the concrete some more, then dialed her number again. He left a longer message. 'You lied to me.' Five minutes later, he called once more. 'Or at least you told me only part of the truth. Why would he do this over shoes? Call me.'

As he got out of the car, his phone rang. He snatched it to his ear. 'Did he even steal your Jimmy Choos?'

There was silence. Then Dan Peters said, 'My Jimmy *whats*?'

'Goddammit,' Kelson said, and hung up.

Breathing hard, his eye twitching, he walked out of the parking garage and went up to his office. The computer training company that shared his floor had just finished a session, and a bunch of business casuals brushed past him on their way to the elevator. He unlocked his office door, let himself in, and yelled, 'Yah!'

Genevieve Bower sat in the client chair. She wore white yoga pants, which were a mistake, and a clingy white shirt, which wasn't.

'Like a super hot ghost – with lips,' Kelson mumbled, then asked, 'What are you doing here?'

She looked at him as if he'd missed the obvious. 'Waiting for you.'

'How did you get in?'

'Building security – Steve. Cute. I told him I had an appointment with you.'

'I just called you.'

'Three times. You sounded incoherent.'

'Why didn't you—' But another worry flashed through his mind. He went to his desk and checked the bottom drawer. His Springfield XD-S remained where he'd left it. He checked under the desktop. The KelTec hung from its mount.

Genevieve Bower said, 'What if you bump it with your knees? Would you shoot yourself in the nuts?'

Kelson glared at her. 'You—'

'I got bored waiting,' she said. 'I looked around.'

'You lied to building security. And you lied to me. Whatever you had going with Jeremy Oliver involved more than shoes.'

'I didn't lie. He stole them. I want them back.'

So he hit her with it. 'Jeremy Oliver's dead.'

She looked at him as if he'd come late to a party. 'I know.'

'You do?'

'Why do you think I'm here? You seemed to be doing nothing, so I went by his place. I found him on the living room floor.'

'You mean sitting on the couch?'

'The floor. I put him on the couch. He kept a .22 in his sock drawer. I put it in his hand.'

'You did what?'

'If the cops think he killed himself, they'll move on. If they think someone killed him they'll start poking around and I'll never get my stuff.'

'That was stupid in about a hundred ways.'

'I thought it was pretty clever. I came right here. If I'd stood outside your door, people would've wondered about me. So I flirted with the security guard – to save us both from trouble.'

'Why would someone kill Oliver?'

'You mean besides him being a jerk? He probably ripped off someone else too. Or maybe he had another sideline going. Drugs? Maybe his DJ music sucked.'

'Or maybe you did it,' Kelson said.

'Yeah, I shot a man who has sixty thousand dollars of mine in shoes. Because once he was dead he would, what, give them back?'

'I've seen people do dumber things.'

'I didn't kill him.'

'What aren't you telling me?'

'Do you treat all your clients as if they're guilty?'

'Only the ones I don't trust.'

She considered that for a moment. Instead of arguing, she said, 'Do you *need* to trust me to do the job?'

'It would be nice to know what I'm getting into.'

'Ask me anything,' she said. 'I'll try to tell the truth.'

'What exactly did you do when you went to Oliver's house this morning?'

She tugged on a sleeve, adjusting her shirt. 'I parked on the street, two doors down. I walked to the back of the house and went up the stairs. I went inside.'

'Was the door locked?'

'No.'

'Was that usual?'

'I don't know. We only dated for nine days. But I sensed something was wrong.'

'Was *that* usual – for you to go into a place when you knew you shouldn't?'

'Pretty much,' she said. 'I called Jeremy's name. When he didn't answer, I went to his bedroom. His job kept him out late and he would go to after-parties. Sometimes he slept until three or four in the afternoon. But I didn't find him in the bedroom. I went to the living room and found him. Dead.'

'Where?'

'By the front window.'

'There's something you aren't telling me.'

She gave him a blank stare.

He asked, 'Did you take anything from the house?'

She hesitated. 'Yes.'

'What?'

'His laptop.'

'May I have it?'

'No.'

'Why not?'

'It has – pictures on it.'

'You dated him for nine days, and he has nudies of you?'

'Yes.'

'Videos?'

She said nothing.

'You got right down to it, didn't you?' he said. 'You should delete them.'

'I plan to.'

'And then you'll give me the laptop?'

'No.'

'What else is on it?'

Again she said nothing.

'You know, when I found Oliver dead, I called the police,' he said. 'I'll need to talk to them sooner or later. When they ask questions, I won't be able to stop myself from telling them about you.'

'I didn't kill Jeremy.'

'After I tell them what I know, you'll need to convince them yourself.'

'Will you keep looking for my things?'

'I don't trust myself. I tell the truth as far as I understand it. But that doesn't mean I'm totally honest with myself. My therapist warned my ex-wife and my daughter that my perceptions of the truth might differ from reality. I might tell you you're pretty and I might think I'm just describing a fact of nature – the way I might say a giraffe is tall or a hamburger is medium rare – while I really want to go to bed with you.'

Genevieve Bower waited to make sure he was done, then said, 'Which is your way of saying you'll stay on the job.'

'Yes. But if you—'

His phone rang.

Caller ID said *Dan Peters*.

'That's a cop,' Kelson told her. 'You want to explain yourself now?'

'Could you hold them off for now?'

The phone rang again.

'For now.' He silenced the ringer. 'I've worked with this guy before. He's mostly reasonable, but once he gets a thought in his head, it's hard to shake it. I'll try to keep from putting thoughts in his head.'

'Thank you.'

The phone vibrated – Kelson had a message. 'He thinks I'm an idiot.' He touched the phone key for voicemail, then touched the key for the speaker.

Dan Peters's voice said, 'What the hell, Kelson?'

'See?' Kelson said.

Peters said, 'Blood on the floor. Blood on the rug. Blood on the couch. But no body. Is this your idea of funny?' The message ended.

Kelson stared at Genevieve Bower.

'I don't know,' she said.

So he dialed Dan Peters's number.

Peters answered after the first ring. 'What the hell?'

'What do you mean, "no body"?' Kelson said.

'I mean, no body. Blood smears. Spatter on the floor. A hole in the wall by the shelves – small caliber. No body unless you stuck him under the floorboards.'

'He was sitting on the couch,' Kelson said. 'A .22 in his hand. A gunshot wound above his left eye.'

'You're telling me a guy killed himself and then got up and left?'

'He didn't kill himself. He died on the floor – but then he was on the couch. The gun in his hand – he didn't pick it up. It probably doesn't match the bullet in his skull – or the wall.'

Peters sounded worn out. 'Are you screwing with me?'

Kelson told the truth, as always. 'I have no idea.'

'Tell me what happened,' Peters said. 'What you saw.'

Kelson told him about parking in front of the North Hermitage bungalow, stepping on to the front porch, stepping off it, walking to the back of the house, climbing the back steps, climbing back down—

'Just what you saw inside,' Peters said.

Kelson described the kitchen, the eggshells in the kitchen garbage, the bedroom, the red velour bedspread and half pint of Hennessy—

'The body,' Peters said. 'Tell me about the body.'

Kelson told him about Jeremy Oliver's body in bloody detail.

'Come down to the station,' Peters said. 'You need to give a full statement – background and that kind of thing. *Not* to me. I'll get someone with typing skills and a couple reams of paper.'

When they hung up, Kelson promised Genevieve Bower he would keep looking for her stolen fakes. She promised to call right away if she heard anything about Jeremy Oliver or if she sensed a personal threat or even felt uneasy.

Kelson said, 'Oliver's death probably has nothing to do with you. Whoever killed him took him by surprise. At least he seemed calm when I talked with him last night. But by moving his body, you put yourself into the middle of whatever happened. And now the body's gone. Where? Why?'

If Genevieve Bower knew any answers, she didn't share them.

SEVEN

K elson picked up Sue Ellen at Nancy's house at six thirty that evening. Dressed in dentist scrubs, Nancy waved from the door as their daughter ran down the front walk to his car.

Nancy and Kelson met in police academy, but she quit the department and went to dental school when Sue Ellen was born. Now she pulled teeth and, in her spare time, practiced taekwondo and jujitsu. Since she'd started dating again – a man whose name she wouldn't tell Kelson, and even Sue Ellen wouldn't spill – she seemed happier than he'd ever known her, at times almost affectionate, a development Kelson considered a turnoff. Still, just last week she'd said a mixed martial arts promoter had encouraged her to join the amateur competitions he staged in a southside warehouse on the first Monday of each month. So there was hope.

At Taquería Uptown, Kelson liked the bare walls and the *carne asada*. Sue Ellen liked the guacamole, the *limón* soda, and the chance to play Stump Dad when they sat side by side on the counter stools. A white-shirted, white-hatted counterman welcomed them as they came in.

Sue Ellen and Kelson sat, and before the counterman even set a *limón* soda in front of her, she started the questions.

'Favorite food,' she said.

'Eggs,' Kelson said.

'Eggs?'

'Scrambled – with glazed donuts.'

'That's just weird,' she said.

'Eggs.'

'Fine. What's your weirdest dream in the last week?' she asked. 'In three words or less.'

'Eggs, eggs, eggs,' he said.

'Really?'

'You know I never lie. Let's just have a conversation tonight, OK?'

She didn't bother to shake her head. 'Tell me an embarrassing childhood memory.'

Kelson nodded at the counterman. 'He doesn't want to hear this.'

'*Sí*, I do,' the counterman said.

'An embarrassing childhood memory,' Sue Ellen said.

'This is just mean,' Kelson said.

'And don't say "eggs".'

As he told it, mild disgust crossed her face, though the counterman listened with open-minded interest. 'That's gross, Dad,' Sue Ellen said.

'Don't ask what you don't want to know,' he said. 'Had enough?'

'Are you kidding?' she said. 'This is just getting good. What did you do today in six words or less?'

'You first,' he said.

Sue Ellen took the challenge. 'Homework sucks, homework sucks, homework sucks.'

'Not much of a plot,' he said.

'That's because homework sucks. Your turn.'

'Big-boobed client loses Eighties DJ corpse.'

Sue Ellen counted with her fingers. 'First of all, that's seven. Second of all, a dad shouldn't say "boob" to an eleven-year-old.'

'Is "big-boobed" one word or two? And you made me.'

Kelson ate his tacos, Sue Ellen her tostadas. They went out for coffee afterward, and he treated her to a double espresso.

'You know, this will keep me awake all night,' she said.

'I know,' he said. 'My gift to your mom.'

EIGHT

The next morning, Kelson drove to his office and tracked the purchase history on Jeremy Oliver's credit cards. He looked for self-storage rentals, payments on a commercial property lease, even check-ins at motels – anything that might show where Oliver hid Genevieve Bower's stolen fakes. He found mostly a record of cheap meals at fast food restaurants and expensive drinks at late-night dance clubs. Oliver needed to store his DJ equipment somewhere, and Kelson wondered if the shoes might be with it. He opened the JollyOllie website and clicked through the images until he found one of an outdoor party. Behind a couple in matching madras shorts, he saw a yellow cargo van emblazoned with a JollyOllie logo.

He made a property search of the address where Oliver lived and found that Oliver rented the attic from a Bruce McCall. He dialed McCall's contact number, over-explained himself to the woman who answered, and got put through to an impatient-sounding man.

'Long story short,' Kelson said, and started into the long story of how he found Jeremy Oliver's body and then the body disappeared and then—

'I'm sorry,' McCall said, 'why are you calling?'

'The garage behind the house,' Kelson said. 'Did Jeremy Oliver rent it?'

'Yes,' McCall said. 'Why?'

'Did he keep his van there?'

'Sure, his van and his sound equipment.' Then he made the mistake of asking, 'Who exactly is this?'

Kelson told him about the bullet he'd taken in the head as an undercover narcotics cop and started to work sideways from there.

'Look,' McCall said, 'I've already talked with the police. If you need more information, get it from them.'

'Just one more thing. When I found Oliver's body, the garage looked empty. Do you know where he kept the van when he didn't have it in the garage?'

'Far as I know, he either drove it or kept it in the garage. That van was his whole life.'

They hung up, and Kelson did a vehicle registration search and then called a woman he knew at the Auto Pound. Beatrice O'Malley was the gruffest cop he'd ever met, but he once saw her cry when they found a thirteen-year-old drug lookout dead in the trunk of a stolen BMW. Now he rehearsed what he would say and, when she answered, spit it out all at once. 'If you tow a yellow van that advertises a DJ business called JollyOllie, will you let me know?' He gave her the license and registration numbers and added, 'Do me a favor and don't ask why.'

'OK – *why*?' she said. She talked like she had tobacco in her cheek.

'Jimmy Choos. They might be in the van.'

'Huh?'

'Case I'm working. Stolen shoes.'

'Funny. How's that head of yours? Still seeing double?'

'I never saw double.'

'Your daughter?'

'Sue Ellen's good, thanks.'

'The cats?'

'How did you hear about the cats?'

'Word gets around. You tell one guy, that guy tells another guy, that other guy tells me. You know I can't tell you about vehicle recovery, not unless it's your van. I hear you're hanging with a good-looking one-armed guy.'

'Only a few people can outtalk me, Beatrice,' Kelson said. 'Let me know about the van if you've got it in your heart.'

'You know I got no heart,' she said.

Next, Kelson put the battery back into Jeremy Oliver's phone. Oliver had set a password, and Kelson tried everything from 'jollyollie' to 'olliejolly' to 'jeremyO' to variations on Oliver's Hermitage Avenue address to 'crappy80stunes'. He got nowhere. He stared at the screen and said, 'You bastard.' The screen stayed silent, so Kelson said, 'We've got ways to make you talk.'

*   *   *

At eleven, he joined Rodman, Marty, and Neto at a table at Staropolska, a Polish restaurant where Rodman knew the owner. Kelson handed Jeremy Oliver's phone to Marty and said, 'I can't get past the password.'

Marty didn't ask whose phone it was or why Kelson wanted to break into it. He said, 'Time me.'

Kelson looked at his watch, and Marty went to work, his thumb beating the screen as if keeping time to music. When he held up the phone to show he'd gotten in, Kelson checked the time. 'Forty-three seconds.'

Marty grinned. 'Still got it.'

Neto rolled his eyes. 'Old man.'

'Yeah? Fuck you.' Marty turned off the phone, turned it on again, and gave it to Neto. 'Money where your mouth is.'

Neto grinned. 'Time me.'

'Do it one handed, fuckhead,' Marty said.

Neto tucked a hand behind his back and went at it with the other. When he held up the screen to show the others, Kelson checked his watch. 'Forty-one seconds.'

Neto pointed at his uncle. 'Eat it, Marty.'

Marty looked scornful. 'Youth.'

They ordered the family dinner, which started with potato pancakes, soup, and salad, shot through beef stroganoff, sausages, and sauerkraut, and finished with pierogi and sweet cheese blintzes. They ate and drank, talked and laughed, waiting for Neto's call from G&G.

Rodman told Neto, 'We'll follow you wherever they send you. If they pull something, we'll be on top of them before they know we're there.'

'Like a brick,' Kelson said.

Neto said, 'Nix. I'll go alone.'

Kelson said, 'Who the hell says "nix"?'

Marty said, '*I* do.'

Rodman nodded and said, 'He does.'

'I'm good,' Neto said.

'You aren't good, you're cocky,' said Kelson.

'Says the man whose phone I just hacked,' Neto said.

'Sam's right,' Rodman said. 'Anyone who scares your uncle needs watching.'

'I guarantee I can outsmart them,' Neto said. 'No problem, no worries. I'll call if I change my mind – I won't change my mind.'

'I guarantee that kind of attitude will get you killed,' Kelson said. 'I saw it happen when I worked narcotics. It almost happened to me.'

'Listen to the man, Neto,' Marty said.

Neto gave Kelson a superior smile. 'A man with a hole in his head? No thanks.'

'I respect guts,' Kelson said. 'I hate cockiness.'

As if the G&G people respected the lunch schedule, Neto's phone rang as he chewed his last bite of blintze. He answered, exchanged a few words, and hung up. 'Rogers Park Branch Library,' he told the others. He quoted the caller – 'Alone.'

So they wished him luck, and he said luck was for suckers and left – alone – to do the job.

Rodman and Marty let him get out the door, then exchanged a look. Rodman asked Kelson, 'You want to watch the arrogant prick with us, or play point?'

'I'll stay by my phone,' Kelson said.

So Rodman and Marty followed Neto to the northside library.

Kelson sat in his car outside Staropolska and looked through Oliver's phone. Call history showed over a dozen missed calls from Genevieve Bower, ending two and a half days earlier, along with two calls Oliver had made to her. She'd texted him another dozen times, pleading with him to return her things and threatening to cut off his balls – sometimes both in one message. He'd texted back, demanding to see cash. Only one exchange confused Kelson. After Genevieve Bower said she couldn't raise the fifteen thousand dollars, Oliver wrote, *Get it from her*, and she wrote back, *Screw you*.

'That's telling him,' Kelson said to the phone.

He scrolled through Oliver's contacts – over two hundred of them. None stood out.

He looked through Oliver's pictures and videos. Mostly, he had shots and clips of his DJ jobs, though he'd saved a whole album of selfies of himself getting high. 'Dumbass,' Kelson said. When he found a series of shots of Genevieve Bower doing things with her breasts he didn't know breasts could do, he said, 'Yikes,' selected the pictures, and deleted them.

He checked Oliver's web browsing history. 'Surprise me for once,' he said when he saw that Oliver spent several hours every day on Pornhub watching videos he found by searching the phrase 'big tits' and a few others he found with 'big daddy'. In the past week, Oliver had also searched the Jimmy Choo website thoroughly and looked at websites tied to the counterfeit shoe trade.

On Google, Kelson discovered that the Chinese played hard in the fake shoe market, selling sneakers and sandals for under ten bucks a pair. Phony Nikes were big. A Sabrina's Closet link listed 'Seven Ways to Spot Fake Jimmy Choos'. Kelson learned that unless Genevieve Bower also had authentic-looking Jimmy Choo shoeboxes, authentic-looking dust bags for the shoes, and zipper tabs with the Jimmy Choo name engraved on them, her fakes would sell for much less than she said they would – more than ten bucks a pair but nowhere near list price. 'Liar,' he said.

Returning to Oliver's web browsing history, Kelson saw that JollyOllie also seemed to eat a lot of pizza, searching for restaurants throughout the city and suburbs. 'Probably near his DJ jobs,' Kelson said. But one search surprised him. A month and a half ago, Oliver had searched the name 'Genevieve Bower'. According to her when she hired Kelson, she'd met Oliver only four weeks ago at a cousin's party, starting a nine-day whirlwind of dating and imprudent video recording.

'The hell,' Kelson said, and he got out his own phone and called Genevieve Bower.

She answered, 'Do you have the shoes?'

He said, 'I have questions. Tell me how you met Jeremy Oliver.'

'My cousin Susan had a party. Her fortieth birthday. Jeremy did the music. We started talking, and—'

'Did you start talking with him, or did he start talking with you?'

'Why?'

'I'm trying to understand,' he said.

'I was at the bar. He came to get a drink. He said something corny. I'm a sucker for corny.'

'Do you remember what he said?'

'Yeah. "I prefer blondes."'

'Like a gentleman.'

'All I know is he looked at my face, not my chest, which is what most men look at, you included.'

'But he was thinking about your chest, and you fell for his act. Then what?'

'Has anyone told you you're a jerk?'

'Yes. What happened then?'

'I told him I hated Duran Duran and Milli Vanilli and Styx – pretty much everything he played before he came to the bar. I asked why didn't he play Madonna.'

'What did he say?'

'Nothing. He got his drink and walked away. But in the next mix, he played "Like a Virgin" three times in a row. Everyone booed. Not me – I loved it.'

'So you left the party with him?'

'He met me at my house after he packed up.'

'For nine whirlwind days of sex and rock 'n' roll.'

'More or less, yes.'

'And then he stole the shoes.'

'Yes.'

'What else did he take?'

'What do you mean?'

'The shoes aren't worth sixty thousand dollars – or even the fifteen thousand he asked for. What else did he take?'

'Do you know how much Jimmy Choos cost?'

'I don't wear furry shoes,' he said. 'But I know how much they cost at the Jimmy Choo store on Oak Street. I also know I can buy a pair of knockoff bunny slippers online for three bucks. So I'm guessing I could get some fancy fake Jimmy Choos for about seventy or eighty. But you've got a hundred pairs, and that's wholesale. Forty bucks a pair at most. Four thousand dollars total.'

'You've got no idea—'

'Could Oliver have known who you were before the party?'

'What? I don't think so.'

'How close are you to Susan?'

'She's my cousin. I don't get along so well with my family, but I always liked her.'

'Why don't you get along with your family?'

'I don't see how that has anything to do with getting my stuff back.'

'What's Susan's last name?'

'Centlivre. Why?'

'I'm making a checklist. Who's *her*?'

'What?'

'*Her*. Someone you know – someone Oliver thought might help you out. Seems to have money to throw around.'

'Where did you get that idea?'

'Oliver's phone. Funny story about how I got into it.'

'Look, Jeremy did Susan's party. He knew she's my cousin and knew she had enough money to hold a birthday bash for herself. He thought she'd lend me the fifteen thousand if I asked. But I hired you to do a job. If you can't—'

'I *can*. But I could do it better if I understood what it's really about.'

'You know what it is,' she said. 'Find my stuff. Get it back for me. That's all. Find it. Can you keep that straight?'

NINE

Kelson drove to his office. He took his Springfield from the bottom desk drawer. He unstrapped his KelTec from his under-desk rig. He released the magazines, rolled them in his palms, snapped them back, and returned the guns where they belonged. 'Ask Dr P about it,' he said. He stared at his bare desktop. 'She'll say, *Sure, you got shot in the head – what do you expect? A little OCD never hurt anyone.*' He laughed then – at nothing, or at himself, he didn't know.

He took out his laptop and searched for Susan Centlivre. She ran a fragrance and candle shop called The Wick in Highland Park, twenty-five miles north of the city on the lakefront. Her Facebook page showed a wide-faced, longhaired woman who wore long batik dresses and liked horses. 'The hippie cousin,' Kelson said. He clicked through her photo albums – showing her on vacation at a house in the woods, made up in heavy rouge and period ruffles for a costume party, picnicking with longhaired friends in a field of wildflowers. Nine pictures showed her birthday party, including one with Genevieve Bower kissing her on the lips. 'Because you never know,' Kelson said.

He dialed the number for the fragrance and candle shop.

The woman who answered sounded vaguely British. 'The Wick.'

'Right. Can I talk to Susan Centlivre?'

'Speaking.'

'I thought you'd sound like a stoner.'

'I'm sorry?'

'Why do you talk that way?'

'What way?'

'Like you're having tea with the queen.'

The shop owner hung up.

'Shit,' Kelson said. He breathed deep, in and out. He made a mental script. Then he dialed again.

'The Wick.'

'Not quite Monty Python, but close.'

She hung up.

He waited five minutes and dialed once more.

'The Wick.'

'Hi,' Kelson said, 'my name's Sam Kelson and I'm looking into the death of a man you recently employed for a private party. Jeremy Oliver.'

'I'm sorry?'

'JollyOllie.'

'He's dead?'

'I'm afraid so.'

'What happened?'

'That's what I'm trying to figure out. Someone shot him. It isn't clear who or why.'

'That's terrible. But why are you calling me? I only had him play music—'

'Did you know he hooked up with your cousin?'

'Genevieve? I saw them talking at the party. What does she have to do with it?'

'I don't know that either,' Kelson said, 'but I'm working for her. How did you end up hiring him?'

She hesitated. 'He DJ'd a party for my sister's business. I liked his music.'

'He play the Grateful Dead?'

'I'm sorry?'

'You know, the whole hippie-dippie thing.'

'No, actually I *don't* know.' Her voice couldn't sound less hippie-dippie.

'Would you mind telling me where you're from?' Kelson asked.

'I was born fifteen miles from here. I've lived here most of my life.'

'Huh,' he said, and, after they hung up, 'a hell of a lot of good that did.'

Twenty minutes later, DeMarcus Rodman called from the Rogers Park Branch Library and said, 'You should see this. Neto's burning up the keyboard – it's like watching piano. The kid's fingers are a blur.'

'No trouble, then?'

'Not unless watching Beethoven is trouble. They've got a table of something like ten computers. All these homeless guys and retired types plinking at the keys. Neto's like Barry Bonds coming to the plate in peewee league. I mean, this boy's on steroids.'

'Anyone from G&G watching him work?'

'Everyone's watching – human fingers don't move that way. But no one that looks like a problem.'

'Does he know you're there?'

'I don't think so. He's in a zone, man. Marty could sit on the monitor, and the kid would brush him off like a fly.'

'Good deal,' Kelson said. Then he told Rodman about his conversations with Susan Centlivre and Genevieve Bower and his conclusion that the stolen shoes weren't worth the fifteen thousand Oliver demanded for them.

'Sounds like the Neto show is more exciting,' Rodman said.

'Call if anything happens – maybe Neto will sprain a finger or the keyboard will combust from the friction.'

Kelson put away the laptop, turned his chair, and smiled at the picture of Sue Ellen, then made faces at the picture of the kittens. Sue Ellen's frozen expression and the kittens' frozen motion

looked like life and death all at once – a girl and her pets caught
in a crystal glacier where they could remain for hundreds of
years – thousands – without losing their beauty. 'Funny that way,'
Kelson told them.

He was still staring at them ten minutes later, as if he could
will them to blink, when his phone rang.

Beatrice O'Malley was calling from the Auto Pound. 'You like
your engine parts blackened or just well done?' she said. ''Cause
Jeremy Oliver's van's got both.'

'What happened?' Kelson said.

'Someone torched it. Behind a building on West Hubbard. We
towed it in twenty minutes ago.'

'Wow. Any signs of violence?'

'Sure, the fire beat the hell out of it. More than that, I don't
know.'

'Can I come look?'

'Forensics is coming later. They'll take it downtown. If you
want, you can have a peek, but you can't touch.'

The Central Auto Pound was located two levels below the surface
streets on Lower Wacker. Beatrice O'Malley oversaw the operation from a white portable trailer behind a long white fence.
If she walked out of the portable and looked up, she saw a sky
constructed of steel beams and concrete. The place felt like a
deep cave and smelled of auto fumes and engine oil.

O'Malley walked Kelson across the lot to a pen and unlocked
a chain-link gate. The burned hulk of a once-yellow Chevy
Express cargo van stood alone in the pen. The tires were gone,
the melted remains of synthetic rubber clinging to the wheel
rims. The JollyOllie logo looked like phantom lettering. Someone
had broken out the windshield, or maybe the heat had exploded
the glass. The windows on the rear doors were gone too.

'Looks like it got in a fight with a dragon,' O'Malley said.
'Remember what the lap dancers tell you – *Hands off.*' She left
him there and went back to the trailer.

Kelson peeked in through the windshield. The seats and interior
might once have been red, but only flecks and patches of pink
remained, like grimy wounds, among the charred fabric and seat
springs.

Kelson moved around to the driver's door. Somehow the outside rearview mirror had survived. He glanced into it and recoiled at the sight of the man who stared back, as if Jeremy Oliver – or Oliver's killer – was ambushing him. 'Don't do that,' he said to his reflection, and went to the back of the van.

Through the broken rear windows, he saw the burned scraps of a digital mixer, four large speakers, coils of audio cable, an amplifier, and a turntable. He also saw the papery skeleton of a wooden crate large enough to hold a washing machine. Shoes – melted, swollen, twisted with strands of liquefied plastic that looked like wet glue – bulged from the sides and bottom. 'Yeah,' Kelson said, as if he'd heard bad news. He stuck his head through the window and breathed the stink of gasoline and burned plastic and rubber. 'And barbeque,' he said. 'Burned leather?'

He stepped outside the pen and called Genevieve Bower. She answered on the second ring, and he said, 'Sorry. They're gone. The cops impounded Oliver's van – burned. The shoes were in it.'

Genevieve Bower barely said, 'Damn.'

'Yeah. Sorry.'

He seemed to expect her next words. 'Was there anything else in the van?'

'His sound equipment.'

'Anything of mine?'

'Like what?' he said.

She faltered. 'A thumb drive. Red.'

'I don't know. The van's at the pound. It's evidence – I can't search it. I can't even touch it.'

'Look for a red thumb drive.' A kind of pleading.

'I can't – I'm sorry.'

'Please.'

'What's on it?'

Halting. 'Videos.'

'Of you and Jeremy Oliver?'

'No.'

'What—' But even his cross-firing brain told him to ask no more. 'I can't,' he said.

'*Please.*'

He mumbled something about doing what he could, and they

hung up. He stood alone, surrounded by rows of impounded cars on the grimy lot. Beatrice O'Malley was back in the trailer office. 'Such a bad, bad idea,' he said. 'A dungeon, not a cave. Dragons, for God's sake.' He went back to the van – to the passenger side door, invisible from the trailer office. He touched the handle – and hesitated. Then he gripped it. The fire had melted something in the release mechanism. He yanked. The door opened.

He checked the glove compartment, what remained of it. Oliver had stored a glass pipe, a pocketknife, a screwdriver, and a pack of condoms. No thumb drive.

The center console produced another pipe, a filthy coffee cup, and, at the bottom, a bunch of quarters, dimes, and pennies. No thumb drive.

Kelson got out, eased the door shut, and went to the back of the van. 'Bad, bad, bad,' he said. He pulled the back doors open, climbed inside, and shut them behind him. The stink of the fire cut at his nose and throat, but he lifted the lid off the shoe crate. The boards that rimmed the top of the crate crumbled. 'Dammit,' he said, and set the lid on the cargo bed. He dug a hand into the melted mess and jumble of shoes, poking his fingers into filthy holes filled with ash and flakes of strange substances, expecting – 'nothing,' he said. He dug his other hand in and crammed it into a melted crevice. The sides of the crate collapsed, spilling destroyed shoes across the back of the van. Kelson yelled – then, realizing that yelling made his situation worse, hissed. Nothing he could do to put the crate back together, so he rummaged through Oliver's electronic equipment. 'Worse and worse and worse.'

No thumb drive.

He climbed out of the van, shut the doors, and brushed the soot and grime off his pants and jacket. He left the holding pen, closed the gate, and snapped the padlock shut.

He went into the trailer. A large man in a Chicago Blackhawks hat was hollering at O'Malley about a Lexus he'd parked in a fire lane only long enough to rush inside for a take-out order. O'Malley had crossed her arms over her chest the way she did when she wanted to build up maximum pressure before letting a jerk have it. Kelson tapped the large man on his shoulder and said, 'You don't want to do that.' Then he smiled at O'Malley, said, 'Thanks,' and left.

Sitting in his car, he dialed Genevieve Bower again.

Her phone rang and rang, and when the call went to voicemail, he hung up.

He drove back to his office under a graying afternoon sky, parked in the parking garage, went up to his desk, and called Rodman.

Rodman and Marty LeCoeur were drinking beer at Silvana, a bar up the street from the Rogers Park Library. 'Neto spotted us,' Rodman said. 'He sent Marty to get him a Red Bull. Then he kicked us out. G&G gave him a six o'clock deadline. He says he'll meet us here at five. The kid is good – maybe even as good as he says. We're going to get him drunk, and then he's buying us rib eyes. Meet us at Gene and Georgetti at eight?'

'Yeah, I'll pass,' Kelson said. 'That kid bugs me.'

When they hung up, Kelson checked his pistols. He said good night to the picture of Sue Ellen, stuffed his hands in his pockets instead of petting the picture of Payday and Painter's Lane, and left his office.

As he drove his Challenger from the parking garage, he rolled down his window by the booth, and said to the attendant, 'Never play with matches.'

The attendant said, 'One of these days you're gonna let me drive that car.'

'You're my kind of man,' Kelson said.

He drove home through heavy traffic, talking to the people in the other cars – the ones who cut him off, the ones who let him in at a corner, the woman who stared at him a moment too long as they waited at a red light – as if they sat next to him in his passenger seat.

When he let himself into his apartment, the kittens raced across the carpet and rubbed against his ankles. He lay down inside the door and let them crawl on to his chest and sniff his chin. They purred as they worked their little claws on his shirt and purred louder when he stroked their backs. 'When all else fails,' he said to Painter's Lane.

At five o'clock he felt an impulse to join his friends at Silvana for an evening of drinking and steak. He put on his jacket and started out the door. Then Painter's Lane meowed at him, and he felt another impulse. He took off his jacket, went to the kitchenette, and poured a bowl of milk for her and another for Payday.

He was sitting on the floor watching the kittens lap the milk when his phone rang.

Caller ID said *DeMarcus Rodman.*

Kelson answered, 'Do a shot for me. If Neto's paying, make it top-shelf.'

Rodman said, 'Turn on the news.' In all the years Kelson had known him, Rodman had never sounded agitated. Now he sounded agitated.

'What happened?' Kelson said.

'I don't know. We heard it from the bar. It shook the damn walls. When we went outside, we saw smoke.'

'I don't understand,' Kelson said. 'Where? What happened?'

'The library,' Rodman said. 'The goddamned library.'

'What happened? Is Neto OK?'

'That's what I'm saying,' Rodman said. 'I think he's dead.'

TEN

Neto wasn't dead.

The blast had shredded the left side of his body. It had punctured his left eye. It had pocked his head and body with metal and molten plastic.

'Very critical,' said the doctors at the University of Chicago Trauma Center. 'If he wakes up . . . we don't know if he'll wake up – we don't know what will remain of him if he does – what function, what cognitive . . .'

Two others died. 'Neto's one of the lucky ones,' said a nurse, and Rodman had to hold Marty to keep him from punching her.

The dead – a homeless man working at the computer two seats down from Neto, and a young mother at the computer between Neto and the homeless man. A baby girl in a stroller between the woman and Neto survived with only abrasions. 'A miracle,' the same nurse said. The mother's body shielded her girl from the blast. It partly shielded Neto too.

Including the woman's baby, ambulances carried six people to hospitals around the city, the most critically injured to the Trauma Center. Now, Marty LeCoeur, Rodman, and Kelson had one of the internal waiting rooms to themselves. The lights were soft, the paint the golden color of an autumn sunset, the chairs upholstered in earth tones. The room seemed to whisper *Peace, Patience, Forbearance*. When the doctor left, Marty stared at the walls as if they were closing in on him and said, 'Fucking makes me sick.'

Then he called his brother, Neto's father. He started gentle but in a minute was yelling into the phone, 'You get the fuck down here *now*,' and in the hush of the room the voice of Neto's father – who'd kicked Neto out around the time of the Banco Santander Río trouble – came through the earpiece – 'The hell if I will.' Marty swore at the man, the man swore back, and when Marty hung up, he had tears in his eyes. He stared at Rodman and Kelson and said, 'I'm his only family. *We* are.'

'I don't even like the kid,' Kelson said.

Marty glared at him.

'Sorry. Anything you need. Anything I can do.'

'Yeah,' Marty said, and he wiped his glazed eyes with the back of his hand. 'You can find out what the fuck happened.'

After a while, Marty's girlfriend Janet came. They went to a corner and mumbled, and she put a big paw on his little shoulder, but when they came back to Rodman and Kelson, she sat apart as if afraid she would break him if she got close. They all were quiet except when Kelson's thoughts leaked out of his mouth.

Just before midnight, the doctor returned. 'We think we've stopped the internal bleeding,' he said. He gave them the details about the procedures they'd performed – a whining blur of information that hurt Kelson to think about, and he told him so. 'I'm sorry,' the doctor said. 'So sorry.'

'Everyone's sorry,' Kelson said. 'Me. You.'

'What fucking good?' Marty said.

'He's stable for now,' said the doctor, and added a string of clichés. *Touch and go. Only time can tell. Resting peacefully. Looks like a fighter. Hope for the best.*

'I'm a numbers guy,' Marty said. 'Give me the numbers.'

'You've got power of attorney?' the doctor asked.

'We've got each other's back. What're the odds?'

The doctor hesitated. 'I really can't say—'

'Give me the fucking numbers,' Marty said. 'What's his chances?'

The doctor frowned. 'Twenty percent?'

Marty nodded and said, 'I could fucking kill you.'

An hour later, Rodman and Kelson left. Janet had fallen asleep, breathing thickly from her thick throat. Marty sat with his eyes wide and hard, digging at the fabric on his pants with his fingers.

A little after one a.m., Kelson and Rodman got into Kelson's car and spun through the radio stations, searching for news.

So soon after the explosion, the police and FBI were releasing few facts and just starting to eliminate possibilities.

The blast occurred at four fifty-four p.m.

It might have come from a backpack the homeless man set on the table by his computer.

No gas lines ran through or under that part of the library.

Standard computer electronics and the network between the machines had no explosive components.

Five people were hospitalized. The baby girl went home with her dad.

No one had claimed responsibility for the blast.

There was no reason to think foreign or domestic terrorists were responsible.

There was no reason to think they weren't.

The police were releasing no names.

The mayor, the governor, and the president were demanding answers.

'Blah, blah, blah,' Kelson said.

'It's too soon,' Rodman said.

'Blah, blah, blah.'

They drove north through the city, wending through late-night streets toward the Rogers Park Library, and stopped before a line of blue barricades on Clark Street. Cops guarded the barricades, holding back a crowd of spectators. A dozen news trucks and vans had parked at angles on the street, their microwave transmission masts poking at the sky like stingers. Grim-faced reporters, blinking under artificial light, talked to the news cameras. Beyond the barricades, shattered window glass shimmered on the sidewalk and street. Part of the front wall had burst outward. Broken brick rubble and wooden framing were piled over a mangled book-return box. Electrical wires hung from the wall over the blown-out hole. The air was still and cool and smelled of smoke and dust.

Kelson and Rodman shouldered through the crowd and approached a young uniformed cop.

'Who's the officer in charge?' Kelson asked.

The cop stared at him as if he'd spoken another language.

'My name's Sam Kelson – ex-CPD, Narcotics.'

'Ex?' the cop said. 'You need to step back, sir. We have our hands full tonight.'

'Who's in charge?' Kelson asked again.

The cop seemed to look through him.

Rodman stepped forward. The top of the barricade came to his thighs. He leaned down at the cop. He let his eyelids hang lazily over his eyes and gave the cop a gentle smile. 'My friend,' he said, 'asked you who's in charge.'

The cop looked annoyed but also scared. 'Lieutenant Jillian Richard's got lead.'

'Who else is here?' Kelson asked. 'Dan Peters? Venus Johnson?'

'Richard has about half of the homicide unit with her. All I know, I keep my mouth shut and eyes open. That means you're keeping me from doing my job.'

'Check for Peters and Johnson,' Rodman said.

The cop looked up at the enormous man. Anyone could see he wanted to object. But Rodman gave him more of his gentle smile, more of his lazy gaze, and, like most men facing a polite monster who seemed capable of extraordinary violence, the cop did as he was told. He talked on his radio to a commander. Then he told Rodman, 'Yeah, Venus Johnson's working the scene. No, I won't ask to talk to her. No, you can't go in and find her yourselves.'

So Kelson and Rodman stood with the rest of the crowd, watching and listening, breathing the heavy air as if making it a part of them would help them understand what had happened. After a while, a very dark-skinned, solid-legged woman in a blue jacket stepped into the street from the far side of the library building. Kelson thought he recognized Venus Johnson, and he yelled, 'Venus,' but the woman disappeared around the other side. He yelled again – and again – until people in the crowd stared at him, and Rodman put a hand on his shoulder to quiet him. Then three officers dressed in white forensics suits came out of the ruined front of the library. 'Snowmen,' Kelson said, and more people stared at him. Twenty minutes later, when Venus Johnson came back out from the side of the building, Kelson yelled again, 'Venus.'

She turned toward his voice, then seemed to think better of it and walked toward a mobile command truck.

Kelson yelled louder. 'Venus Johnson—'

When Johnson spun back toward Kelson, she looked as if she wanted to vent her fear, anger, and sadness – all of the emotions that had roared into her during the terrible evening.

She crossed to the barricades and said, 'You're a goddamned vulture. What the hell are you doing here?'

'Was it the homeless man?' Kelson asked.

'I said, what the *hell*—'

'A friend's nephew was in there,' Kelson said. 'He's hurt. Bad. I promised to find out what I could.'

Johnson blinked, and her energy seemed to drain. 'Ah, shit,' she said. She turned away, then turned back, as if she would apologize. Instead, she yelled at the crowd. 'Vultures.' She walked off and disappeared into the command truck.

ELEVEN

K elson slept for three hours and woke with a raging head-ache. He popped two Percocets, and the sharp pain dulled to a throb and then became a heavy cloud. He showered and poured three bowls of Cheerios – one for himself and one for each of the kittens. He added milk and laid a slice of ham over the top of the kittens' bowls. He set the bowls on the dining table, put the kittens on the table by them, and sat for breakfast. Payday's tail swung in time with her lapping tongue. Painter's Lane closed her eyes as she ate.

After washing the dishes, Kelson checked the news.

The dead homeless man's name was Victor Almonte – thirty-one years old, an army vet who served a tour in Afghanistan, born in St Louis to a local girl and her Dominican boyfriend, in Chicago since leaving the army. The dead woman's name was Amy Runeski – twenty-four, unemployed, separated from her husband, living with her two-year-old daughter in a friend's Rogers Park apartment, using the library computers as she went through divorce proceedings.

'The husband?' Kelson asked Payday. His stomach turned as he imagined a man hurting his daughter. 'If so, I'll kill him.' Then, to reassure Painter's Lane, 'Not literally.' Then, to Payday, '*Maybe* literally.'

But an unnamed FBI source pointed at the homeless man's backpack. The pack – the little that remained of it – may have had a suspicious object in it. An FBI lab was testing it.

Still, no one had claimed responsibility. The mayor warned the public against jumping to conclusions. 'At this point, we don't know,' he said. 'We're investigating all possible causes, including accidental.'

'I don't like accidents,' Kelson said to Painter's Lane. 'Or chance.' He looked at Payday. 'Or even statistics – much. Twenty percent chance Neto will live? No, he either lives – a hundred percent – or dies – a hundred percent.'

Payday meowed at Kelson.

'Yeah,' Kelson said, 'I'll shut the hell up.'

So he dialed Rodman's apartment and, when his friend picked up, asked, 'You asleep?'

'What's sleep?' Rodman said.

'Any word on Neto?'

'He's hanging on. Marty's a wreck. I'm heading over to give him a break.'

'I'll see you there,' Kelson said.

An hour later, he walked into the internal waiting room at the University of Chicago Trauma Center.

Janet was eating a Hostess berries and cheese Danish from a vending machine.

Rodman was staring out a window at a little garden.

Marty had pulled two armchairs so they faced each other. He

stretched on his back between them, his short legs splayed over the armrests. His eyes were wide and hard, staring at the ceiling tiles.

Kelson said, 'Hey.'

Janet kept eating.

Rodman kept looking out the window.

Marty kept staring at the ceiling, but he asked, 'Why'd G&G send Neto to that library? Did they do this?'

'Why would they blow up their own operation?' Kelson said. 'Seems like the worst thing they could do. But it's a bad co-incidence that Neto was there – and I don't like coincidences.'

Rodman turned from the window. 'The mayor says it could be a problem in the building.'

'Do you believe that?' Kelson said.

'No.'

Janet said, 'It's the homeless guy.'

Rodman said, 'What kind of homeless guy blows up a library?'

'He comes back from Afghanistan messed in the head,' she said. 'He's living outside. He's mad at the government. I've got a cousin went to Afghanistan.'

'Your cousin blows up libraries?' Kelson said.

'He manages a Long John Silver's. But he has bad dreams.'

'The homeless guy didn't do it,' Rodman said.

'It *isn't* the girl,' Janet said. 'She's getting a divorce. She's got a baby. Why would she kill herself?'

'The husband,' Kelson said.

Rodman nodded his big head. 'Maybe the husband.'

Janet put the last of the Danish in her mouth. 'The bastard.'

Marty sat up on the chairs. He seemed to have heard none of the conversation. 'Why'd G&G send Neto there?' he said again, then asked Kelson, 'Will you talk to them? See what's what? If DeMarcus goes, they'll see this big black dude and they'll worry. But you, you're – you look . . .' He searched for the word.

'Ineffectual,' Janet said.

'You, they don't worry so much,' Marty said.

Janet tapped her forehead. 'Hole in the brain. You don't fool no one.'

Kelson said, 'Anything for you, Marty.'

*   *   *

G&G kept third-story offices in a business park in Mundelein, forty miles north of the city. Skinny tinted windows squinted from between scrubbed white concrete panels on the outside of the building. The inside – the lobby, the elevator, the third-floor hallway, the G&G reception area – smelled like floor polish.

When Kelson asked the receptionist if Sylvia Crane, Harold Crane, or Chip Voudreaux could talk with him about Neto LeCoeur, she raised her eyebrows and phoned into the inner offices.

A minute later, a man in a navy blue suit, barely pink shirt, and blue tie came out to reception. He wore his curly brown hair short, had watery gray eyes, and had done something to his teeth that made them unpleasantly white. He offered to shake Kelson's hand, said, 'Chip Voudreaux,' and asked Kelson to follow him to his office.

Another man, in his late sixties, with a beakish nose and sharp blue eyes, came to the office door across from Voudreaux's and glared at Kelson as he walked past. Voudreaux ignored the man, sat at a dark-wood desk, crossed his fingers on top, and asked, 'How can I help you?'

'Did you blow up Neto LeCoeur?' Kelson said.

A faint smile appeared on the man's thin lips. 'I don't know who—'

'I'm friends with Neto's uncle, Marty LeCoeur. Long story short . . .' He explained his past as a narcotics cop, his current work as a private investigator, how he knew Marty LeCoeur, and how he met Neto.

After a few minutes, Voudreaux interrupted him. 'I could deny I've ever met Neto or his uncle.'

'But you won't?'

'If I did, no one could prove otherwise. We're exceedingly careful. No company-related phone records. Nothing on paper. Nothing anyone but the very best analysts could track electronically. If you look for the LeCoeurs here, you won't even see their ghosts.'

'So why don't you deny you know them?'

Voudreaux frowned again. 'We have a bigger problem.'

'Bigger than two dead and five people blown apart?' Kelson said.

'Depending on whose perspective. It seems that just before the explosion at the library, your boy diverted our funds.'

'He did what?'

'Every penny,' Voudreaux said. 'He initially transferred the money as we instructed him to, but as he finished, he did – something. The money disappeared from our clients' accounts. We can only assume it reappeared in an account of his own.'

'How much?'

Voudreaux pressed his lips together, then said, 'Thirty-seven million.' He was sweating behind his tie. 'Give or take.'

'Ha,' Kelson said.

'You know the kind of people he stole from?'

Kelson grinned at him. 'The kind who hire fools like you.'

Voudreaux seemed to consider the suggestion. 'I suppose so. The kind who make rules work for them, and if the rules stop working they break them and make new ones. The kind who brook no interference with their plans and dreams.'

Kelson still grinned. 'They "brook no interference"? How did Neto even do this?'

Voudreaux glared at him. 'That's what we expect Neto to tell us. If not Neto, his uncle. If they don't . . .' He left that hanging.

'Seems to me you're in more danger than he is,' Kelson said. 'Your clients will come after you. They gave you the money. You lost it.'

'We expect the LeCoeurs to return the money. Within twenty-four hours.'

'Or else? You pull out the hunting knife?'

Voudreaux allowed himself a smile. 'That was a joke. I bought it as a gift for my father. But you're right again. Our clients will come for my blood and the blood of my colleagues. But they'll want more.'

'Nice business you're running.'

'I hear Neto is still unconscious. I recommend that his uncle get right to work. Find the money. Give it back. Maybe the investors can remain ignorant of Neto's indiscretion.' Voudreaux stood up from his desk to let Kelson know he was done talking to him.

Kelson said, 'You never answered my question. Did you try to kill him?'

Voudreaux stared at him with his watery gray eyes. 'I assure you, we did not.'

TWELVE

K elson drove back to the hospital. The staff had moved Marty, Janet, and Rodman to a smaller room, without a window. Kelson gave Marty Voudreaux's demand, and the little man said, 'Fuck *him*.'

Kelson agreed. 'He seems like a fool.'

'He's a fucking *prick*,' Marty said.

'You'd better do it, though,' Kelson said. 'Voudreaux said G&G will go after Neto if they don't get their money – and go after you too.'

Rodman said, 'I should've gone with. Talked sense into Voudreaux.'

'Wouldn't've made a difference,' Marty said. 'These guys mean it.'

'Can you get the money?' Rodman asked.

'Fuck if I know how. Neto's got tricks I never learned. Million-buck three-card Monte. I'm good – he's something else.'

'Then you should give this to the cops or the feds,' Kelson said.

The little man looked furious. 'Don't be an asshole. I go to the cops, I'm done. The cops kick my ass. Or they listen, and I testify, and then if I'm lucky – if I get a great fucking lawyer who gets me a great fucking deal – they throw me in a single-wide in Phoenix. 'Cause I knew a guy – lasted two months before he hanged himself in his closet.'

Rodman let his lazy eyelids hang low. 'Then you better get to work. You have all you need?'

'I don't know what I need,' Marty said. 'I've got to go to G&G and find out. They've got the info about the accounts and the passwords Neto used to get into them.'

'You should stay here with Neto,' Janet said.

'What fucking good?' Marty said. 'I do more for him if I clean this mess.'

'I'll go with,' Rodman said. 'Maybe they need to see what *they're* up against.'

Janet agreed to stay and relay updates on Neto. Kelson agreed
to look into the dead victims – Victor Almonte and Amy Runeski.
So Marty and Rodman drove to Mundelein, and Kelson drove
to the Harrison Street Police Station.

No, said the man at the station desk, Venus Johnson wouldn't
talk to him.

'Try Darrin Malinowski from Narcotics,' Kelson said. 'He
used to be my boss.'

'You're wasting my time,' the deskman said, but he dialed
the extension for the narcotics unit and explained what Kelson
wanted.

Instead of having the deskman send Kelson back, Malinowski
came out to talk.

Kelson said, 'That look on your face – it's what people do
when they meet someone they feel bad for.'

'Take it how you want,' Malinowski said.

'I need to talk with Johnson.'

'You know that won't happen right now.'

'I've got information for her. Neto LeCoeur is one of the
victims – he's at the U of C Trauma Center.' Then, because
Malinowski stared at him with flat incomprehension and
because Kelson couldn't help himself, he told him what he'd
promised to keep secret. 'Neto got tangled in a big financial scam.
He's got a record for this kind of thing going back to when he
was a teenager. He was doing it again when the library blew up.'

Malinowski twisted his lips. 'How do you know this?'

'I'm pals with Neto's uncle. Sort of.'

'Jesus, Kelson, what are you mixed up in now?' But the
commander dialed the homicide unit on the deskman's phone.
He got Venus Johnson on the line and told her she should give
Kelson a minute. Then he ushered Kelson into the department.

Johnson met them at the door to the homicide room.

'You look wiped out,' Kelson said.

'Yep.'

'Ragged.'

'Lousy to see you too, Kelson.' She walked him to her cubicle.

Styrofoam coffee cups, a Coke can, and a couple of paper
plates with the remnants of delivery food littered her desk. An

architectural rendering of the Rogers Park Library showed on her computer screen.

She said, 'Sit. Talk. Then get out.'

'Tell me about Victor Almonte,' he said.

'Don't even think it. Malinowski said you have information about one of the injured.'

'Neto LeCoeur,' Kelson said. 'What about Amy Runeski's husband? Any chance he did it?'

'Did *what*? We haven't determined if—'

'Bullshit,' Kelson said. 'You put out the details. Homeless vet. Divorce. The news will name one of them as a suspect by tonight.'

'Watch the news then,' Johnson said. 'Malinowski said you've got something. If you don't, leave. I'm running thirty hours without sleep, and unless things break cleaner than they're going to, I'm looking at another thirty.'

Kelson said, 'A holding company called G&G Private Equity hired Neto LeCoeur to transfer funds into their clients' accounts. Some of the accounts might be legal, but most probably aren't. It's offshore money laundering, but I don't know the details. Neto was sitting next to Amy Runeski when the place blew. He's sleeping in a hospital bed now. The doctor says eighty percent chance he'll never wake up, though I don't believe in odds.'

'Hold on,' Johnson said. 'A company hired him to do this from a library?'

'I know. G&G uses public computers for their distributions. I guess that keeps their own machines clean. They move around a lot of money. Millions. Tens of millions.'

Johnson breathed in deep through closed teeth. 'They had a guy – called *Neto* – move millions – we're talking about dollars?'

'Yeah.'

'Neto moved these millions from a rat-shit computer at a rat-shit library?'

'You want to write this down?'

Johnson closed her eyes.

Kelson said, 'You need to talk to a man named Chip Vou—'

'Yeah, I'll do that,' Johnson said. 'Meantime, I've got a shitload of work. And next time you have a story for me, *you* write down the details, OK? All the details.'

She stared at him. He stared back.

She said, 'Take your time – write it neat. Use big letters – easy to read. Use goddamned crayons. Then take the paper and wipe your ass with it. Flush it down the toilet. Don't come and stink up my life with it.'

The news that night said that eleven months after Victor Almonte returned from Afghanistan the police charged him with arson for torching a sofa at his sister's house. Since then, they'd arrested him twice, once for trespassing and once for shoplifting. After the library blast, the police found a mangled coil of wire and part of a radio transmitter in his shredded backpack. Fox News added a scoop – in Afghanistan, Almonte served as an ordnance disposal specialist, disarming IEDs. And CBS interviewed Emma Almonte, Victor's sister, outside a little tan-brick house on North Keeler. 'My brother couldn't do this,' she told the camera with a slight Dominican accent. 'No, no, no, no, no.'

'Huh,' Kelson said.

NBC aired a news conference where Amy Runeski's husband Tom clutched his baby daughter to his chest. He asked for everyone's prayers. He was tall and blond and wore wire-rimmed glasses. He'd slapped a Looney Tunes Band-Aid on one of his daughter's cheeks.

Kelson said, 'Picture perfect.'

The baby daughter worried him, so he turned off the TV and called Sue Ellen. Her voice made him happy.

'What's new, honey?' he said.

'I hate polynomials.'

'Tough day at school?'

'Polynomials suck.'

'You hear the one about the polynomial?'

'No *dad jokes*,' she said.

'But where would we be without polynomials?'

'Good night, Dad,' she said.

'Stay away from libraries, OK?'

'What?'

'Watch YouTube. Play online poker.'

'Dad . . .?'

'Just thinking – books are overrated, you know?'

'Really?'

'I mean, I want you to watch out for yourself. Be safe.'

'You're weird, Dad.'

'I know.'

At eleven o'clock, he turned out the light. Lying in bed, he realized he'd never heard back from Genevieve Bower. He turned on the light again and called. Her line rang and rang, and when it went to voicemail, he said, 'Huh' again, and hung up. Then he said, 'I've got to stop saying "huh".' He turned off the light and closed his eyes. With Payday sleeping by his feet and Painter's Lane on the pillow by his face, he dreamed of fire.

THIRTEEN

I n the morning, the FBI released the video from the Rogers Park Library security camera. Lying in bed, Kelson watched it on his phone.

A grainy image with washed-out colors showed a wooden table with ten computers on it. Ten people – old, young, well-dressed, disheveled – sat at the table. A scruffy-haired, brown-skinned man in an orange T-shirt sat with his back to the camera at one end of the table. A gray-green backpack rested by his computer. A round-shouldered white woman in jeans and a green sweatshirt sat next to him. The baby girl whose father Kelson had seen in a press conference sat in a stroller next to the woman. After a moment, the woman – staring at her computer screen – dangled a wrist into the stroller, and the girl reached with the tiniest of hands and held her mother's pinkie. Kelson's stomach fell. 'Ah, shit,' he said. Next to the woman, Neto's fingers touched the keyboard keys as if his mind had fused with the electronic circuitry. 'Like a pianist,' Kelson said, as Neto clinked the enter key, raised his hand, let his fingers play across the other keys, and clinked enter again. 'Even a kind of joy.'

Then, in an instant, the scene disintegrated. An obliterating dust shot through the room, the image melted and ripped, and the video went dark. 'Like a bullet in the head,' Kelson said. He watched a second time, trying to freeze the video at the moment of the blast. 'How do they know it's the backpack?' he said. He watched a third time and said, 'No.'

He got out of bed. 'No *what*?' He went into the bathroom, followed by the kittens. 'Just no.' He looked down at Payday. 'No.' As he stood at the toilet, he said, 'No, no, no, no, no, no, no.'

He showered.

He went to the kitchen.

'No appetite,' he told Painter's Lane. But he poured three bowls of Cheerios, topping the kittens' bowls with sliced salami. 'No headache either, though,' he told Payday. 'The fire must've burned it out.'

Before clearing the dishes, Kelson called Genevieve Bower's number again. Again her line rang and rang. 'No one.'

He drove back to the U of C Trauma Center.

Rodman sat alone in the little waiting room, his eyes closed, his enormous back spread over the chair. As Kelson came in, Rodman opened his eyes and reached for his hip. He had no gun on his hip.

'Get yourself hurt that way,' Kelson said.

'Old habits,' Rodman said.

'Where's Marty?'

'Still at G&G. You know what those people are.'

'You let them keep him?'

'He decided to stay. He knows he's got to fix the wreck Neto caused. They gave him some codes and passwords and set him up with all kinds of computers. Tell the truth, if he'd wanted to leave they could've kept him anyway. I'll fight big guys like me with or without a gun. But little white people in suits intimidate the hell out of me. They push a button, and sixteen security guys pop up. They make a call, and twenty suburban cops drop in. You know, G&G have a file on Marty an inch thick. After yesterday, I'll bet they have files on you and me.'

'You met Chip Voudreaux?'

'And Sylvia Crane. She does this act, except it isn't an act. Voudreaux kids around with the hunting knife. Sylvia Crane is the real thing.'

Tough women excited Kelson – and he said so.

'You,' said Rodman, 'are one messed-up dude.'

'Any word on Neto?'

'Still sleeping,' Rodman said. 'Bleeding from the brain again. They do some kind of reflex test on the eyeball – Neto doesn't have it. Marty needs to decide.'

'Nothing's worse.'

'Doing nothing about it is worse.'

Kelson considered that. 'Want to get out of here for a while?'

They drove out to Emma Almonte's address on Keeler Avenue and parked at the curb behind a Ford Focus with a *Proud Family of a Veteran* sticker on the bumper. Emma Almonte's tan-brick house had pinched little windows with little metal awnings over them. A double security floodlight faced the street from under a gutter. An American flag stuck from a metal bracket below the security light. Burglar bars covered the front door. A wide ribbon embroidered with roses hung from a nail between the door and the bars. It swung in the breeze when Kelson knocked. Emma Almonte made him and Rodman explain who they were and why they'd come for ten minutes before opening and letting them in.

Beyond the little entry hall, the front room smelled clean, though the white rug showed threads in the middle. Most of the furniture looked old and worn.

'Except the couch,' Kelson said, as he and Rodman stepped inside.

'I'm sorry?' she said.

'New,' he said. 'After your brother . . .' He mimed lighting a match.

Her cheeks colored. 'Yes.' She was about five and a half feet tall, with a wide, olive-brown face and coral lipstick.

'You've got great lips,' he said.

'I'm sorry?'

Rodman cut him off. 'Victor stayed with you when he came back from Afghanistan?'

She watched Kelson as if he might bite but said, 'Until last week.' She gestured toward a closed door. 'I gave him a room.'

'So he wasn't really homeless,' Kelson said.

'Can we look?' Rodman asked.

She opened the bedroom door. 'Victor didn't have much,' she said. 'Changes of clothes. A phone. What he brought back from the army. It makes no sense.'

A roll-down shade hung over the single window. A blue cotton spread stretched over the bed, the sides and corners tucked so the top looked flat and springy. A striped rectangular throw rug, its long side aligned perfectly with the side of the bed, lay on the floor. Kelson crossed the room to the dresser. Almonte had arranged a few of his possessions in a row on top. A black, big-toothed comb. An electric beard trimmer, its cord coiled. A Timex, its band stretched out. A pair of aviator sunglasses.

'Neat freak,' Kelson said.

'Even before he went into the army,' Emma Almonte said. 'More when he came out.'

'He looked dirty in the library video.'

'It makes no sense.'

Kelson touched the top dresser drawer. 'Do you mind?'

'Go ahead. There's nothing.'

Two pairs of underwear and two pairs of black socks lay in one corner of the top drawer, two shirts and a sweater in the second drawer. The third drawer was empty. Neatly folded sweatpants and a pair of pajama shorts lay in the bottom drawer.

'He left without saying goodbye,' she said.

Kelson looked at the things on top of the dresser. He picked up the watch.

'He never wore it after he came home,' she said.

Kelson glanced around the almost bare room. He looked at Emma Almonte's lips. 'He was proud,' he said.

She had a sad smile. 'Very.'

'And hurt.'

'Bad.'

Rodman spoke, his voice a low purr. 'Who came to see him in the days before he left?'

'Victor had no friends,' his sister said. 'When he first got back, a couple guys he served with would check on him. They would call. Then they stopped calling, and he sat in his room alone.'

'Why would he go to Rogers Park?' Rodman asked.

'He wouldn't,' she said. 'He liked to be alone. He liked to stay home. Mostly he locked himself in his room.'

'He had electrical wire and a transmitter in his backpack,' Kelson said. 'Did he like to play with—'

'You aren't listening.' Her dark eyes showed heat. 'Victor didn't own a backpack like that. I never saw it, and I would've seen it. Do you know how he came home from Afghanistan? He and his best friend were taking the detonator out of an IED in Jalalabad. Victor went back to the truck, and the IED exploded. Victor had trouble after that. The army gave him a discharge and sent him back to me. He used to have friends. He used to be funny and smart. Do you really think he'd play with wire and radio transmitters? Do you think he'd even *touch* them?'

'Then why'd he burn your sofa?'

Again her cheeks colored. 'I don't know. He said it was an accident. The fire department inspector said it was arson. It was a small fire – it wrecked the cushions. Victor called nine-one-one himself. He threw the cushions out on the front walk before the firetrucks even came.'

'Cry for help?' Rodman said.

'I don't know what he was thinking,' she said.

Kelson and Rodman thanked her for talking with them, and Rodman gave her his phone number and said, 'If you think of anything.'

Kelson gave her his card and looked at her lips. 'If you need to talk.'

But as they moved toward the front door, voices from outside the house stopped them. Then a fist pounded on the front door. A moment later, another fist pounded in the back. A megaphone told Emma Almonte to open her door.

Kelson went to the front window and looked.

A joint team of FBI agents and Chicago Police officers had parked cars and special operations trucks up and down the street as far as Kelson could see. Men and women dressed in assault gear crouched low behind the vehicles. They'd fastened a black metal cable to the front-door burglar bars on one end and the front of a tactical truck on the other. The rose-embroidered ribbon, torn from the door, lay on the lawn.

'I guess you'd better,' Kelson told Emma Almonte.

She opened the door. Six men on the sidewalk below the front step pointed assault rifles at her. One of them lowered his rifle and said – politely – 'Ma'am, we have a warrant to search your house.'

FOURTEEN

'What the hell are you doing here?' Venus Johnson asked Kelson on the street in front of the house. Kelson, Rodman, and Emma Almonte stood facing a black FBI truck, their hands cuffed behind their backs. FBI agents and CPD officers poured in and out of the house.

'You think it's Victor Almonte,' Kelson said. 'It isn't.'

Rodman told Emma Almonte, 'Get a lawyer. The cops'll hear what they want. They'll twist it. I've been there.'

Her eyes were steely. 'I have nothing to hide.'

Venus Johnson faced Kelson. 'What fucked-up logic convinced you that coming here made sense? You used to be a cop – Malinowski says a pretty good one. You know better than to step into shit this deep.'

Kelson looked at her. 'How did Victor Almonte even end up at the Rogers Park Library?'

'Took the damned El, I'm guessing.'

Rodman said to Emma Almonte, 'Get a lawyer. The cops break everything. They break whole families.'

Kelson turned from Venus Johnson. 'They broke DeMarcus's. He used to have a brother.'

'My family's already broken,' Emma Almonte said.

Venus Johnson put a hand on the back of Kelson's neck. 'I'm talking to you.'

Rodman glared at her. 'You don't want to do that.' His voice was gentle. Nothing else about him was.

She took her hand off. 'If you screwed up this investigation, I swear to God I'll—'

'None of that either,' Rodman said.

Emma Almonte smiled at Rodman and said to Johnson, 'I don't know him, but getting him mad seems like a bad idea.'

Kelson said to her, 'I like you.'

Venus Johnson eyed each of them, one after the other. 'Goddammit,' she said – then she turned to another cop and, gesturing at them, said, 'Separate cars. Downtown.'

FBI Special Agent Cynthia Poole visited Kelson in the interview room at the Harrison Street Police Station. She wore a charcoal-gray pantsuit with a white blouse and had tied her brown hair in a neat ponytail. She wore thick-framed glasses.

'Christ, what a cliché,' Kelson said. His hands were chained to a metal loop on a metal table.

'Excuse me?' She sat down across from him.

'Let me guess. Your dad was a cop. You grew up idolizing him, but he said no daughter of his would go into law enforcement. So you one-upped him by going FBI. You played sports in high school. Softball? Volleyball? In college, you studied criminal justice and minored in something useful – Spanish – no, *chemistry*, since they put you on a bomb investigation. You met your boyfriend at Quantico. Or your girlfriend. Girlfriend, right?'

'Has anyone told you to shut the fuck up?'

'Happens all the time. See, I took a bullet in my head, and I can't help—'

'I read your file,' she said.

'Then don't be too hard on me.'

'Don't make excuses for being an asshole,' she said. 'Why were you at Victor Almonte's house?'

'*Emma* Almonte's house,' Kelson said, 'where Victor was living. Same reason as you. Since leaving the department—'

'Getting fired,' she said.

He stared at her, speechless for a moment.

'Keep your facts straight,' she said.

'Since *getting kicked out on disability*,' he said, 'I've worked as a private investigator. One of my friends asked me to look into this after his nephew—'

'The nephew being James "Neto" LeCoeur,' she said.

'That's the one. I told Venus Johnson about him. He's—'

'A juvie hacker who grew up into an adult screwball –

unemployed for the past eight months after a series of short-term programming jobs which left almost all of the clients unsatisfied and some of their companies in disarray.'

'That's more than I knew.'

'Civil lawsuit pending from Vanguard Machines, where Neto rearranged the accounts payable system – without permission or authorization.'

'So you can read a report.'

'Why are you being a jerk?'

'Nancy – she's my ex – says it comes naturally. But I think it's because you cuffed me and dragged me downtown, and now you're treating me like a punk.'

'We could treat you worse. We've got cause.'

'Because I'll bet you found a load of bomb-making materials between Victor Almonte's two pairs of underwear? Maybe a couple kilos of C-4 in one of his socks? And that sister of his, you'd better watch out – she's got international terrorist connections coming out of her—'

'Enough.'

Someone knocked on the door, the door swung open, and a man came in. His brown street shoes were clean but worn, his slacks unpressed, his blue button-up shirt the same. He carried a manila folder. A tag hanging from a lanyard around his neck identified him as FBI Special Agent David Jenkins.

'*He* knows how to dress,' Kelson said. 'But *you* . . .'

The woman agent gestured at Kelson's face and said to the new man, 'See that scar on his forehead? He got shot in the brain when he worked on the narcotics squad.'

Jenkins eyed the scar. 'Cool.'

'It turned him into an asshole,' she said.

'I'm just open about my thoughts,' Kelson said. 'I've got what the doctors call disinhibition.'

'I see,' Jenkins said, and he took a third chair. He opened the manila folder, ignored the sheets of paper clipped together, and pulled two photographs from an envelope. He set the photographs on the table so the faces looked at Kelson. One was of Sue Ellen. She stood outside Nancy's house smiling at the photographer – maybe Nancy. The other was of Nancy. Dressed in dentist scrubs, she stared at the photographer as if thinking of yanking the photographer's incisors.

Kelson caught his breath. 'Which is to say, you're threatening me. That was quick. Where'd you get the pictures?'

'Your old supervisors had them here. Probably got them from your ex. I guess you've been in trouble before? Something that made your coworkers want to know what your family looked like if bad stuff happened to them.'

'And now I want my lawyer.'

'We're showing you the pictures so you know what's at stake,' Jenkins said. 'No threat. But it could've been them at the library. It could've been anyone. Your old boss says you mean well. But meaning well differs from doing well. You need to stay out of our way.' He picked up the photos of Sue Ellen and Nancy and gazed at them. 'Because next time it could be them.'

'No threat?' Kelson said.

'No threat.'

'I want my lawyer,' Kelson said. 'His name is Ed Davies.'

Jenkins put the photos in the envelope and put the envelope in the folder. 'You can go.'

'I can?'

'Why would we want to spend more time with an asshole?' Cynthia Poole said.

'How about my friend, DeMarcus Rodman?'

'We released him ten minutes ago,' Jenkins said. 'He's waiting for you outside.'

'Emma Almonte?'

'Let us worry about her.'

'She's innocent.'

Jenkins smiled as if Kelson was in over his head. The two agents left then, and Venus Johnson came in with a key for Kelson's cuffs.

'Nice people,' Kelson said, 'if you like that kind of people.'

Johnson released his left wrist.

Kelson said, 'The kind who twist your testicles and say, *Glad to meet you. Let's be friends.*'

Johnson released his right wrist.

Kelson said, 'Don't ever let them touch a picture of Sue Ellen or Nancy again.'

'For a weak guy, you talk tough,' she said. 'It's kind of cute.' She opened the interview room door to let him go.

Rodman was waiting for him on the sidewalk outside the station. The smell of car fumes and burning wood hung in the cool air. The big man looked at him hard. 'You all right?'

'Sure,' Kelson said. 'You?'

Rodman tipped his head in a nod. 'Fuckers.'

'They mean well,' Kelson said.

'Sure they do.'

Kelson pulled out his phone and dialed his lawyer. 'You need to find someone for me.'

'I thought that was *your* job,' Davies said.

'She's in the system. Emma Almonte.'

'The bomber's sister?'

'He didn't do it.'

'The news says—'

'Turn off the news, and listen to me. The FBI has her. Maybe at a CPD station, maybe someplace of their own. She's done nothing.'

'You sure about that?'

'Do I ever lie?'

'That's not what I asked.'

'You know what they'll do if they convince themselves. She won't have a chance.'

'I'll make some calls, and if no one will tell, I'll file a habeas corpus. But, you know, if they really want to hold her . . .'

'Yeah, I know.'

FIFTEEN

Kelson and Rodman took a cab back to Keeler Avenue to pick up Kelson's car. The FBI and Chicago police vehicles were gone, leaving only a trampled lawn in front of the tan house and a four-inch scratch on the driver's door of Kelson's Dodge Challenger. Someone had folded the rose-embroidered ribbon and set it on the steps to the front door.

Kelson drove toward the U of C Trauma Center, jabbering nonstop about Emma Almonte – her innocence, her standing up to Venus Johnson, her amazing lips – and about Johnson's failure to see what was what, though she should know better. Then he talked about the FBI agents' threats – if they *were* threats, and not warnings about what really could happen – with a few words here and there about the kittens and Sue Ellen, until Rodman started to hum.

'Am I saying too much?' Kelson said.

'No. It's like a weird rap. You should put it to a beat.'

'Sorry.'

'Never say you're sorry to me, man.'

Kelson dropped Rodman at the Trauma Center entrance and drove toward his office. He turned on the radio for the two o'clock news. When it came on, he learned only that he already knew more than the reporter did.

In a joint operation, the radio said, the FBI and Chicago Police raided the northwest-side house of Victor Almonte's sister. They took three or four individuals into custody, including Emma Almonte, age twenty-eight. 'With great lips,' Kelson told the radio reporter. A neighbor said the officers carried several boxes from the house. She said Emma Almonte was always 'so nice'. Victor 'kept to himself' and also was 'nice'. In the meantime, an unnamed source said the other dead victim, Amy Runeski, and her husband Tom were battling for custody of their daughter when the library blast killed Amy. 'Ah,' Kelson said, and he pulled to the side of the road. 'He's still in the mix.' With cars flashing past him, he spent ten minutes searching Google on his phone before finding an address for Tom Runeski at the corner of North Damen and Argyle. Then he cut back into the afternoon traffic.

The address took him to a courtyard apartment complex – three floors, plus basement rooms the realtor would call garden apartments. Across the street, Winnemac Park stretched out over sixteen city blocks, with muddy baseball fields, a soccer field surrounded by a running track, and a lot of open space.

Kelson parked, walked into the building courtyard, and found the intercom button for Tom and Amy Runeski. After he touched it a third time, a woman's voice answered.

'Tom Runeski?' Kelson said.

'He's done talking to reporters,' the woman said.

'Me too,' Kelson said.

When she said nothing more, he touched the button again.

'What?' A different woman's voice.

'My name's Sam Kelson. I do private investigations. The private part is kind of a joke. I used to be a cop, but now the police think I'm—'

'Go away,' the new woman said.

'They're coming,' Kelson said. 'Bombs scare the hell out of them. They'll have guns and tactical gear. They'll knock down the door if they need to. Or maybe a couple of them will come alone. They'll buzz the intercom, like me. They'll stand and talk with you – polite. By the time they're done, you'll have told them something you shouldn't have, and they'll put it on the news, and maybe they'll drag you downtown and lock you up because it's just enough, and you'll start thinking you would've preferred if they'd just knocked down the door because at least that would be honest.'

'Who *are* you?'

'Sam Kelson. I do private—'

The door buzzed.

'Thank you,' Kelson said, and went in.

Two women stood at the top of the first flight of stairs.

'Like trolls at a bridge,' Kelson said, then pointed at the older of them and said, 'His mother,' and the younger, 'His sister.' He asked the older one, 'Your son's inside?'

She said, 'You have no shame?'

'Tons and tons,' Kelson said, and started up the stairs.

The older woman blocked the top. 'Why should he talk to you?'

'I always tell the truth,' he said. 'And I have an open mind. The open mind's another joke – more like a hole in the head.'

'Please leave him alone,' the younger one said. Except for the six studs around the rim of her right ear, she looked a lot like her mother.

He said, 'Except for the studs in your ear—'

She said, 'Tom talked to the police. They know who did it. The homeless—'

'They're starting to doubt themselves,' Kelson said. 'They'll come back, and this time—'

A man spoke from inside an open door behind the women. 'Let him in.'

They frowned, but moved aside. As Kelson stepped past the older woman, she clutched his arm and said, 'I'm warning you.'

Tom Runeski stood in a bright living room holding his daughter, as if he'd just stepped off camera from the previous night's press conference.

'Are you for real or are you still posing?' Kelson said. 'Sorry, that's not fair. I have a daughter too.'

The man looked bewildered. He wore his wire-rimmed glasses tight against his face, his blond hair uncombed. His mother gazed at him like she wanted to hold *him* to her chest. He asked Kelson, 'What do you want?'

'First,' Kelson said, 'I need to know what you're like. When I worked as an undercover narcotics cop, we used an Asshole Test on the street dealers. We poked and picked at them – just enough to see how they took it and how we should handle them. On a one-to-five scale, anything above three we needed to watch out for.'

Runeski's sister took a step back. His mother started to object. But Runeski got a sad smile. 'Amy sometimes said I was an asshole. Look, we had a hard time. After Samantha was born, Amy became unhappy. With me. With' – he waved at the living room furniture – 'this.'

'She was divorcing you.'

'She said she outgrew me,' Runeski said.

'When my ex kicked me out, she said I shrank.'

Runeski gave him more of the sad smile.

'I really did,' Kelson said. 'I shrank – a part of me, gone. What's this about a child custody battle?'

Runeski looked like he was in shock, and Kelson wasn't helping. 'Amy wanted to move back to Wisconsin, where her parents live,' he said. 'We were working out the details.'

'When we did the Asshole Test, we also worried about anybody who was a *one*,' Kelson said. 'They weren't assholes. We called them victims.'

Runeski spoke softly. 'I'm no one's victim.'

'Don't be too sure,' Kelson said. 'When the police and FBI come back—'

'The homeless guy didn't do it?'

'If he did, he had help. But the police and FBI are still talking to reporters about your marriage problems, and that means they've got an eye on you. When they come, volunteer nothing. They need quick answers, so they'll take anything you tell them and stretch it to fit every possibility they can. They'll stretch it until it breaks, and maybe you'll break with it.'

'For an ex-cop, you're suspicious about other cops,' the man said.

'They're doing their job,' Kelson said. 'Most of them do it well. But doing it well sometimes hurts people – especially people who are already hurt.'

Runeski held the baby tighter.

Five minutes later, Kelson went downstairs and out through the courtyard. As he stepped on to the sidewalk, Venus Johnson and Special Agent David Jenkins got out of the front of a black SUV. Two men in squarely tailored gray suits got out of the back.

'Man, I'm good,' Kelson said.

'What the hell?' Johnson said.

Kelson gazed at the new men. 'Do they have special catalogs for you guys? Stores where only you can shop? Everything cut at right angles? A bunch of Lego people who work there?'

'I told you to stay away,' Johnson said.

Jenkins said, '*I* told you.'

'Yep, you both told me. Now you can go tell Tom Runeski whatever you want to tell him. You can tell his mom and sister too. You can put them wherever you're keeping Emma Almonte. You can even lock up the baby.'

'You know what?' Venus Johnson said. 'I hate the sound of your voice.'

'Funny, my friends think it sounds like music.'

The four officers jogged into the courtyard, and Kelson got in his car and called Rodman. He told him about Tom Runeski, his sister, and his mother. 'Cute baby,' he added.

'A cute baby makes him innocent?'

'It might,' Kelson said. 'Runeski didn't admit too much and didn't protest too much. Either he's a great faker or he's one of the walking wounded. How's Neto?'

'The doctor wants his organs.'

'Damn.'

'He says Neto's still got a chance – says never stop hoping. But he says it's the kind of chance where you need to decide what to do with the organs. The hospital wants Marty to sign off. Thing is, he isn't answering his phone.'

'Damn,' Kelson said again.

'Maybe he's so deep in the G&G computers, he can't hear the phone ringing. Maybe the G&G people took it away.'

'I'll go to G&G,' Kelson said.

'And do what?'

'Talk to them. I'm good at talking.'

Rodman laughed. 'Yeah, right – take a gun.'

So Kelson drove to his office to get one, rapping about Tom Runeski, babies, and G&G Private Equity as he moved through the streets.

He parked his car outside his building and rode the elevator to his office. Conversations buzzed inside the rooms where the company that shared his floor held training classes.

He put his key in the lock, but it met no resistance.

'Huh,' he said, and turned the knob.

Genevieve Bower sat in his client chair again. Bruises covered the right side of her face. Her right eye was swollen and black. She'd dug his Springfield from his bottom desk drawer and unstrapped his KelTec from its hidden rig. She'd set the KelTec on the desk, and she gripped the Springfield with both hands. She looked terrified as Kelson stepped into the office. He forced a smile at her, and her face eased. 'Oh,' she said, 'it's you.'

SIXTEEN

'One question,' Kelson said. 'How did you get in here this time? Another question. What happened to your face? And would you please keep your hands off my guns?'

For a moment Genevieve Bower stared at him. Then tears ran from her eyes, the good one and the swollen one. When she cried, her breasts quivered.

'Oh, don't do that,' Kelson said helplessly.

'They came for the thumb drive,' she said.

'The – who did? The one in Jeremy Oliver's van?'

'You said it wasn't there.'

'That's what I mean. The one I looked for.'

She sobbed, her body heaving.

'Please stop that,' he said.

'They beat me,' she said. 'They only let me go because I told them I would get it. I lied.'

'Who are they?'

'I–I can't tell you.'

The tears, the confusion, the quivering and heaving – Kelson felt the beginning of a headache. And a twitching eye. And an erection. He went to his desk and sat across from her. She put the Springfield into his outstretched hand. He popped the magazine, checked the ammunition, snapped the magazine back in place, and put the gun in its drawer. He left the KelTec on the desk. He breathed in deep and exhaled long, the way Dr P taught him. He said, 'I can't help you if you don't tell me who they are and why they want the thumb drive so badly. You said it has videos on it. Tell me about them.'

Her sobbing stopped, though her eyes remained wet and her bruises glistened. 'I shouldn't have come here,' she said. 'I knew . . .' She got up and started for the door.

'Come back.'

'Why? All I want is the thumb drive.' Her tears started again. 'The rest of it's mine to worry about – not yours or anyone else's.'

He pointed at the chair.

She came and sat.

He rubbed his forehead until the twitching stopped. He closed his eyes, as if he could free himself from his headache in the dark. He said, 'Your old boyfriend Marty LeCoeur has a nephew, Neto. Neto got blown up in the thing at the Rogers Park Library. Now Marty's in trouble. Maybe I am too.'

'I'm sorry,' she said, like she meant it.

'All I'm saying is, I've got a lot going on. I don't know what I can do for you.'

'Just find the thumb drive,' she said.

'I don't know where to start.'

'Jeremy had it.'

'First he had your shoes. Then he had your thumb drive.'

'I'll pay you.'

He breathed in deep and breathed out long. He took a pad of paper and a pen from the top desk drawer and slid them across the desk to her. 'Who were Jeremy's friends? Who did he trust? Anyone he might've given the drive to?'

She wrote two names Jeremy Oliver had mentioned in the short time they knew each other – Zoe Simmons, a friend of Oliver's since high school, and Rick Oliver, his cousin. 'They all grew up in Oak Park,' she said. 'Maybe you can find them.'

Kelson said, 'Let's say I tell you I'll do this, what happens to you next? You walk out of here, and these people grab you and put you in a room and hit you some more?'

She forced a little smile. 'They won't find me. I rented a motel room on—'

'Don't,' Kelson said. 'If anyone asks, I'll tell.'

'You'll look for the thumb drive?' she said.

The pain in Kelson's head pierced like a needle, from above his left eye back to his left ear. 'New rules,' he said. 'No coming into my office when I'm out. No touching my guns. No lying.'

She started to object.

'If you can't tell me something, say you can't,' he said. 'But no lying.'

'OK,' she said.

'And please cut out that quivering, heaving thing. It messes with my brain.'

'I've never met a man like you before,' she said.

'About a hundred fifty years ago, there was a railroad worker named Phineas Gage. An iron rod shot through his head. The rod ripped up his left frontal lobe, but less than a month later he was walking. A few years ago, a kid in Florida got shot through the brain with a fishing spear, but he seems to be fine now. But, yeah, we're a little club. You don't want to join.'

He showed her to the service elevator and explained how to leave through the back of the building. Ten minutes later, he tucked his KelTec into his belt, walked out of his office, and went to his car. He drove out of the city and inched northward through early-evening traffic toward G&G Private Equity. As he drove, he chatted with the radio reporters. When music came on, he sang along with the lyrics he knew. He made up the rest. Then he called Sue Ellen and asked about her day at school.

She said, 'I love polynomials now.'

'What did they do to change your mind?'

'Now I hate graph functions. Can I come over to play with Painter's Lane and Payday?'

'I'm working tonight, honey.'

'Good,' she said, 'I won't have to talk to you.'

'Funny,' he said.

Before they hung up, she said, 'Love you, Dad.'

'Love you too, honey. That's what hurts, right?'

'Nope,' she said.

'You're a smart kid.'

Kelson pulled into the G&G parking lot a few minutes before six. In the evening light, the late-May leaves on the little trees that dotted the edges of the parking lot looked so green they might burst. The white concrete panels on the outside of the G&G building, shadowed by the lowering sun, looked grimy.

Kelson went inside and rode the elevator to the third floor.

The receptionist gave no hint that she recognized Kelson from his last visit.

'Marty LeCoeur?' he asked her.

She had a pleasant smile. 'No one by that name works here.'

'Chip Voudreaux? Sylvia Crane or Harold Crane?'

'Of course.'

'Tell them Marty's friend Sam Kelson wants to talk to them.'

She raised her eyebrows. '*Marty's* friend.' She dialed into the inner office.

A minute later, Chip Voudreaux came out in a navy blue suit, pale-yellow shirt, and blue tie. He smiled at Kelson with his too-white teeth and said, 'Ah, Sam,' as if Kelson was a favorite client.

'Everyone here seems so *happy*,' Kelson said.

Voudreaux had a chummy laugh. 'Come . . .' He led Kelson to his office.

A thin-faced woman with expensive blond hair sat on a brown leather sofa against one of the walls. She wore a blue skirt and matching jacket, and the way she crossed her legs made Kelson think she wanted to kick someone.

Voudreaux introduced them. 'Sam Kelson – Sylvia Crane.'

'My pleasure,' she said, without apparent pleasure.

'Don't kick me,' Kelson said.

She made a little square of her mouth and glanced at Voudreaux. Voudreaux asked Kelson, 'What can we do for you?'

'Let me talk with Marty LeCoeur.'

'I don't see what good that would do. He's working on our problem. We're treating him well. Feeding him coffee. We even gave him a little pillow for his back. He asked for his girlfriend, but we didn't see how that would help.'

'So you locked him in a room with a computer and you won't let him talk to anyone?'

'Why would we lock it? We have security personnel to keep him where he belongs.'

'Be careful about angering him.'

Voudreaux's smile turned ironic. 'I think our men can handle him.'

'I've never seen it, but my friend DeMarcus says when Marty gets angry, he turns into a bull shark.'

The ironic smile grew. 'We'll take that risk.'

Sylvia Crane said to Voudreaux, 'We could hold this one too.'

Now Kelson smiled. 'Believe me, I'd annoy the hell out of you.'

'He has a point,' Voudreaux said.

'Only one way to get rid of me,' Kelson said. 'Let me see Marty.'

'Oh, there's more than one way,' Sylvia Crane said.

That made Kelson grin. 'You're tough – or you *try* to sound tough. I like hard women. My ex-wife Nancy's the toughest person I've ever known. She—'

'Stop,' Sylvia Crane said.

'She could kick your ass,' Kelson said. 'And mine. And' – he pointed a thumb at Voudreaux – 'she could knock his shiny white teeth out. But *you're* faking it. Tough talk. And the way you sit, you look like you want to boot someone. But I can tell.'

She uncrossed her legs and stood up. Kelson took a step back in case.

Voudreaux said to her, 'Maybe we let him see LeCoeur. Put his mind at rest.'

'Why do we want anyone's mind at rest?' she said. 'They need to know what happens.'

'What happens happens,' Voudreaux said. 'No harm in easing LeCoeur's worries – clearing his mind so he can work.'

Sylvia Crane glanced from Voudreaux to Kelson and back. She looked unhappy. 'Fine,' she said.

Kelson stared at her with a new understanding. '*You* call the shots here?'

They took Kelson down a narrow hall to a door guarded by a thick-shouldered man in khakis and a black-logoed G&G golf shirt. He had no gun.

'But you don't look like you'd need one,' Kelson told him.

The man nodded to Crane and Voudreaux and opened the door.

Marty sat at a white table in an all-white room lit by fluorescent ceiling strips. He worked on two side-by-side big-screened laptops. He seemed to have tightened into his small body. As he keyed numbers on to a big field of other numbers, he mumbled, 'Fuck, fuck, fuuuck.'

Voudreaux put on his toothy smile and said, 'Marty, my man, how's it coming?'

Marty jerked from the table and stared at Voudreaux and Crane like a feral cat. Then he noticed Kelson.

'Hey,' he said. 'How's Neto?'

Kelson hated to say it. 'Bad, Marty. Sorry.'

'Goddammit.'

'Yeah.'

'He need me?' Marty said.

'Not much anyone can do,' Kelson said. 'The doctor wants to know about his organs. You know, about donating them.'

Marty shook his head. 'That boy never gave away anything he could sell – never bought anything he could steal either.'

'The hospital wants your OK before they pull the plug.'

'Hell if they're getting it. Neto's a fighter. You watch – he'll—'

'The doctor says—'

'What the fuck's the doctor know?'

'He says—'

'Does he know Neto? *I* know Neto. The kid's a survivor. I ain't pulling the plug.'

Voudreaux said, 'Great reunion here – and pity about Neto – but we have zero time for this.'

Marty stared at Voudreaux's eyes like he would eat them.

Kelson stared at Voudreaux's too-white mouth. 'Your teeth look like they'd hurt,' he said. 'My ex-wife's a dentist, and she—'

Sylvia Crane said, 'Are you making progress, Mr LeCoeur?'

'Fuck if I know. This system you're using, any halfway smart high school kid with a bag of Cheetos could hack it. You give it to a guy like Neto, and you're asking for it. I don't blame victims, but you're fucked.'

'Just so we're clear, *you* recommended Neto for the job,' she said. 'We hold you responsible.'

'Why the fuck d'you think I'm here instead of sitting with Neto? But you can hold my fucking balls over a blowtorch, it changes nothing,' Marty said.

'You're a colorful individual, Mr LeCoeur,' Voudreaux said, 'and under other circumstances, we might appreciate color. Right now, we want results. What do you need to get this done?'

'Time,' Marty said. 'Luck. What I really need is Neto. The kid built walls inside walls inside walls.'

'What kind of time?' Voudreaux said.

'Without Neto? Weeks. Maybe a month. Maybe even then I can't do it.'

'We need it *now*,' Sylvia Crane said.

Kelson looked at her. 'When you say "now", do things just happen around here?'

'Almost always,' she said.

Kelson said to Marty, 'We've got to get you out of here.'

'Excuse me?' Voudreaux said.

'I'll stay,' Marty said.

Kelson said, 'D'you know what they'll do if you can't get their money?'

'That's why I'm here,' said the little man.

'Desperate people do dumb things,' Kelson said.

Voudreaux said, 'We aren't desperate.'

'Oh, come on. Look at you. Those teeth.' Kelson turned to Sylvia Crane. 'And you – you know you want to kick me. Everything about this place is frantic.'

Sylvia Crane said, 'Do you always make bad matters worse?'

'*Always*?' he said. 'No.'

For a moment she looked like she *would* kick him, and keep kicking until the police report read 'Unidentified Male' and the lab needed to use partial prints and DNA. Or maybe she'd call in security to do the job. But then she laughed at him.

Kelson frowned. 'That worries me more. Do you ever lose control?'

She turned to Marty. 'Get back to work. Let us know if you need anything – food, coffee, anything.' Then she said to Kelson, 'I'll show you out.'

She led him back through the narrow hall and past the receptionist. She walked him to the elevator and waited with him. When the elevator doors opened, she rested her fingers on his wrist and held him for a moment. 'Some advice, Mr Kelson,' she said. 'Next time you think of coming here, don't. Go to a movie instead. Go out for dinner. Spend some daddy-daughter time with – what's her name? Sue Ellen?'

'How do you—'

'Shh,' she said. 'Be smart, that's all. You can do that, can't you?'

SEVENTEEN

Kelson went home and cooked spaghetti. He poured a glass of wine and popped a Percocet. He told the kittens about his trip to Emma Almonte's house in the morning. He told them about Venus Johnson dragging him down to the Harrison Street Police Station. He told them about his visit with Tom Runeski and Runeski's baby girl in the afternoon. He told them about Genevieve Bower's reappearance.

But when he told them about his meeting with Sylvia Crane and Chip Voudreaux at G&G, he added a warning. 'Be careful. I've known people like them. When they get caught, everyone talks about their greed. But the money's just a side benefit. I think they get off on hurting people.'

After he ate, he let Payday and Painter's Lane lick the butter off the remaining spaghetti. 'Sure, live it up,' he told them.

He poured more wine, and when his phone rang, he said, 'Screw it,' but caller ID said *DeMarcus Rodman*, so he picked up and told Rodman about his trip to G&G.

Rodman seemed distracted. 'The doctor says Neto should make it through the night, but he doubts he'll get through tomorrow. Janet's at the hospital. I came home to shower.'

'What then?'

'I'll hit the streets,' Rodman said. 'Let's say Victor Almonte really did blow up the library. The questions haven't changed. Why'd he do it? Why that library? Why an hour before closing? How'd he get there? Where'd he get the explosives? Who saw him? Who talked with him? Someone always sees and talks. I'll go out tonight. I'll go back out tomorrow. We do what we're good at, right? I'll find every bastard who knows anything about Almonte. I'm lousy at sitting in a hospital waiting for a kid to die.'

'You're a good man, DeMarcus.'

'I don't know about the "good" part,' Rodman said.

Ten minutes after they hung up, Kelson's phone clacked to

tell him someone had sent a text. He ignored it and poured more wine. After another two glasses and another Percocet, he checked the message.

Nancy had texted, telling him she had an early meeting with her staff at the Healthy Smiles Dental Clinic and asking him to give Sue Ellen a ride to school. 'No need to own me if you can rent me,' he said. 'Whatever that means.' He texted back, *Of course.*

When he slept, he dreamed of the seventeen-year-old named Bicho who shot him in the head during a drug bust, gunfire ringing off the alley walls of an icy February night. In the dream, Bicho ate dinner with Kelson and Sue Ellen at Taquería Uptown. Bicho ordered a margarita and became angry when the restaurant wouldn't serve him. When Kelson explained that the counterman was showing no disrespect – the restaurant just didn't have a liquor license – Bicho wouldn't hear reason. He pulled out a black revolver and threatened to shoot the counterman. But then Sue Ellen kissed Bicho on the mouth, and he put away the gun and ate his *sopa de mariscos*.

Kelson woke from the dream in a panic, but after doing his breathing exercises, he closed his eyes again and slept peacefully.

At eight a.m. the next morning, his ringing phone woke him.

'I thought you were picking up Sue Ellen,' Nancy said when he answered.

'Oh shit,' he said.

'Bad answer,' Nancy said.

'Ten minutes,' he said.

'Dammit,' she said.

Eleven minutes later, Kelson pulled to the curb at Nancy's house. Nancy and Sue Ellen were waiting on the front porch.

Kelson jumped out. 'I'm sorry. I—'

'Daddy.' Sue Ellen grinned as if he could do no wrong.

Nancy glared at Kelson and said, 'Go.'

After dropping Sue Ellen at Hayt Elementary, Kelson drove to Rodman's Bronzeville apartment. Rodman, just back from talking with men and women who owned the streets and city parks after midnight, came to the door from the kitchen. His girlfriend Cindi, after a nightshift at Rush Medical, sat on the couch under the portrait of Malcolm X.

Rodman gave Kelson a mug of coffee, brought a cup of tea to Cindi, went back to the kitchen, and scrambled a half dozen eggs. When the three of them sat together at the dining table, Rodman forked a bite into his mouth and said, 'Emma Almonte lied.' He washed down the food with coffee. 'Two blocks from her house, there's a strip of auto body shops, a metal casting company, and a hair salon. A couple men sleep under the awning at an empty warehouse. A couple more drink all night in an alley next to the warehouse. The drunks said they never saw Victor Almonte. So I bought them a bottle of Smirnoff and hung out awhile. Then they said *maybe* they saw him some nights – *maybe* they drank with him sometimes. But Emma Almonte told us he liked to be alone – locked himself in his room. So I shook the sleepers awake and asked them about our man. Sure, they said, they knew Victor. One of them – a skinny guy – said Victor spooked him, talking about what he did in Afghanistan, what he'd seen, what he wanted to do to people who hated veterans. But the other guy said Victor was cool – he just had issues like everyone else. Point is, Victor went out and made the rounds, even though Emma Almonte told us he'd gone a hundred percent homebody.' Rodman paused to eat a piece of toast. 'Next I went to Rogers Park, by the library,' he said. 'Around the corner, there's a school with a playground – great place to get high at three in the morning on a spring night. Two guys and a girl I talked to never saw Victor Almonte. But they pointed me to someone else. So I went over by the railroad tracks a block from the library, and I kicked around in the weeds and bushes on the embankment until I found a little camp. The guy there must've been about a hundred years old, but he was sharp, *real* sharp. Nine-to-five, regular as a banker, he shakes a can for nickels outside the library. He said he saw Victor Almonte twice, once on the day the library blew up and once about a week before. He remembered because the first time Victor stuffed five bucks in his can, and the second time he gave him a twenty, a one, and a pocket of change – the old guy figured it was everything Victor had. The first time, Victor poked around outside the library, went in for a few minutes, came out, and poked around again. The second time, he went right in and didn't come back until the paramedics wheeled him out on a gurney.'

Rodman poured another cup of coffee and said, 'That's it.'

'So he did it,' Cindi said.

'Looks like,' Rodman said.

Kelson said, 'But, as you said, *why*?'

Cindi looked tired. 'He comes back from his tour hurt. More in the head than the body. He can't sleep – spends too much time alone – sneaks out now and then when his sister's in bed or at work. Maybe he goes on the internet or watches TV and sees something that angers him in Rogers Park. Or maybe a girl from Rogers Park broke his heart once. Don't overthink it, 'cause maybe you'll never know. Every night at Rush, we get patients who're so broken inside, the stitches we sew them up with and the pills we give them for the pain don't even start to heal them. If we ask for their story, they take us to crazy places. Sometimes we're afraid to ask. Sometimes we don't want to know.'

Kelson said, 'Where'd Almonte get the explosives? You think he traded the alley drunks a bottle of Smirnoff for them? Everything about this blast makes it look like he targeted a place and time – maybe specific people – and went after them. Unless we find out he thought ISIS wrote library books or the reference librarian ran off with his best friend, we need to know the story.'

Cindi said, 'You know how many times I've heard parents and wives and husbands bawling when the doctors gave them the news and asking, "Why, why, why?"'

Rodman downed his coffee, sat back in his chair, and crossed his big arms over his big chest. He said to Kelson, 'You're right, though. We need the story.'

'You all think what you want,' Cindi said. 'You haven't seen what I have. Sometimes when we try to explain the reasons to the parents and wives and husbands, it just makes the hurt worse.' She carried her plate into the kitchen, then disappeared into the bedroom to sleep.

'She's wiped out,' Rodman said.

'But she's right,' Kelson said. 'We all disagree and we're all right.'

EIGHTEEN

At ten thirty, Kelson drove to his office, listening to the radio. As he pulled into a spot in the parking garage, the news came on. The police and FBI had named Victor Almonte as the certain perpetrator and called the blast a suicide bombing. A man who served with Victor in Jalalabad said everyone in the platoon loved him, though he seemed to blame himself after his best friend died while trying to disarm the IED. Another reporter said that one of the library victims had moved to a rehab facility, three remained hospitalized, and the fifth had gone home. The reporter identified the hospitalized. Vickie O'Brien, eighteen years old, a high school senior planning to go to Roosevelt University the following fall, was in critical but stable condition. Randy Belford, fifty-five and unemployed, had gone home and then returned with an infection. James 'Neto' LeCoeur, a twenty-three-year-old computer technician, was in very critical condition, with life-threatening injuries. 'Bring out your dead,' Kelson said to the reporter. When the news ended and Kelson turned off the engine, the air in the car smelled of exhaust fumes. 'No need to kill myself,' he said, and got out.

He went up to his office, nodded at the picture of Sue Ellen, and turned on his laptop. He needed to put in some hours for Genevieve Bower. The laptop screen lit up, and Kelson said, 'Bruised, battered – and screwy too.' He added without meaning to, 'With truly amazing breasts.' He shook his head at himself. 'One of these days . . .'

He picked up his research where he'd left off – looking for Jeremy Oliver's Oak Park friend Zoe Simmons and his cousin Rick. Oliver might have given one of them Genevieve Bower's red thumb drive. Or they might be able to tell Kelson where else to look.

'What's on it?' he asked the laptop. 'Dirty pictures?' He imagined what Genevieve Bower would like to do, what she might want to try. 'Stop it,' he told himself, and he typed Zoe

Simmons's name into Google, adding other search terms – 'high school', since Genevieve Bower said Oliver had known her since then, and then '80s dance music'.

He discovered that a lot of high school girls named Zoe colored their hair fuchsia, and more than a few did gymnastics. He also discovered that a woman named Zoe posted Pinterest pictures of an old Richard Simmons dance workout.

So he searched 'Zoe Simmons' alongside 'Jimmy Choo'. 'Ha,' he said when a link to a Reddit post appeared. The post – put up eight days earlier – showed a skinny, black-haired woman in pink tennis shoes with what looked like patches of carpet on the sides of them. The post said 'Me and My Jimmys' and added 'You the Best Jolly'. 'Score,' Kelson said – then realized he still didn't know how to find her. 'Or not.'

He searched 'Rick Oliver' and 'Richard Oliver' with the terms 'Jeremy' and 'JollyOllie' and '80s DJ'. Nothing. He searched with 'Jimmy Choo'. Nothing. He searched with 'dead cousin' and 'missing cousin'. Nothing.

He called Genevieve Bower.

She answered on the first ring. 'Did you find it?'

'What did Oliver tell you about his cousin?' Kelson said.

'Just he plays lacrosse – and he's gay.'

'You couldn't've told me that before?'

'I didn't think—'

He hung up before she could finish answering.

Then he searched 'Rick Oliver' with 'lacrosse' and 'Chicago'. A link gave him a registration roster for New Wave Lacrosse, which organized a local lacrosse league. Rick Oliver had signed up for a winter indoor tournament. He listed no phone but gave a northside address. 'Score,' Kelson said again. 'Or *goal*. Or whatever.'

He turned off the computer, put it in its drawer, and headed for the door. Then he turned back and got his KelTec. He tucked the pistol in his belt and said, 'Because I'm not a complete fool.'

Rick Oliver lived with his boyfriend on the bottom floor of a greystone three-flat on Roscoe Street, east of Halsted. Kelson parked behind a green dumpster in an alley a couple doors away, climbed the front steps, and rang the bell. When no one answered, he rang again. When no one answered again, he went back down the steps.

Then the door opened behind him. A thin, barefoot man in blue jeans stared down at him. He looked annoyed. 'Yes?'

'Rick Oliver?' Kelson asked.

The man yelled into the house, '*Richard.*'

Another man – tall and wide – came to the door. He wore a red jersey and matching shorts. Except for pads and helmet, he looked ready to play.

'Yes?' he said – same attitude as the first man.

Kelson said, 'You not only play lacrosse, you *are* lacrosse.'

'Excuse me?'

'Are you Jeremy Oliver's cousin?'

'Are you another cop?'

'I used to be. Then I got shot in the head, and I became more of a liability than an asset – apparently. Now I—'

'What do you want?' he said.

'Genevieve Bower's thumb drive.'

'Whose what?'

'Your cousin dated her.'

'Jeremy? Never heard of her. Why are you here?'

'That's a complicated question,' Kelson said. 'What did the police tell you about Jeremy?'

'He's missing. They found his van.'

'He isn't missing,' Kelson said. 'He's dead. Or he's dead *and* he's missing.'

That worried the man some. 'What are you talking about? They said—'

'I saw him – his body. I called the police. Then I left, and they came, but your cousin was gone – hell if I know where. He got shot right here' – he touched his forehead above his left eye – 'which is where I got shot too, but with different results.'

The boyfriend said, 'You're freaking me out.'

'Call nine-one-one,' Rick Oliver said to him.

'Why?' Kelson said. 'What did I say?'

'I don't know who you are, but the detective who talked to me said nothing about Jeremy being killed.'

'Was the detective's name Dan Peters?' Kelson said.

Rick Oliver squinted at him. 'Yeah.'

'He means well,' Kelson said.

The boyfriend had his phone out. 'Should I?' he asked Oliver's cousin.

'If you do, ask for Peters,' Kelson said. 'Tell him Sam Kelson came by.'

'He'll vouch for you?' Rick Oliver said.

'He'll tell you to chase me away with a stick. But you don't need to. I'll go. But answer two questions first. If Jeremy stole someone's thumb drive, where would he hide it?'

'I don't know why he'd steal a thumb drive, but until his van burned he lived his life out of it and his apartment. Or maybe he'd give it to me to hold on to. I don't know where else.'

'And where can I find Zoe Simmons?'

Rick Oliver looked down at him with contempt. 'Do you really think I'd tell you how to hassle my friends?'

NINETEEN

So Kelson left and drove a half mile from the greystone to the bungalow on North Hermitage where Jeremy Oliver had lived. After finding him dead in the dormered attic, Kelson had talked to Bruce McCall, who'd rented Oliver the apartment and detached garage and who'd also said Oliver ran his whole life from the van. The van was a bust, but Kelson hadn't searched the garage, and he'd given the attic only a quick look before skipping out.

Now, he walked around to the back of the house and went to the garage. He tried the handle on the big garage door. Locked. He went to the little side door and looked through the window into the dark. Like last time, he saw two bikes along the far wall and gardening tools in a corner. He tried the knob. Locked. So he smacked his elbow against the windowpane closest to the knob. It shattered on to the garage floor. 'Bad, bad idea,' Kelson said. He reached through the broken pane and unlocked the door. 'Why do I think this is acceptable?' He stepped inside. 'Or smart?'

The air in the garage was cool and smelled of dirt and motor oil. Kelson left off the light and walked around the open space, peering into the gaps between the two-by-fours on the unfinished walls. He pulled the bikes into the middle of the room, inspected them, and looked at the wall where they'd stood. He took a garden shovel from the corner, laid it on the floor, and did the same with a broom, a rake, and another shovel. He rooted through a basket of spades, clippers, and loppers. Something – the dustlessness, the way the tools rested against each other – made him think another person had come into the garage and searched it. 'But with a key,' he told the broom, as he put it back in the corner.

'Screw it,' he said, and he went back to the door and hit a switch that turned on a single bulb hanging from the middle of the garage ceiling. He gazed at the two-by-four ceiling beams. If a thumb drive lay on one of them, he couldn't see it. Maybe Jeremy Oliver kept a stepladder in his kitchen pantry. Or maybe Kelson would find the thumb drive in the dormered apartment and wouldn't need a ladder.

He left the garage, crossed the yard, and went up the stairs to the attic door. He tried the knob. Locked too. He tapped the window, loud enough for anyone inside to hear. No one heard. He smacked another pane with his elbow, reached inside, and let himself in. 'Here we go again,' he said.

The kitchen looked and smelled as it did on the day when Kelson found Oliver's body. 'Which means nothing,' he said, and opened the pantry.

The pantry had shelves of mac and cheese, Chex Mix, tomato sauce, and instant oatmeal. There were also a lot of cans of green beans. No ladder. Kelson pulled a vacuum out from under the shelves, opened the dirt canister, and stirred the inside with a finger. Dust. 'Figures,' he said. He went to the sink and tried the drawers and cabinets. They held the stuff that kitchen drawers and cabinets hold.

He searched the bedroom closet and removed the dresser drawers in case Oliver had taped the thumb drive to the back of one of them. In the bathroom, he checked the medicine cabinet and stood on the toilet to peer into the exhaust fan.

He said, 'Why bother?' and went into the living room. He checked under the couch cushions – sure now, without good reason, that someone else had gone through the house just as he was going through it. He moved the furniture from the walls, peered under it, and pushed it back where it belonged. Peters had told him about a bullet hole near the shelves. Kelson found it and stuck the tip of his pinkie into it. 'Like a hole in the head,' he said.

He went back through the hall to the kitchen. 'Due diligence,' he said.

He went outside and downstairs into the yard. As he started along the side of the house, a paunchy man in his sixties came out the back door of the house downstairs. He smiled like the kind of man who smiles easily and often. 'Hey there,' he said, 'you a friend of Jeremy?'

'Hardly,' Kelson said. 'Are you Bruce McCall?'

The man smiled. 'Hardly. I heard you upstairs and thought Jeremy came home.'

'Unlikely,' Kelson said. 'Does Bruce McCall live here?'

'I'm his tenant,' the man said. 'Mr McCall owns a bunch of properties in the neighborhood. You mind if I ask what you were doing up there?'

'Looking for a thumb drive,' Kelson said. 'And a stepladder. Do you have one? – I mean a stepladder.'

The smile stayed on the man's face, but he got a look in his eyes that Kelson saw often when talking to strangers. 'Why were you . . .'

Kelson smiled back. 'Do you watch Jeremy's place when he's gone? You see anyone up there lately?'

'No one that doesn't belong,' the man said. 'Except you.'

'Good to have neighbors,' Kelson said. 'I live in a high-rise, and you'd think everyone would watch out for each other, but—'

The smiling man's smile started to fall. 'Is there anything I can help you with?'

'Unless you have a stepladder or want to hold my feet while I do chin-ups on the garage beams, you can tell me where Bruce McCall has his office.'

'No office,' the man said. 'This is like his hobby. He works out of his house. His wife's dad runs some kind of big-money company. What do you want up in the garage beams?'

'A thumb drive. Never know where someone might hide it.'

'I see,' the man said, and, like so many others, he seemed

to dismiss Kelson as harmless and confused. 'Well, I can't help you there.'

'Nope, you've reached your limit.' Kelson turned to leave.

The man sounded as firm as he probably ever could. 'Don't come back unless you're with Jeremy, OK? Or Bruce McCall. Or someone who belongs here.'

'I see no reason I'd want to,' Kelson said. He got halfway to the front of the house before turning back again.

The smiling man was climbing the stairs to check on Oliver's apartment. He stopped when he saw Kelson.

'One more thing,' Kelson said. 'Do you know the name of the company owned by Bruce McCall's father-in-law?'

For some reason, that triggered another little smile. 'Don't remember the name. It's one of those places you know about if you've got the money to know about it. If you aren't loaded, don't knock.'

Kelson said, 'Could it be G&G Private Equity?'

The man's smile widened. 'That's it. G&G. Marry a woman like that or win the lottery – either one'll do for me.'

TWENTY

Kelson sat in his car in front of the bungalow and dialed Genevieve Bower's number.

It rang four times and bounced to voicemail.

'What the hell?' Kelson said to the recorder. 'What's with JollyOllie and G&G? You don't – you don't drag me into something like this without telling me. People like Chip Voudreaux and Sylvia Crane don't care about you and your shoes and your screwball boyfriend and your – Jesus Christ, just call me.' He hung up, stared at his phone, then called her again and managed to stay calm. 'All right,' he told the recorder. 'Part two. I get it now. You told G&G about Marty. That's how they got in touch with him and how he gave them Neto and how Neto got blown up in the library. And Marty mentioned me to you. That's how you called me and I got busted at Big Pie Pizza and all the rest.

So that fits. But how does Jeremy Oliver come into it? I guess what I'm asking is, what's on the thumb drive?'

He hung up again, then looked through his call history until he found Bruce McCall's number. He dialed it.

McCall answered, and Kelson said, 'I talked with you before about Jeremy Oliver and the garage he rented from you.'

'How could I forget?' McCall said.

'Why didn't you tell me your wife's the daughter of the owner of G&G Private Equity?'

McCall sounded impatient. 'What does Sylvia have to do with it?'

Kelson barked a laugh. 'Wait, your wife is Sylvia Crane?'

'Of course.'

'God help you, you like them mean.'

'Excuse me?'

'Me too. The meaner, the better. Sexy, right? My ex-wife—'

'I'm going to hang up now,' McCall said.

But the synapses in Kelson's broken brain were firing free. 'Does her dad look like a weird old blue-eyed ostrich – with a beak of a nose?'

McCall hung up.

Kelson breathed in deep, breathed out long, and dialed again.

'How does the family know Genevieve Bower?' he said when McCall picked up.

'Who?'

'Dammit, you don't see a woman like her and forget her. You just don't.'

McCall hung up again.

'Dammit,' Kelson said.

He called Rodman, catching him in his car, and told him about the connection between Jeremy Oliver and the investment firm.

'Yeah,' Rodman said, 'makes sense.'

'It does?'

'Sure. Marty keeps screwed-up company. He's a great friend, but hanging with him's like climbing into a bag of spiders. His heart's in the right place, though.'

'Next time, remind me not to hang with him.'

'Your heart's in the right place too,' Rodman said. 'What're you up to now?'

'Trying to pull spiders out of my hair. Soon as I can, I'll talk to Genevieve Bower – make her tell me what's on the thumb drive and what this is all about. Meantime, I'll track down Oliver's friend Zoe Simmons.'

'Careful,' Rodman said. 'If G&G's involved in what happened to Oliver, they're showing their teeth.'

'What are *you* up to?' Kelson asked.

'Heading to U of C,' he said. 'Janet called. She thinks Neto's going down for the count.'

'It all crashes,' Kelson said.

'Some days are like that.'

'Some lives,' Kelson said.

Next, Kelson dialed directory assistance and got the phone number to Rick Oliver's greystone on Roscoe. He called and the boyfriend said Rick had gone out. So Kelson talked to the boyfriend for a while. He told him about Genevieve Bower hiring him, about finding Jeremy Oliver dead in the attic apartment, about Genevieve Bower showing up in his office with a black eye and bruises – and about how locating Zoe Simmons might help stop the pain. He told him about Neto taking the G&G job and getting blown up and probably dying at the hospital – and about how locating Zoe Simmons might ease that pain too, since she was connected to JollyOllie and therefore Genevieve Bower, and so on. He told him about Sue Ellen and the kittens spending too much time alone since he was busy with these tangled cases – and about how locating Zoe Simmons might also allow him to spend more time with them.

The boyfriend could have hung up. He could have told Kelson to shut his mouth. Instead, he asked, 'Do most people think you're a dumbshit?'

'Some do,' Kelson said. 'Not many.'

'Zoe lives in the house next door to ours,' the boyfriend said. 'She was watching out the window the whole time you talked to Richard.'

'I didn't see her,' Kelson said.

'I know. Do you miss a lot?'

'Some,' Kelson said.

*   *   *

A half hour later, when Kelson knocked on Zoe Simmons's door, a skinny woman with black hair answered. Kelson looked at her shoes. Pink with carpet patches stuck on the sides. 'Jimmy Choos,' he said.

She laughed. She had a crooked smile, as if something had happened to her jaw.

'You're pretty anyway,' he said.

The crooked smile did something mischievous. 'Not you. What happened?' She gestured at the scar above his eye.

'A kid shot me.'

'Ouch.'

'Yep. Are you Zoe Simmons?'

She did a weird half curtsy. 'Speaking.' She turned and walked into the house, leaving the door open. He followed her into a living room furnished with cheap chairs, a cheap table, and a futon couch of the kind college kids have – and thirty-year-olds still trying to earn enough to replace their college furniture. She sat on the futon and swung her fake Jimmy Choos over the side.

He said, 'I'm—'

'The guy pestering Rick a while ago. I know – I saw you.'

'Rick's boyfriend told me you live here, when I called.'

'Because *I* told him to tell you when he said you asked about Jeremy and Genevieve. I've been friends with Rick all my life. We lived three houses away when I was growing up, and look at us now – next-door neighbors again.' She had the affected, showy voice of a bad actor. 'But Jeremy is only friends with Jeremy. Do I like him? No. But do I want him dead? No. Am I sorry if he really is dead – and by the way, you're the only one who's said so? Sure. Do I want him alive the same way I want everyone else alive, because death sucks? Yeah. But will I cry a lot if he's gone? Not much. Jeremy's always been a jerk. I never talked to him except he wanted something from me.'

Kelson clapped once because he thought she was performing for him. 'Did he ever mention a business called G&G?'

'If it didn't have the word "gimme" attached to it, he didn't say it.'

'When did you last talk?'

'That's why I told Rick's boyfriend to tell you where to find me. Eight days ago, Jeremy came by and I thought right away he wanted something. But he gave me these.' She pointed the toes of the fake Jimmy Choos at Kelson. 'Jeremy never gave me anything before – and then, magic slippers, right?'

'What did he want from you?'

'Nothing – or almost nothing, which freaked me out, like he was going to tell me he was pregnant with my baby. He just wanted me to hold on to a thumb drive.'

Kelson blinked. 'Give it to me.'

'What?'

'Sorry. Is it red? Can I see it? It's Genevieve Bower's. She hired me to get it back.'

'That's the thing. He changed his mind. I asked what was on it, and he got squirrelly and said he'd keep it. He didn't even ask for the shoes back. That was a new Jeremy. Next thing I knew, he disappeared, and now you say he's dead.'

'He didn't let you see what was on it?'

'He didn't even let me touch it.'

Kelson pushed for information about where Oliver might have hidden the thumb drive, and when she said she didn't know, he gave her a card and asked her to call if she thought of anything. Then she invited him to a performance of Chekhov's *Cherry Orchard* at the Rat and Thimble Theater in the Back of the Yards neighborhood. She was playing Anya. All of the actors were wearing black leather, and Anya's love interest Peter Trofimov would ride on to stage on a Harley-Davidson.

Kelson walked out to his car. He leaned against the hood and dialed Genevieve Bower.

Again the call went to voicemail.

'Part three,' he said to the recorder. 'I'm waiting for your call. I want to know about you and G&G. No lies. Part four. I talked to Rick Oliver and Zoe Simmons about the thumb drive. Unless you can give me something, I'm looking at a wall.'

He got into the car and started the engine, but before he could pull from the curb, his phone rang.

He snatched it to his ear. 'About time. Tell me about G&G.'

But Rodman spoke to him – gentle, calm, sad. 'Neto's gone, man.'

'Shit,' Kelson said, and cut the engine.

'Yeah, shoulder deep.'

'Marty needs to know.'

'I should do it,' Rodman said, 'but I've got to stay here awhile. Janet's in pieces.'

'I don't want to picture that,' Kelson said. 'I'll tell him.'

'You sure you're up to it?'

'I know I'm not.'

TWENTY-ONE

Forty minutes later, Kelson walked back into the G&G office and told the receptionist, 'I need to see Marty LeCoeur.' When she picked up the phone to tell Chip Voudreaux and Sylvia Crane that he'd returned, he stepped around her desk and went up the hallway toward Voudreaux's office and the internal room where Marty was working. 'The things I do,' he said. The receptionist shouted after him, but he rounded a corner and then another and startled the thick-shouldered guard at the door to the internal room.

'Message for Mr LeCoeur,' Kelson said.

The guard said, 'Uhh . . .'

'Thick-headed too?' Kelson said. 'This is life and death. Or just death.' He opened the door and walked past the guard into the room.

Marty's fingers did something to the keyboard that sounded like a little drum.

'Marty,' Kelson said and, when the little man said nothing, only leaning into the screen of one of the side-by-side laptops as if he would join himself to it, said his name again. 'Marty—'

'Shh.' His eyes on the screen. 'I *got* it – maybe. I . . .' His fingers drummed the keys. Then he stopped typing, checked one screen against the other, and started again. Something like bliss showed on his face.

'Beautiful,' Kelson said, 'in its own strange way. Almost like love, right?'

'Be' – Marty's fingers swept across the keyboard, and new

numbers appeared on the screen – 'fucking' – his fingers pattered and pattered – 'quiet.'

Kelson watched for a few moments, then said what he needed to say. 'Neto's dead.'

Marty's fingers broke rhythm, as if reacting to a muscle spasm. He seemed to try to force himself through Kelson's words back into the work he was doing.

Kelson said, 'I'm sorry.'

Marty stopped typing. He stared at the screens as if the numbers were disintegrating. 'Neto?' he said.

'Yeah,' Kelson said. 'DeMarcus called. I'm sorry.'

Marty's hand hung above the keyboard as if phantom muscles might go back to work, unwilled by his mind. Then his little body seemed to contract. Kelson expected him to cry. But Marty gripped one of the laptops and flung it against the wall.

Kelson went to it and toed the screen, which had detached from the base. Still wired, it displayed four columns of numbers and dates.

He looked at Marty and said again, 'I'm sorry.'

The little man burst from his chair in a rage unlike any Kelson had ever seen. He picked up the other laptop and hurled it against the same wall. It burst into pieces.

The thick-shouldered guard rushed in and tried to restrain him. But Marty seemed to turn into a muscle – all torque and spring. One of his little legs flashed out and smashed the guard in the thigh. Then he did something vicious to the guard's ear with two of his knuckles, and the guard crashed to the floor.

'Really?' Kelson said.

Marty stared at the damage – the wrecked laptops, the downed guard. 'I need to see Neto,' he said. 'Let's get the fuck out of here.'

'Seems like a good idea,' Kelson said.

TWENTY-TWO

J anet was crying in the private waiting room when Kelson and Marty walked in. Draped over the side of her chair, she was mashing her head and body against Rodman, who sat next to her. Her face was blotchy and wet.

She looked up at Marty, groaned, pulled herself from Rodman, and consumed the little man in her big arms. 'Jesus Christ, Marty,' she said, 'I wanna kill someone.'

'Yeah, baby, me too,' he said.

After a while, a grief counselor came in and took Marty and Janet to see Neto.

Kelson sank into the chair where Janet had sat. 'He's a hard little man,' he said.

'He hurt anyone at G&G when he heard the news?'

'He knocked out a guard about twice his size.'

'They got off easy.'

'He didn't say a word on the drive here. I thought he'd cry, but his eyes turned to ice.'

'I've seen it,' Rodman said. 'I watched him take down a bunch of big guys at Streeter's Tavern once. I sat back and waited for him to ask for help. He hit the last of them over the head with a stool, then dragged the stool – covered with the guy's blood – over to the bar and ordered a piña colada. Marty drinks beer and whiskey. Hates everything else. But he ordered a girly drink to make a point. And he drank it like he liked it.'

'A hard little man,' Kelson said again. 'G&G will come after him. You think he can handle them?'

'Even a volcano's got limits.'

'Can you take him home with you – keep him safe?'

'Sure,' Rodman said, 'though the G&G people know who I am too.'

'Do they want to take on *two* volcanoes?'

Rodman lowered his eyelids halfway. 'Me? I'm the gentlest man I know.'

Kelson left Rodman to deal with Marty, and he drove to his office. As he walked out of the parking garage he said to the attendant, 'Cherish every moment.'

The attendant said, 'Sometimes I wish you'd keep your thoughts to yourself.'

'Me too,' Kelson said.

In his office, he strapped the KelTec under the desktop and checked the Springfield in its drawer. He considered the picture of Sue Ellen, considered the picture of the kittens, considered the picture of Sue Ellen again, and said, 'Hi, honey.'

Her picture stared at him with those eyes he loved.

'Some days like this,' he said. 'Some lives.'

He sat and stared at his closed office door. He asked it, 'Who next? What monster?'

He unstrapped the KelTec and laid it on his desk, the barrel facing the door. 'Really?' he asked it. He took its silence to mean . . . *maybe*.

Then his phone rang, making him jump. Caller ID said *G&G Private Equity*, and a sound like *henh* came from his mouth. He answered, 'Sam Kelson – as if you didn't know that.'

A man identifying himself as Sylvia Crane's assistant asked if Kelson would come to G&G to discuss a possible job.

'What kind of job?' Kelson said.

'I imagine that's what Ms Crane would like to discuss with you,' the assistant said.

'I'm not big on half answers,' Kelson said.

'Ms Crane isn't big on employees who ask too many questions and fail to do what they're told.'

'Sounds like a bad fit,' Kelson said, and hung up.

A minute later, his phone rang again. Sylvia Crane herself.

'What the hell's your problem?' she said.

'That's a long list, Ms Crane.'

'Will you or won't you come to my office?'

'I doubt it,' he said. 'You people scare me – sending Neto out on a little chore that gets him killed, locking up Marty LeCoeur in a workroom. Bad things happen around you. Sometimes you make them happen. How do I know I'll walk out of your office again if I walk in?'

'The job pays well.'

'Oh, then sure – you can stick a gun in my mouth if you promise to tuck a few bills in my panties.'

'You wear panties?'

'A metaphor. I suffer from disinhibition, not a lack of imagination.'

'The job has nothing to do with the LeCoeurs or the money Neto LeCoeur stole. You're safe with me.'

'I doubt that,' he said, then realized. 'It has to do with Genevieve Bower?' When she said nothing, he said, 'Sometimes I impress myself. I lost a lot when I got shot in the head, but I think I make these leaps better. My therapist says that's my brain compensating.'

'Will you come to talk about the job?'

'Will you and your people keep your hands to yourselves?'

'If you don't want the job you can walk away and we'll never see or talk to each other again.'

'I don't trust you,' he said. 'How's the security guard Marty punched?'

'Fired. Other than that, bruised and humiliated. Are you coming?'

'I'll tell you what – you want me to work for you, you can come here to talk about it, and you can leave your security thugs behind.'

She hesitated, then said, 'If those are your wishes.'

An hour later, Sylvia Crane sat in Kelson's office. She glanced past him at the pictures of Sue Ellen and the kittens. 'Cute,' she said.

'Unnecessary small talk,' he said.

'You don't care for it?' She seemed to be working hard to make her angular face look friendly.

'I care for *every* kind of talk. But right now, I'd like you to tell me what the job is and then leave.'

'You're a strange man, but I'll overlook that,' she said. 'I understand you're a former police officer. G&G has a history of positive dealings with law enforcement. We demonstrate our appreciation for the police, and they find ways to work with us. We prefer cooperation to force. Do you?'

'What's the job?'

'We're missing a copy of some files.' She stopped trying to look friendly, and that made Kelson like her better. 'From what my husband Bruce tells me, you know about this copy. We'd like to pay you to retrieve it.'

'Genevieve Bower's thumb drive.'

'As I'm sure you know, we can outbid her for it.'

'One problem. She already hired me. I sold my services.'

'What's she paying you? A couple thousand?'

'More or less,' Kelson said.

'What if we add a zero? Would that eliminate questions about professional ethics? Say, twenty thousand for a week's work? Double it if you need more time? Double it anyway, as a reward for your quick work?'

'Let's say that would do it for me,' Kelson said. 'I could justify taking the job. Genevieve Bower has lied and told me half truths. But I still have a problem. If I took your money and cheated her out of hers, I would give all the details to anyone who asked – and a lot of people who didn't. That's the disinhibition talking. Then, if new clients asked if they could trust me, I would tell them *no* – or I'd tell them *yes*, but only if no one offered me a better deal. You see how that would wreck my business? What's on the thumb drive?'

'We want it back because it's private and compromising. We want to hire you instead of going to the police because – again – it's private and compromising.'

'"Compromising" is a funny word. It can mean embarrassing or it can mean illegal.'

'Let's say it means both. Nothing *I've* done personally. But the videos on the drive would affect me and those I love in damaging ways. I would like to stop that from happening. I would like you to help.'

'Who's Genevieve Bower to you?' he said. 'I looked online but couldn't find a connection. Why does she want the videos? Why do you?'

Sylvia Crane crossed her legs. 'You understand, for the same reasons of privacy, I can't talk about her.'

'Sorry, that won't do. Everyone wants to keep secrets from me, but I can't work that way.'

Sylvia Crane frowned. 'Let's say Genevieve Bower appears on one of the videos along with someone I care deeply for.'

'Huh – she's got a bad habit with cameras, doesn't she? Who's Jeremy Oliver to you?'

'My husband says Oliver rents an apartment from him, and there've been problems – he disappeared. Bruce says you told him he's dead.'

'Are you really going to do that?'

'What?'

'I told you I could almost justify taking your job because Genevieve Bower lied to me, and now you give me this crap. Oliver stole the thumb drive from Genevieve Bower, so he knew or found out what was on it. Now he's dead – I saw him. And someone torched his van, and – I tell you this because you're really annoying me – someone searched his apartment. I'm guessing that person was looking for the same thumb drive you and Genevieve Bower want. But you're saying you don't know of a connection to him?'

Her face flushed. 'I'm sure there must be one, but I don't know of it.'

Kelson stood up at his desk. 'You can leave now.'

'Just like that?'

'Just like *what*? I told you why – and no one *ever* says I tell them too little.'

'We're talking about people's lives,' she said.

He laughed at her. 'From what I see, you screw with people's lives every day – moving money around in secret, hiring guys like Marty and Neto LeCoeur to do your dirty accounting.'

'My *family's* lives,' she said. Something in her angular features seemed to be splintering.

'Someone's threatening you?'

'The *way* we live.'

'Nothing about the way you live looks worth sacrificing much to save.'

'I've made sacrifices too.' Her eyes looked as incapable of tears as Marty LeCoeur's. But they showed pain. 'Sacrifices you can't imagine.'

Kelson stared at her, then lowered himself into the chair again. 'I don't want to hear about your sacrifices. I swear, if you tell me about a pony you gave up when you were a poor little rich girl because your daddy made a bad investment, I'll punch myself in the face.'

'Will you at least keep looking for the thumb drive?' Sylvia Crane asked. 'And will you tell me if you find it? *Before* you give it to Genevieve Bower?'

'What good would that do?'

'I can prepare myself – and those around me.'

'All these secrets. Most of the time I wish I could keep them, but sometimes I'm just pissed off at people like you who've got them.'

Regret edged at her voice. 'I seem to piss off a lot of people.'

'I'm with you there,' he said. 'What're you going to do about the money Neto sent to parts unknown?'

For a moment, she seemed distracted. 'You don't need to worry about it.'

'You're holding Marty accountable for Neto. Maybe you'll hold Marty's friends accountable too. I like to know who thinks I owe them.'

'We'll get the money back,' she said, almost apologetically. 'Every dollar. Every penny. We have to, you see? Our reputation depends on it. We'll decide who shares blame, and we'll do what we need to do. In the meantime, my father will make the company a personal loan.'

'Beaky?'

'Excuse me?'

'He can spare thirty-seven million?'

'Maybe.' She seemed to consider Kelson. 'Like you, he has an unusual sense of the world. Before I leave, I want you to meet him.'

'What do you mean? Where is he?'

'Downstairs in the car with our driver – he likes to stay close to me. It'll take only a minute.'

'I told you to come alone.'

'That's not quite what you said. And are you really worried about a little sixty-eight-year-old man?' She took out her phone, straightened her face as if the phone could see, and touched the keys. 'Hi,' she said. 'I'm with Mr Kelson. Will you come up?' She listened to the response, then hung up with a tired smile.

'Why do you want me to meet him?' Kelson said.

'So you can see what I'm dealing with.'

'Why would *I* want to?'

'Oh, everyone should meet my father at least once.'

A minute later, the short man with the beakish nose and intense blue eyes knocked. He wore gray slacks, a yellow dress shirt, and red suspenders.

When Kelson let him into the office, the man moved as close as a boxer looking to clench. Kelson stepped back, bumping against his desk.

Sylvia Crane used more of that tired smile. 'Sam Kelson, this is my father, Harold Crane. Daddy, this is Sam Kelson – he's still considering whether to help us.'

Harold Crane reached a well-manicured hand to shake. It seemed big for the body that supported it.

When Kelson gripped it, the man's fingers were flaccid.

Seeming to take pleasure from Kelson's expression, the man shot a glance at his daughter.

She eyed him the way you do a child who likes to knock down bottles at the grocery store. 'Mr Kelson speaks his mind.'

'Always,' Kelson said.

'Seems like a dangerous habit,' Harold Crane said. He dropped into one of Kelson's client chairs. 'I'm glad you're thinking of helping. My daughter's used to getting her way.'

'I haven't agreed to anything,' Kelson said, 'but I'm used to having tough women get their way with me.'

The man cackled. 'Me too, me too. Sylvia's mother was the toughest bitch I ever knew, God rest her soul. I have unconventional beliefs, and I behave in unconventional ways, Mr Kelson. If I said or did the same as everyone else, who would pay attention? They would go to Goldman Sachs. Our clients are looking for the unorthodox. If we don't surprise them once or twice a year, they'll find another firm that will – though it's also true that as long as I keep the green river flowing, everyone's happy. Do you know the green river, son? Have you been down it?'

'Cash?' Kelson said.

'Smells better than lilacs,' the man said.

'That river can dry up,' Sylvia Crane said, with the tired smile.

Her father pointed a finger at her and told Kelson, 'She's a tough bitch too. That's why I love her – and why I keep her near.' He got up, adjusted his suspenders, and seemed about to offer Kelson another handshake, but crammed his hands into his pockets. 'Nice meeting you, Mr Kelson. I hope to see you again.' He nodded toward his daughter and added, 'If you date this one, watch out – she's eaten up two husbands, she's working on the third, and she shows no loss of appetite.' He went to the office door, opened it, and stared back at his daughter. 'Come, dear.'

Kelson looked at her. 'Why don't you lock him up?'

She smiled. 'My father earns his clients over fifty million dollars a year. He gets a quarter of that. Don't you wish you were so crazy?' She followed her father to the door. 'You'll tell me if you find the thumb drive?'

Kelson felt something between pity and revulsion toward her. 'I'll think about it.'

TWENTY-THREE

Often lately, Kelson dreamed about the kittens. In one recurring dream, he and Sue Ellen entered Payday and Painter's Lane in a cat show at McCormick Place Convention Center on the lakefront south of downtown. Other pet owners brought Siamese cats, Persians, weird long-backed Abyssinians, and mouse-faced Sphinx cats – fragile, haywire breeds. Kelson and Sue Ellen had the only mutts. Payday and Painter's Lane won no ribbons, but Sue Ellen laughed and grilled Kelson with Stump Dad questions as the crowds walked past. In another dream, Payday and Painter's Lane wandered into a mass of kittens – hundreds of them, thousands – and Kelson's anxiety over losing them crumbled under his pleasure at all the kittenish fur and mewling.

But on the night after he talked with Sylvia Crane and her father, he dreamed that a sparrow had gotten inside his apartment. Payday and Painter's Lane stalked the bird as it flitted from a lamp to the dining table and then batted its tiny wings against the window. When it landed on his bed, the kittens pounced and tore the sparrow apart. Kelson yelled, 'No, *no* – don't do that – *don't*,' as they ripped off the little legs and bit into the tender belly. Payday looked up at him, feathers hanging from her mouth, and, using Marty LeCoeur's voice, said, 'It's what we fucking *do*.'

Kelson's phone rang, knocking him halfway out of the dream. He grabbed at it, answering, 'Thank God.'

'*What*?' It was Dan Peters.

'They were killing the bird.'

'Spit out the Percocet, Kelson,' the detective said. 'Meet me at the Canal Street Marina.'

Kelson shook free of the dream. 'What's going on? Since when do you call me?'

'Since we found your friend Jeremy Oliver – what's left of him.'

The Canal Street Marina was a triangular boatyard nested between the rusting base of the Canal Street lifting bridge, the South Branch of the Chicago River, and four lines of railroad tracks. By late May, most of the people who dry-docked their boats through the winter and spring had brought them upriver to the harbors, readying them for the first warm days of June. A chain-link fence topped with coils of barbed wire surrounded the remaining dry-docked boats.

Kelson parked outside the marina at three in the morning. He told a uniformed cop that Dan Peters had asked him to come, and the cop let him through the gate, pointing him across a concrete lot to a forty-foot sailboat on a wooden cradle. Crime tape looped around the boat, and inside the taped ring, Dan Peters, a couple of forensics detectives, and a few other cops Kelson didn't know worked in the hot white glow of pole-mounted floodlights. Outside the crime tape, a man in an untucked flannel shirt and filthy jeans sat on a plastic crate staring at the ground while a cop with a clipboard asked him questions.

Kelson cut wide around the interview and went to Peters, who nodded back at the man in flannel and said, 'His name's Demetrius – one of the drunks who live in the neighborhood. Around midnight he decided he wanted some of the yachting life, or at least a vinyl cushion to help him sleep off a bottle of Bacardi. He squeezed through a hole by the street gate, said eeny meeny, and climbed aboard. He found more than he was looking for.'

'Why do you want me here?' Kelson said.

'First, you can identify Jeremy Oliver. Second, you can tell me everything you know about him and how he took up dryland sailing in the afterlife.' He said to another cop, 'Give him a look.'

The cop stood on a wheeled metal platform that the marina used when servicing boats.

Kelson climbed a ladder and looked into the open cockpit.

The decaying remains of Jeremy Oliver, his legs tucked up to his chest like a sleeping baby's, lay on a brown plastic sheet. All the parts of him seemed to be there, though one hand looked as chewed up as the sparrow in Kelson's dream.

'Tell me,' Kelson said.

'Five lawn bags, one inside the other,' the cop said, gesturing at the brown plastic. 'Forensics cut them away, all but a hole that rats already chewed through.' He motioned at Oliver's hand and said, 'I hate rats. The drunk climbed up, looking for a place to put his tired head, but he smelled something bad. The bags must've kept the stink down for a while, but you can't keep rats from dinner. They chewed the hole and started on the fingers. So the drunk skedaddled down and flagged a cruiser, and now here we are.'

'Peters woke me out of a bad dream,' Kelson said. 'I liked the bad dream better.' He climbed down the ladder and went back to Peters. 'Yeah, it's him. Can I go home?'

'You can tell me everything you know,' Peters said.

'Who owns the boat?' Kelson asked.

'You know how much I like it when you do that? I ask you a question, and you act like I offered to give you a secret password. What do you know about Oliver?'

'Last week, I went to Big Pie Pizza on North Avenue to meet a client named Genevieve Bower. My friend Marty – who's more DeMarcus Rodman's friend than mine – gave her my name. She said she's missing her shoes. I got arrested after that, but it turns out she's missing more than—'

'*Just* Oliver,' Peters said. 'The short version.'

'Which do you want – everything or the short version?'

'Give me everything, but make it short.'

'All right. Jeremy Oliver, aka JollyOllie. Thirty-four years old, white. Grew up in Oak Park. Worked as a DJ, spinning Eighties hits. Lived on North Hermitage. Had a Chevy Express cargo van – burned.'

'I know all this,' Peters said.

'I think you're unsure what you want,' Kelson said.

'What did you find out when you dug into him?'

'How do you know I dug?'

'As much as I think you're an idiot, I think you're a persistent one.'

'Huh,' Kelson said. 'Along with Genevieve Bower's shoes, Oliver stole a thumb drive. It's supposed to have videos on it.'

'Of what?'

'I haven't seen them. I think there's some sex involving Genevieve Bower. I've asked around. The people who know are slow with specifics, and most people don't know. Oliver played rotten music and had a worse personality. No one liked him, except Genevieve Bower, who dated him for nine days – until he ripped her off, so then she didn't like him either.'

'Would she have killed him?' Peters asked.

'She couldn't even find him. She has ideas about cutting off the balls of guys she's mad at, but I think she's just looking for love.' He added, 'Like the rest of us.'

Peters stared at him, waiting for more.

Kelson said, 'So she comes into my office with a black eye and bruised face, and I get the feeling she took the beating because of the thumb drive and whatever happened to Oliver. I ask, but she won't say much. Now she's hiding at a motel.'

'Can you get in touch with her?'

'I can try.' Kelson took out his phone and dialed her number.

As had happened before, her line rang and rang and bounced to voicemail.

He talked to the recorder. 'I need to talk to you. The police need to talk to you. *Everybody* needs to talk to you. Call me.' He hung up. 'Nope,' he told Peters. 'Also, Oliver rented his attic from the husband of a woman whose family runs a private equity firm called G&G.'

'What am I supposed to do with that?'

'Anything you want. You asked for details – I'm giving them to you. Want the rest?'

Peters considered what Kelson had told him and seemed to decide that if he asked anything more he'd get a lecture on kittens. 'It's always bad at three a.m.,' he said.

'It's never good when you're dead,' Kelson said.

'I suppose. Go home and sleep.'

'Did I give you anything that couldn't've waited for morning?'

'I guess not,' Peters said. 'But I've got to ask.'

'And if you do, I've got to tell.' Kelson walked toward the gate.

Peters called after him. 'We already left a message for the boatyard manager. To find out who owns the sailboat.'

Kelson nodded and kept walking. Then he called back to him. 'Let me know if it's Harold or Sylvia Crane – or Chip Voudreaux.'

TWENTY-FOUR

Kelson drove to the Golden Apple Grill, a twenty-four-hour diner where he landed on especially bad nights – and especially good ones – and ordered a waffle with a side of sausage and a side of bacon. 'Put the bacon in a bag, please,' he said to his regular waitress.

'For the kittens?'

'Can't have them eating sparrows,' he said.

She was used to him, mostly, and tried to humor him, awkwardly. 'Save the birds – that's my motto.'

'Or the hand of a dead man.'

'Keep it to yourself.' She had limits.

He read the news on his phone while waiting for his food.

The *Tribune* had a profile of Victor Almonte and biographical sketches of Amy Runeski and Neto.

Almonte's profile included pictures of a smiling four-year-old boy, a high school kid with his soccer team, and a man in a soldier's uniform. Under a headline that asked WHAT WENT WRONG? two unnamed demolition technicians who served with him said no one could be a better, more loyal, or more reliable friend. Never in a million years, they said. Always had our backs. Something must've gone horribly, horribly wrong.

Kelson exited the article and dialed his lawyer Ed Davies. He left a voicemail – 'Did you find Emma Almonte? Did you spring her? I need to talk with her.'

Then he opened the *Tribune* site again and read about victim number one, Amy Runeski – her upbringing in Kenosha, Wisconsin, her dancing at the Kenosha Academy of Dance, Music & Drama, and her first date with Tom Runeski at the Pub 'n' Grub.

The sketch of James 'Neto' LeCoeur called Neto 'precocious', 'fun loving', and, according to his seventh-grade math teacher, 'a young man with a bright future'. Neto's father, who'd refused to come to the hospital when Marty called, said Neto was 'quite a boy'.

'Which could cut either way,' Kelson said.

The waitress, delivering his food, said, 'What could?'

'Fathers and sons,' Kelson said.

'Mothers and daughters too,' she said. 'Mine kicked me out when I was seventeen. I never understood until I had one of my own.'

'Sad,' Kelson said.

'Just the way it is.' She put a sticky-bottomed bottle of syrup on the table. 'It's what we do.'

'I've heard that before,' he said.

'Sure, it's common wisdom.'

When she left, he cut a bite of sausage, opened the *Sun-Times* site on his phone, and forked the sausage into his mouth.

Then his phone rang.

Caller ID said *Ed Davies*.

When Kelson chewed a hello, Davies said, 'Why the hell are you calling me at four thirty in the morning?'

'If it's too early, why the hell are you calling me back?' Kelson said, and hung up. He realized his mistake and dialed.

'What?' Davies said.

'Did you bust Emma Almonte out?'

'Don't call in the middle of the night unless you have an emergency,' Davies said, and *he* hung up.

Kelson stared at his phone as if it might change its mind, then said, 'Crank,' and ate his waffle.

*   *   *

At seven thirty, after returning to his apartment for a shower, he drove to his office. He checked his guns, winked at the pictures of Sue Ellen and the kittens, sat at his desk, and called Genevieve Bower. Again, her line went to voicemail. 'Now you're worrying me,' he said.

He dialed Dan Peters, who answered after the first ring.

'Genevieve Bower's missing,' Kelson said.

'And *I* haven't slept – and I'm up to my ass in paperwork – and the coffee in the department sucks,' Peters said, and then, sounding as if he was trying to care, 'in what sense missing?'

'The only sense. I tried calling a bunch of times. No answer.'

'Maybe she doesn't want to talk to you. I sympathize.'

'Last time someone went missing, he turned up in garbage bags in a boatyard. Last time I saw Genevieve Bower, she had bruises and a black eye.'

'Right.' Peters sighed into the phone. 'If this is a waste of time – even a second of it . . .' He let Kelson imagine the rest.

So Kelson spent twenty minutes re-describing Genevieve Bower, the conversations they'd had at Big Pie Pizza and in his office, and her plans to hole up in a motel. 'You could get some beat cops to look at places with cocktail lounges,' Kelson said. 'She's the type who'd want a lounge.'

'What type is that?'

'She comes off as cheap – you know, in a good way.'

Someone knocked on Kelson's office door – soft, as if the person was worried about disturbing him.

Phone to his ear, he went to open it, saying to Peters, 'I think whoever killed Jeremy Oliver will—'

He opened the door.

A heavy man in a red nylon jacket cradled Genevieve Bower in his arms. She looked too drunk for anyone to *want* to hold. Her bruises had started to yellow as they healed. She wore a thin pink pajama shirt and matching shorts that hardly contained her. She gazed at Kelson through half-open eyes, gave him a lazy-lipped smile, stuck the tip of her tongue through her teeth, and said, 'Hey there, muffin.'

Kelson spoke into the phone. 'Never mind.'

'Never mind what?' Peters said.

'Never mind Genevieve Bower. Never mind any of this. Never mind *me*.'

Instead of waiting for Peters's anger and questions, Kelson hung up.

He looked at Genevieve Bower. 'Hi,' he said. He looked at the man holding her. 'Hi.'

The man gritted his teeth under the strain. 'Can I put her down?'

Dick Avakian owned a grocery store called Genty's on North Lincoln, three blocks from a strip that included the Apache Motel, the Diplomat Motel, the Summit Motel, and the O-MI Motel. When Avakian and his wife arrived to open the store a few minutes after six, they found Genevieve Bower slumped in the shadows of the entryway. At first he tried to sweep her out to the sidewalk the way he did the street people who sometimes camped in the space on spring and summer nights. But the story she told – about men breaking into her motel room and threatening her with blades – made him bring her inside and give her coffee.

Now, she slumped and shivered on one of Kelson's client chairs, her head lolling, her pale skin damp and sagging, her eye shadow smeared, her bleach-blond hair tangled.

Kelson stared at her sideways. 'If you ran out from the motel like this, where'd you get the booze?'

She pursed her lips as if she would razz him but said, 'Kindness of strangers. Coupla frat boys looking for company – I told 'em I don't do it for money. Guess they felt sorry for me. One of 'em wanted to give me his socks.'

Avakian said, 'She would not let me call the police, but she said you are her friend. My wife had me bring her here.' He had an Eastern European accent. 'I will leave her now, OK?'

'Do you have to?' Kelson said.

The man smiled and gave Kelson a business card for Genty's, which carried a 'full selection of Armenian foodstuffs'. 'If you come to the neighborhood,' he said, and he left.

Kelson gazed at Genevieve Bower, who seemed about to fall asleep. 'What trouble did you get yourself into?' he asked.

She licked her lips and looked nauseous.

'If you throw up on the carpet, I'll add it to your bill,' he said.

She belched, her eyes widened, and something worse seemed

about to follow. Kelson reached under his desk for the waste-basket, but when he came up, she'd already settled. She closed her eyes.

'Before you slip off on me,' he said, 'you need to answer some questions. Who broke into your motel room, and why?'

Again, nausea rose to her face. 'Told you they'd come after me,' she said. 'They want—'

'Who? No screwing around.'

She licked her lips. A line of saliva shined on her chin.

Kelson set the wastebasket on her lap. 'Who?'

She worked her flabby lips. 'They would've cut me. They said they'd kill me. I locked myself in the bathroom. They kicked down the door, but I climbed out the window.'

'Who?'

She frowned. 'Stevie Phillips and Greg Cushman.'

'Who are they?'

She spit into the wastebasket. A string of drool hung from her lips. 'They sent Stevie and Greg . . . for me. I think . . . Stevie did Jeremy.'

'The police found Jeremy's body last night.'

'I know.'

'How?'

'Stevie said.'

'How did they even find you at your motel?'

'I called – my cousin. Yesterday. Susan. She had the party – where I met Jeremy. I trusted – no one else but her.' Her pale skin had a green tinge.

'Did you tell Susan where you were staying?'

'I might've.'

'So you called her when you shouldn't have, and you told her where you were, which you also shouldn't have. But when *I* called you, you didn't answer, and you didn't call back.'

'I didn't want to talk to you.'

'Score one for Dan Peters.'

'You ask questions I don't like.'

'I ask good questions. Here's another – what do you know about G&G Private Equity?'

Her eyes widened, and she threw up.

TWENTY-FIVE

'I'm hungry,' she said, after she wiped her mouth. She'd mostly hit the wastebasket. 'I want pizza – or . . .' Her eyes got heavy as she thought. Then she passed out. Sitting upright in the chair – more or less.

'Hanging this way, hanging that,' Kelson said.

She started to snore.

'At least you won't choke on it,' Kelson said.

He carried the wastebasket out of his office to the garbage chute at the end of the hall and crammed it in. Then he went back and opened the window to clear the smell.

'The things I do for love,' he said. The last word, which came out before he thought it, surprised him. 'Love of the work? Of . . .? Of the – hell, I don't know.' He stared at the snoring woman. Her breasts were truly impressive. 'You're truly impressive,' he told them. A chunk of something stuck to her chin. 'Not love of *you*,' he said. 'Not by a long shot.'

He went to his desk and called a friend and former client named Doreen Felbanks. Until recently she'd traveled a lot, but he knew she'd be around – she wore an ankle monitor and had a court order to stay in the city. She was an ex-escort, told by the judge to take no money for sex work while she was out on bail. Depending on one's view, she either was or wasn't responsible for the deaths of a handful of men, which made her job hunt difficult. After Kelson had finished working for her, he'd slept with her once – not for money.

Now his call woke her, and she answered with a thick throat.

'I like your sleep voice,' he said.

'When you wake someone with an early call, you say, *Sorry for waking you.*'

'It's after eight o'clock, and your sleep voice is incredibly sexy.'

'In what world is eight o'clock daytime? Next time, wait till noon to flirt with me.'

'How are the job interviews going?'

'I had one yesterday. They said my ankle monitor was a turnoff.'

'They said "turnoff"?'

'They said "inappropriate in a classroom of kindergarteners".'

'You applied to be a kindergarten teacher?'

'Teacher's aide. I can't pay the rent unless I start escorting again.'

'They'll throw you in jail.'

'Jail or the street. At least jail has a roof.'

'How would you like to make some money from me?'

'You don't need to pay me for it.'

'That's the second time I've heard someone say something like that in the last half hour.'

'Must be your lucky morning.'

'I want you to work as a guard – or more like an adult babysitter. I've got a drunk woman in pajamas who needs watching. You can keep her at my apartment. Put her in my bed – let her sleep this off.'

'What am I going to do if she acts up? Take away her teddy bear?'

'You're tough, and she's passed out, and when she wakes she'll have a rotten hangover. Raise your voice and she'll cringe and beg you to be gentle. It's lousy work but better than having her throw up on your shoes. She got that out of her system.'

'You know the nicest people.'

'If she annoys you, you can tell her your pay is coming out of her pocket. I'm billing her.'

'I'll be there at noon – when I get up.'

'Ha.'

'An hour, then. Christ, you're hard on a girl.'

As he waited, he researched Susan Centlivre on his laptop, wrote down an address for her house and another for her fragrance and candle store, The Wick, and then tucked his KelTec in his belt.

When Doreen called from a cab downstairs, he draped his jacket over Genevieve Bower, hoisted her into his arms, and stepped out of his office door. The computer training company clients, milling in the corridor, stared at him as if he was kidnapping her. 'She isn't even my girlfriend,' he told two bald men. When the elevator came, he got on with a tall woman in a long skirt. The woman gave him an ironic smile. 'You think this is bad,' he said, 'try singing some Joan Jett around me.'

When he came from the building, the cabdriver saw the passed-out woman and refused the fare.

Doreen, who was wearing black high-heel pumps, pink leggings that clashed with her bright red hair, and a black faux-fur zipper sweater, tried to sweet talk the driver, but he still grumbled, so Kelson gave him an extra twenty and said, 'Her tank is empty – no mess, no fuss. When you get to my apartment, help carry her inside.'

'No, no, no,' the cabdriver said, and tried to give back the money.

But Kelson fished out another twenty and gave it to him along with a business card. 'If she wrecks anything, I'll pay.'

The driver still grumbled, but he loaded Genevieve Bower into the backseat.

Kelson said to Doreen, 'Let me know when she straightens up enough to talk. But don't let her make any calls.'

The cab sped from the curb, and Kelson walked to the parking garage. Forty minutes later, he drove his Dodge Challenger through downtown Highland Park. A bakery called Breadsmith, a lingerie shop called Posh, and a skincare store called Cos Bar looked like money and more money. Kelson read a sign in the Cos Bar window. *Parfums*. 'For Chrissake,' he said. He found a parking spot around the corner from The Wick and went into the store, a little brass bell chiming overhead. The smell of lavender, lemon, mint, and vanilla almost knocked him back out to the sidewalk.

'Whoa,' he said to a woman who stood behind a glass counter. In a green cashmere sweater and beige wool slacks, she looked nothing like the wide-faced hippieish woman he saw in Facebook pictures when he first researched Genevieve Bower's cousin. 'Do people like this?'

'Excuse me?' she said.

He waved at the shelves of candles, gels, soaps, bath beads, and diffuser oils. 'All *this*?'

'Quite a bit, yes,' she said. 'You look like *you* might enjoy cedar.'

'You can tell just by looking at me?'

'Close your eyes and imagine a pine grove.'

'I like the smell of engine oil,' he said. 'City streets.'

She smiled. 'We have nothing like that.'

'Is Ms Centlivre in?' he asked.

'Susan works afternoons this week. May I take a message for her?'

'Some messages are better in person,' he said, and he went out of the store into the fresh air.

Susan Centlivre lived in a large white-brick house at the top of a ravine near the lake. When Kelson knocked on the big door, the wood under his knuckles felt solid. 'Money and more money,' he said.

The Facebook woman opened the door. She wore a blue batik dress. Her long hair hadn't touched a brush in weeks.

Before she could speak, he said, 'You don't get a house like this from selling stinky candles.'

She blinked at him.

'I'm Sam Kelson,' he said.

She blinked some more.

'We talked by phone a few days ago? About Jeremy Oliver's death? Him hooking up with your cousin?'

She blinked.

'Am I talking to a rabbit?'

'I'm confused,' she said. 'Why are you here?' Her voice lilted British, as it did on the phone.

'Why did you send Greg Cushman and Stevie Phillips after Genevieve?' he said.

She blinked.

Her blinking made his left eye twitch.

'That's an irritating habit,' he said, and he rubbed his forehead above the eye.

She stopped blinking and made a decision. 'Come in.' She stepped back from the door to let him past.

'Maybe this is a bad idea,' he said.

Looking amused, she walked up the front hall, and Kelson followed her. She went into a sunny kitchen with French doors that faced a stone terrace and then the ravine. A short, broad-chested man with close-cropped black hair stood by the counter. He wore jeans and a red-and-black flannel shirt, which he'd tucked tightly into his pants. A tall, thin version of him stood by the refrigerator. He wore jeans and a gray sweatshirt with a Chicago Bears logo.

Susan Centlivre gestured at the short man and then the tall one and said, 'Greg Cushman and Stevie Phillips, this is Sam Kelson. Sam Kelson, this is—'

Kelson slipped his KelTec from his belt. 'I told you this was a bad idea.' He aimed his pistol at the short man, then the tall man, and then Susan Centlivre.

None of them looked worried. 'What are you doing?' Susan Centlivre asked.

But Kelson spoke to Phillips. 'Why did you break into Genevieve Bower's motel room?'

The tall man seemed unsurprised by the question but said, 'We didn't.'

'Why did you beat her up?'

Now the man glanced at the short one and back at Kelson. 'She said *we* did that?'

'More or less,' Kelson said.

Susan Centlivre said, 'She got in a fight at a bar – with another woman.'

'Now *I'm* confused,' Kelson said, and asked the men, 'who exactly are you?'

The men glanced at Susan Centlivre. She said, 'They work for the family.'

Kelson asked, 'The Centlivre family?'

Her eyes turned icy for a moment. 'The Cranes,' she said.

He laughed. 'Are *you* a Crane?'

'Before I married. But once a Crane, always a Crane – though I left the family business in my early twenties.'

'Looks like the family business bought you a nice house. Genevieve Bower's your cousin – that makes her a Crane too?'

'Her mother is my aunt – my dad's sister. It's in the blood, like it or not.'

'And your dad is Harold Crane? Sylvia Crane's your sister?'

'Like it or not.'

Kelson wiggled a finger at her, as if a thought was coming to his lips, but he asked the short man, 'Why does Genevieve Bower say you broke into her room?'

The man glanced at Susan Centlivre, and she answered for him again. 'How much do you know about Genevieve?'

'Looks like there's a lot to know. She dated a little one-armed friend of mine named Marty – that's how she hired me. Then she dated a DJ named Jeremy Oliver – JollyOllie. JollyOllie stole her shoes and a computer drive, and I think that's how he got shot in the head.'

Susan Centlivre's lower lip hung open. 'I'm confused again.'

'It's very confusing,' Kelson said.

'Look,' she said, 'Genevieve has had problems. For much of her life – since she was a teenager. That's when I ran away too, though I guess I never ran very far. As you say, I have my house and my store. As far as I went, I never gave up my safety net. I love Genevieve. I admire her for cutting the strings. But cutting causes pain too.'

'What's on the computer drive?'

'You're quick, aren't you?' She said it with a smile, but something in her tone seemed to shift the mood in the room, and Stevie Phillips and Greg Cushman tensed.

'What's on it?' Kelson asked again. 'Genevieve said there's a video of her, but there's got to be more for it to matter so much.'

'It's proprietary information,' she said. 'I'm afraid I can't discuss it.'

'Big words for a hippie candle dealer. And what's with the British accent?'

'I went to school in England.'

'You didn't grow up here with your family?'

'I went for a semester – my runaway time. I got pregnant, had an abortion, tried to become a junkie, got hepatitis instead, dabbled with Buddhism. It was a very formative four months.'

'Then you came back and opened a candle shop.'

'I came back and got into cocaine. I dropped out of school, got married, got divorced, and kicked coke. Then I opened the candle shop, yes.'

'Nice to have money,' he said.

'It smooths the edges,' she said.

'What's on the thumb drive?' he said.

She smiled, and now there was no tension. 'I would like to

find Genevieve,' she said. 'The whole family would. For her sake. If you—'

But he talked over her. 'So you sent Pipsqueak and Stretch here to get her from the motel when she called you?'

She smiled at the interruption and continued. 'If you can find Genevieve and bring her to me safely, I would be more than happy to pay you for your work.'

'I can, but I won't,' he said. 'Sylvia already tried to hire me, and I told her the same – I'm working for Genevieve.'

'I'll be very sorry if Genevieve gets hurt,' she said, and again her eyes hardened. 'My family has hurt her enough. It's what my family does, I'm afraid – especially if we feel threatened.'

'I didn't have much of an opinion about you at first,' he said. 'Now I'm starting to dislike you.'

She glanced at Stevie Phillips and Greg Cushman again, and the glance made Kelson tighten his fingers on his pistol grip. She asked him, 'Where is she?'

'Dammit,' he said. 'Don't ask questions that—'

'Where?'

The words came. 'Tucked in my bed.'

She frowned. 'Don't be a smartass. Stevie and Greg can—'

'She's there with a hot redhead,' Kelson said.

'Cute.' She nodded, and the two men moved toward Kelson with the suddenness of cats.

Kelson swept his pistol across the room, and the men froze. He backed toward the hallway. 'I got what I came for,' he said.

Susan Centlivre glanced at the two men. Neither moved. 'What was that?' she asked Kelson.

'I wondered what kind of person would send thugs after a woman who reached out for help.'

'I told you, you have that wrong,' she said. 'I want to help her. I'm the only one who does.'

Kelson said, 'You wear your hippie costume, and you do your English runaway act, but you talk like the rest of your family. You're as rotten as they are.' He turned and jogged up the hall and out of the house.

TWENTY-SIX

Kelson drove downtown toward his office. He eyed the rearview mirror and saw only a parade of drivers minding their business – bored, talking on their phones, tapping their steering wheels to radio music. He gazed up through the windshield at the May sky, where clouds scudded on a stiff spring wind. 'Family is everything,' he said. He eyed the mirror again, then shifted lanes, cutting close to a silver SUV, which honked at him. 'Or is that health?'

By the time he pulled into the parking garage, his mind – and his monologue – had wandered from the Cranes to Sue Ellen and back. He walked out to the sidewalk, just missing the garage attendant, who scurried away when he saw him coming, went into Ricky's Red Hots, and ordered a hotdog and fries, then carried his lunch into his building.

When the elevator reached his floor, the computer training company classes were in session and the corridor was empty. He put his key in his door, but the lock tumbler had already turned. 'This happens too often,' he said. He set his bag of food on the floor, pulled his KelTec from his belt, and eased the door open.

Stevie Phillips sat in Kelson's chair behind the desk. Greg Cushman sat in one of the client chairs. They looked pleased with themselves.

Kelson used a foot to nudge his bag inside, stepped in after it, and closed the door. He pointed his pistol at Cushman's chest and said, 'Pipsqueak,' then at Phillips's head, 'Stretch,' and then back at Cushman.

Cushman smiled up at him. 'See, we don't need to knock down doors – in motel rooms or offices. Stevie's good with a pick.'

Phillips said, 'My daddy taught me.'

Cushman said, 'In the time it takes you to order a hotdog, Stevie's inside and reading your mail.'

'I'm *that* good,' Phillips said.

Cushman said, 'It's why the Cranes hired him.'

Kelson asked him, 'Why'd they hire *you*?'

'I've got a pleasant smile?'

'Tell that pleasant smile to pick your ass up off my chair and carry you out of here,' Kelson said.

Phillips also tried a smile. 'We could work together.'

Cushman said, 'We have a shared interest.'

'What would that be?' Kelson said.

'Your continued well-being,' Cushman said. 'The Cranes could knock you down. They could make you go away. But you're an ex-cop, right? You've been in the paper and on the news. The Cranes like to keep things quiet, but if you don't co-operate, they're willing to make noise.'

Phillips said, 'We've got nothing against you. Why should you get hurt?'

Kelson laughed at that. 'You guys are a kick. Breaking into my office. Talking like movie toughs. But here we are. Me with a gun. And you – well, you looking like a couple of jagoffs who don't know better than to talk tough to a man pointing a gun at you.'

Phillips reached into his lap and drew Kelson's Springfield pistol up so it pointed at him. 'Yeah, here we are.'

Kelson said, 'What good is a locked door if everyone just walks through it? Why stash a gun if everyone just grabs it?'

'Life's mysteries,' Cushman said.

'What's your deal?' Kelson said. 'Do you do regular security for the Cranes? Or do they hire you special to twist arms and do break-ins?'

'Here's the thing,' Cushman said. 'The Cranes are smart. Smarter than anyone you ever met. Stevie and me, we're dumb next to them, but we're still smarter than you because some of it rubs off. So I'll say this again. No one needs to get hurt. We can do this together. Like friends. You put away your gun. Stevie puts away your *other* gun. Maybe you offer us some french fries – maybe not. But we work this out together.'

Kelson stepped toward him, aiming his pistol at the short man's chest. 'A couple years ago, I got shot in the head. Brain damage – too much for the cops to keep me on the force. I function fine now. I work. I eat. I get from one day to the next. But I have problems with impulse control. My therapist says I'm getting better, but sometimes it seems I'm getting worse. I say a lot that I shouldn't. And sometimes' – he stood close to Cushman now – 'I *do* things. I take unnecessary risks. I show bad judgment.'

Cushman smiled up at him, but said to his partner, 'Put down the gun, Stevie.'

Phillips laid the Springfield on Kelson's desk – in reach, but out of his hand.

'A gesture of good will,' Cushman said.

'Thank you. Now get the hell out of my office,' Kelson said.

'Not till we talk,' Cushman said.

'We just talked – at Susan Centlivre's house.'

'*She* talked. *You* talked. *We* listened.'

Phillips said, 'Our words matter more than hers.' He touched the Springfield barrel, spinning the pistol on the desktop. When it stopped, the barrel pointed at Kelson. 'Or yours.'

Kelson said, 'Is that because when you talk, your words are Harold and Sylvia Crane's?'

'Yeah, you're quick,' Phillips said. 'You lying about the brain damage?'

'I always tell the truth,' Kelson said.

'Susan Centlivre is a nice lady,' Cushman said. 'Sylvia isn't. And Mr Crane? You don't even want to know.'

'We've got ideas about him,' Phillips said.

'Mr Kelson doesn't want to hear our ideas,' Cushman said.

'Sure I do,' Kelson said.

Cushman smiled at him. 'I can tell you're quite the conversationalist. Well, d'you want to be loved or feared?'

'Loved by family and friends,' Kelson said, as if the question was a riddle. 'Feared by enemies – and you.'

'Exactly. But with Mr Crane it's all fear, and always has been.' Cushman's smile widened.

Phillips told Kelson, 'Our job is to give that fear to you. Quietly if we can. Keeping you out of the news if possible.'

'Got it,' Kelson said. 'Did you beat up Genevieve Bower? Did you give her the black eye?'

'Let's say we did,' Cushman said. 'Let's say Susan's story

about the bar fight's a lie we told her because she's a nice lady. If you think about what we *could* do, a little beating doesn't seem so bad. It might be a gentle message.'

'Did you go to her motel room last night to hurt her?' Kelson asked.

'Let's say we did that too.' Cushman smiled. 'Let's say she ignored the gentle message. Let's say the beating didn't make a deep enough impression. Does that help you understand why we're here?'

'It does, thanks,' Kelson said. Then he turned the KelTec in his hand and smacked the pistol grip into Cushman's cheek. The metal cracked against bone, and a bright line of blood rose from the split skin. The silence that came from his mouth was like the silence of a baby who, suddenly injured, revs up to scream.

Phillips snatched the Springfield off the desk and aimed at Kelson. Kelson turned the KelTec and aimed at him.

Cushman's voice squeaked. 'You cocksucker.' Blood streaked his face.

'We came to talk,' Phillips said. 'To ask for your cooperation. Why'd you need to turn it into this?'

'Impulse control,' Kelson said. 'Anger management. I don't like anyone bragging about beating up people who can't defend themselves.'

'Now we've got a problem.' Phillips had his finger on the trigger.

'What was it before?'

'It was an opportunity, maybe. You could've made money. Mr Crane needs men like you. But now you went and did this to Greg, who never did anything but smile at you with his winning smile.'

'Everyone keeps offering me money. I like money. I wish I could take it.'

'Yeah, it's too bad.'

'So what happens now? You shoot me, and I shoot you, and Pipsqueak crawls back to Harold Crane?'

Phillips stared at him, then eased his finger from the trigger and set the gun on the desk. 'No, now you take us to Genevieve Bower. Mr Crane has bigger guns than these. He'll have us come after you on his own schedule if and when he's ready for that

kind of fight. You can think about that. And think about this –
Mr Crane is fine hurting innocent bystanders. To tell the truth,
I think he likes it. Hurting them makes a point. So when you're
with the people you want to love you – your friends, your
family . . .' He gestured at the picture of Sue Ellen on the wall.
'Is that your kid?'

Kelson flipped his pistol in his hand again and smacked the
grip against the other side of Cushman's face.

Cushman screeched. Phillips snatched the gun from the desk
and said, 'What the hell was that one for?'

'Never threaten my family. If Sue Ellen ever—'

Phillips shook his head in disbelief. 'Her name's Sue Ellen?'

Kelson threatened to hit Cushman again.

Cushman cowered and yelled at Phillips, 'Shoot him.'

Kelson swung around and aimed at Phillips, and they were
back where they started.

Phillips said, 'You're a fucking idiot.'

Kelson said, 'Heard it before.'

Then a hand knocked on the outside of the office door.

'Disturbed the neighbors,' Kelson said.

Phillips aimed at Kelson's chest. 'Ignore it.'

The hand knocked again.

Phillips said, 'Shh.'

A voice spoke through the door. 'Kelson? It's Dan Peters.'

'Ah,' Kelson said. 'The cops.'

TWENTY-SEVEN

'We've got two choices,' Kelson said to Phillips. 'Either
we put away my guns and I open the door and try
to pretend we were talking about a job that doesn't
involve beating up and killing people, or we shoot each other
and Detective Peters arrests Pipsqueak for being in the wrong
place at the wrong time. I vote for option number one.'

'You fucked up big,' Phillips said, but he opened the bottom
desk drawer and laid the Springfield inside.

Kelson stuck his KelTec in his belt and said to Cushman, 'Wipe your face.'

The short man wiped his bloody cheek with his sleeve.

'You made it worse,' Kelson said.

'Fuck you,' Cushman said.

'I try to help,' Kelson said, and opened the door.

Dan Peters stepped in and looked from man to man.

Kelson turned to Phillips. 'Thanks for coming in,' he said. 'I'm sure we'll be in touch – whether or not I want to be.' Then he offered to shake Cushman's hand, saying, 'You really do have a winning smile.' Cushman glared at him and followed Phillips into the corridor.

Peters closed the door. 'What was that about?'

Kelson had prepared for the question. 'They wanted me to do a job.'

'Why was one of them bleeding?'

Kelson could prepare only so much. 'I hit him.'

'Yeah? Why?'

'He bragged about hurting people who can't defend them-selves.'

Peters eyed him funny. 'Great customer relations. I see why they're lining up at your door.'

'Funny thing is everyone wants to hire me lately.' Kelson went to his desk. 'What's going on?'

Peters seemed to shake off the image of the bloody-cheeked man. 'We traced the boat where we found Jeremy Oliver. A man named Jim Fitzpatrick owns it.'

'Never heard of him.'

'Fifty-year-old broker. Lives in Bannockburn. Money. Fits the profile of a rich doofus who's got nothing to do with a murder. Just a schmuck whose boat had the bad luck of getting a body dumped in it.'

'Except?'

'Except a name comes up that you mentioned as you walked away last night. Turns out the broker's got a background at the Mercantile Exchange, but for the past five years he's worked for a company no one seems to know much about, called G&G Private Equity, which is owned by a man named Harold Crane. A friend of yours?'

'I met him for the first time yesterday.'

'Tell it,' Peters said.

'All of it?' Kelson felt his resistance crumbling.

'Every detail.'

'You know better than to do that,' Kelson said. Then he told it. He talked for more than an hour. He told him about Genevieve Bower's stolen Jimmy Choos, melted in the back of Jeremy Oliver's burned-out van, and about the thumb drive everyone wanted but no one would explain. When he detoured into Sue Ellen and Taquería Uptown, Peters guided him back. So Kelson told him about Oliver renting the attic apartment from Sylvia Crane's husband Bruce McCall, about Sylvia being Harold Crane's daughter, about Harold's other daughter, Susan Centlivre, taking a year-long head-trip to England but then returning to the family fold more or less, and about the family relationship to Genevieve Bower. He started to tell him about Genevieve Bower dating Marty LeCoeur, which led to Neto, which led to – but Peters nudged him back to Jeremy Oliver. So he told him that the men who'd left the office when Peters arrived *might* have killed Oliver or know who did. He told him about meeting the men at Susan Centlivre's house and finding them at his desk when he returned. He finished with a blow-by-blow account of their faceoff.

Peters looked furious. 'You didn't think you should tell me about them before they got in the elevator?'

'I have no evidence they killed Oliver, or even met him,' Kelson said. 'But it seems like something they would enjoy.'

When Peters left, Kelson yanked open the desk drawer where Phillips had put the Springfield. He wiped the pistol grip and barrel, released the magazine, checked the rounds, and popped the magazine back in place. He put the gun back in the drawer. He took out his laptop and turned it on. Phillips and Cushman had spent only a few minutes in the office before Kelson came in, but he checked his work history to see if they'd opened any files. As far as he could tell, they hadn't.

Then he yelled at the walls. He swore at Phillips and Cushman. He swore at Susan Centlivre. He swore at the Cranes and Chip Voudreaux. He started to swear at Genevieve Bower – then stopped and swore at Phillips and Cushman again.

Someone rapped on the door.

He swore at the door.

Someone rapped again.

He went to the door and tugged it open.

Steve from building security stood outside. 'Is everything OK, Mr Kelson?'

For a moment, words tangled in Kelson's mouth. Then he said, 'Have you been letting a woman named Genevieve Bower into my office?'

Steve's body looked like Genevieve Bower's would if her breasts sank to her stomach. He blushed. 'Yeah.'

'Don't ever do that again,' Kelson said, and slammed the door.

He swore at the walls about Steve.

Then he called DeMarcus Rodman and told him about Phillips, Cushman, Susan Centlivre, the Cranes, and Steve. He also told him about Genevieve Bower vomiting in his wastebasket. He told him about the thin office walls, which kept him from yelling without disturbing others on his floor.

Rodman listened until Kelson spent himself, then said in his gentle voice, 'Maybe you're yelling at yourself. Maybe you're upset because you let this get away from you.'

'You think you're smart, don't you?' Kelson said.

'Yeah, I do.' Gentle. Smooth. 'Good-looking too.'

Kelson breathed hard. 'Thanks for listening, though. What's happening outside my own echoing head?'

'Marty's arranging Neto's cremation for as soon as the cops release the remains. Meantime, Venus Johnson pulled him into the station for a couple hours this morning. When the cops picked him up, Janet freaked out and called me. So I called Ed Davies, and he went down and threatened them with his legal magic. Anyway, he busted Marty out. Marty says Venus Johnson grilled him about Neto – if Neto knew explosives the way he knew computers, any reason he'd blow up a library, any reason he'd hang out in Rogers Park?'

'I thought the cops settled on Victor Almonte,' Kelson said.

'Seemed like it, didn't it? But Marty says Johnson hit him hard, left and right. She knew about Neto hacking the Argentinian bank when he was a teenager and about some other stuff the kid did that Marty'd never heard about. But you know Marty. Johnson must've thought she could roll over him. He says he insulted and picked at her until she got mean. When Davies came to the station, she chucked Marty at him – probably glad to get rid of him before she did something that got her in trouble.'

'What else?' Kelson said.

'Davies says he sprang Emma Almonte late last night. The FBI had her. I'm going to drive out by her house and check on her this afternoon. What about you?'

'Doreen took Genevieve Bower to my apartment. As soon as she sleeps off her drunk, I'm going to do a Venus Johnson on her until she explains why the Cranes want her enough to send a goon squad after her.'

Rodman asked, 'You think Phillips and Cushman would go to your apartment too?'

'I don't think so,' Kelson said, though as soon as he said it he felt the possibility. When they were at Susan Centlivre's house he'd even told them Genevieve Bower was in his bed, though no one had seemed to take him seriously.

'Careful with these guys,' Rodman said. 'They sound smarter than they act.'

'I never said they act stupid,' Kelson said.

He hung up with Rodman and dialed Doreen.

When she picked up, she said, 'Hey baby, you need to start hanging out with a better class of friends.'

'What did she do?'

'You said she'd finished throwing up. You underestimated her.'

'My bed?'

'I got her to the bathroom. Pick up sponges on your way home.'

'Is she awake?'

'Snoring like a bear.'

'You need to move her,' he said. 'The men who broke into her motel room last night came to my office. They might check my apartment too.'

'What if I can't wake her?'

'Do what you need to. Drag her down the hall.'

'And into the elevator? And out to a taxi? Now you're overestimating me.'

'Get her down to the building basement. Hang out in the laundry room until I come.'

'Yeah,' she said, 'now you've got me doing your dirty laundry.'

'I'll be there as soon as I can,' he said. 'Call me when you're in the basement.'

Kelson hung up, grabbed his KelTec and jacket, and left his office. As he rode the elevator to the lobby, he pulled his phone back out and watched its blank screen. He went out to the sidewalk, crossed the street to the parking garage, and jogged up the ramp to his car. He put the key in the door and checked his phone again. 'Come on, c'mon,' he said to the screen.

He drove down to the exit, shot out to the street, and cut around a slow-moving truck. He drove two blocks, glanced at his phone, and accelerated through a yellow light. When a red light stopped him two blocks later, he called Doreen's phone. It rang and bounced to voicemail. 'No way,' he said, and hit the gas as the light turned green. Twice more as he drove to his apartment, he called Doreen's number. Each time, it rang and rang and rang.

TWENTY-EIGHT

K elson swung to the curb in front of his building, went into the lobby, and took the stairs to the basement. He went through a low-ceilinged corridor with exposed pipes and rounded the door into the laundry room. A couple were making out in the corner, the woman sitting on a washer that vibrated in spin cycle, the man standing between her legs. Kelson yelled, 'Did you see a big-breasted woman and a redhead?'

The woman pulled her lips from the man's and stared at Kelson. 'Creep,' she said.

'Get the hell out of here, OK?' the man said.

'How long have you been here?' Kelson said.

'This is your business?' the woman said.

'Like five minutes,' the man said. 'Now leave.'

Kelson was already gone. He ran up the corridor to the elevator, muttered at the elevator door until the car came, and rode to his floor.

When he went into his apartment, Payday mewed at him from his bed. He asked her, 'Where are they?' He poked his head into the kitchenette. He stepped into the bathroom. Painter's Lane was sniffing the mess Genevieve Bower made when she missed the toilet. 'Huh,' Kelson said. He shooed her out and closed the door.

He left his apartment and ran down the hall to the stairwell. He took the steps two at a time back to the basement.

When he charged into the laundry room, the couple were still making out. The man had a hand inside the woman's T-shirt. Kelson stared around wildly. Then he kicked a dryer.

The couple jumped, and the woman yelled, 'What the hell?'

'Impulse control,' Kelson said, and he kicked a garbage can. The can spun across the floor and tipped. The lid rolled off, and the garbage spilled out. At the top there was a man's gray sweatshirt with a Chicago Bears logo – Phillips's. One of the shirt sleeves was smeared with vomit.

'Dammit,' Kelson said, and he kicked another dryer.

Outside in his car, he called Rodman. 'Phillips and Cushman have them,' he said.

'Wow,' Rodman said.

'Exactly. I'm heading to G&G.'

'Don't,' Rodman said. 'This has gone too far. Call Dan Peters or Venus Johnson.'

'I'm sure that's good advice.' Kelson turned the key in the ignition.

'You've no idea what's waiting for you there,' Rodman said.

'I have a pretty good idea. But they don't have any idea what *I'll* do.'

'Control yourself, OK? If they killed Jeremy Oliver—'

'If they hurt Doreen and—'

'I'll meet you there. Wait in the parking lot. Don't go in without me.'

'More good advice.' Kelson hit the gas.

*   *   *

He sped out to the Interstate and north to Mundelein. When traffic thickened, he shoved up within inches of the cars in front of him, jerked the steering wheel, and slid into an adjacent lane. When other drivers honked at him, he flipped them off out the side windows or in the rearview mirror. Joan Jett's 'I Love Rock 'n' Roll' began to play deep in his brain. 'No,' he said. 'Just no.' For a half mile before he got off the Interstate, he drove on the shoulder, swearing at the other drivers – and at himself.

When he reached the concrete and glass building that housed the G&G offices, he left his car in the fire lane, ran inside, and poked the elevator call button. When the indicator light showed the elevator stationary at the third floor, he went to the stairwell and ran upstairs. He burst into the G&G reception area out of breath.

The receptionist raised her eyebrows and asked pleasantly, 'May I—'

He went past her, into the hallway leading to the Cranes' offices.

Before the receptionist could get up from her desk and follow him, he ran up the hall and rounded the doorway into Harold Crane's suite.

Harold Crane was there.

So was Doreen.

They sat together on a blue leather couch across from the desk. They were drinking glasses of wine.

Kelson made a sound. Then he made another sound. Then he managed to make a word. 'What?'

Harold Crane gazed up, his beakish nose pointing at Kelson, and grinned as if he'd pulled off a practical joke. 'Ah, Mr Kelson.'

Kelson stared at Doreen. 'What . . .'

She gave him a masklike smile. She said, 'Turns out I know Harry.'

'*Harry*?'

'From before,' she said.

'You mean, as an escort?'

'I went out with Harry to several dinners,' she said. The little man grinned and squeezed one of her knees. 'As his evening companion,' she said.

'Small world?' Kelson said, and the words felt small in his mouth.

'Small city,' she said. 'For a select clientele.' She laid her hand on Crane's.

Kelson remembered the man's flaccid fingers from when he first met him. He stared at Doreen touching him and said, 'Slugs.'

Doreen gave him a warning look. He started to ask her why. But Stevie Phillips, Greg Cushman, and the receptionist rushed into the office. Phillips and Cushman moved toward Kelson as if they would wrestle him to the floor. Kelson dangled his fingers over the pistol in his belt.

Harold Crane said, 'It's all right, boys,' and Phillips and Cushman stopped. 'Mr Kelson is joining us for a drink.' He gazed at Kelson. 'Is wine acceptable, or do you prefer beer? We also have a bottle of Woodford bouncing around. Can you mix alcohol with the opioids you're taking?'

Kelson brushed his fingers over the pistol grip. 'How do you know—' He glanced at Doreen, who shook her head.

Crane said, 'We have a wonderful research department, as the best investment companies do. Would you like to know your credit history? Would you like me to tell you what you ate for breakfast?'

'I'd like to know where you've got Genevieve Bower,' Kelson said.

'You paid for the waffle at the Golden Apple Grill with a Visa card. I tell you this because I want to frighten you.'

'Where is she?'

'We've already moved her somewhere we can keep her safe.'

'You mean where you can keep *yourself* safe from her?' Kelson said. His fingers rested on the pistol grip.

One side of Crane's mouth curled in a smile. 'I assure you that pulling your gun would be the biggest mistake of your life.'

Cushman asked Crane, 'You want me to take it from him?' He'd taped a bandage over his cut-up cheek.

Crane asked Kelson, 'Will that be necessary?'

Kelson said, 'I'm taking Doreen out of here.'

Crane's smile spread. 'I believe the lady's enjoying her wine.'

Kelson said to her, 'Are you enjoying your wine?'

Doreen raised her glass to her lips and downed the rest. 'Very much.' She set down the glass and squeezed Crane's hand. 'Give me a call,' she said.

She got up and joined Kelson. He stared at her, confused. She smiled. 'Are we going?'

As they walked out of the office toward the reception area, he said, 'What the hell—'

She took his hand, squeezed hard, and whispered, 'Shut up.'

In the elevator, he tried again. 'What the hell was that about?'

'She's in a room in the back.'

'What?'

'Genevieve Bower. I got him to tell me – I had to kiss him for it. His goddamned tongue tastes like a turd. If you hadn't come in, he would've wanted more.' She looked like she wanted to spit. 'We used to call him Scary Harry. The things he wanted to do.'

'Did you do them?'

'Do you want me to answer that?'

'No.'

They went out through the lobby into the late-afternoon sun. Kelson stopped before they got to his car. 'I can't leave her here.'

'Wrong,' Doreen said. 'You've got to. You can't go in alone. You saw that place – you heard Harry. When Phillips and Cushman brought us in, they gave her to three other guys. What're you going to do against five men?'

'I can't—'

'Call for help,' she said. 'Get the cops. What good can you do on your own?'

Then a white van ripped across the parking lot. It stopped in the fire lane behind the Dodge Challenger. Rodman stepped out. He looked cool and calm.

He said to Kelson, 'You went in without me, didn't you?'

'I did,' Kelson said.

Rodman shook his head, then looked at Doreen. 'Are *you* OK?'

'Never better,' she said.

'She was getting drunk with Harold Crane,' Kelson said.

'Where's Genevieve Bower?' Rodman asked.

'Still inside,' Kelson said.

'In a back room,' Doreen said.

'They've got five men on her,' Kelson said.

Rodman glanced from Kelson to Doreen, as if searching for

something he didn't see. 'Hell,' he said, 'what are we waiting for?' He went to the lobby doors and disappeared into the building.

Kelson and Doreen stared at each other. 'Hell,' Kelson said, and they followed Rodman.

TWENTY-NINE

R odman went in to the reception area first, Doreen behind him, Kelson behind her. The receptionist looked unhappy to see them again.

'We're here for Genevieve Bower,' Rodman said, the way a deliveryman might say he'd come to pick up a box.

The receptionist fumbled with her phone. 'I'll call Mr—'

'No, you won't,' Rodman said, gentle, and he took the phone from her. Then he moved past her desk into the hallway.

Kelson pulled out his pistol, and he and Doreen went into the hallway after him.

Stevie Phillips was coming from a doorway at the far end. He saw the three of them and froze at the sight of Rodman. Then he yelled, 'Cushman.'

Greg Cushman popped out of a doorway across from him, followed by a man in a gray sport coat who looked enough like him to be his brother.

When a freckled man came from a doorway halfway down the hall, Rodman backfisted him in the face, and the man stumbled back into the room and stayed.

Cushman's lookalike reached inside his sport coat, and Rodman said, 'No, no, *no* – bad idea.' Kelson stepped around Doreen, training his pistol on the man. The man dropped his hand to his side.

Phillips ducked back into the room he'd come out of and slammed the door.

'Silly,' Rodman said and, as Kelson held his pistol on the other two men, went to the door and tried the knob.

It was locked.

Rodman punched a spot above the knob with the heel of his hand. The door flew open.

He stepped in, and a gun fired at him, twice – a small-caliber *pop*, *pop*.

He jumped back out, hugged the wall, and looked at his belly and legs to make sure nothing had hit. He nodded at Kelson, and they switched places – Rodman watching Cushman and his looka-like, Kelson moving for the door.

Kelson went in, his finger on the trigger, his eyes blurring with fear.

The shooter – a guy who parted his long blond hair from over his left ear – was inspecting a little pistol, as if unsure whether it had misfired or he'd had bad aim. Genevieve Bower sat in a chair at one end of a conference table. She no longer looked drunk. She looked terrified. Phillips stood behind her and, when Kelson came in, locked his arms around her head as if he might snap her neck.

'Put it down,' Kelson said to the blond guy.

The guy hesitated.

Kelson shot a bullet into the wall beside him. 'Please,' he said.

The guy laid his pistol on the floor.

Kelson aimed at Phillips. 'Move away from her.'

'You're out of your goddamned mind,' Phillips said.

'Yep,' Kelson said, and shot again – into the wall beside Phillips.

Phillips tightened his arms. 'If you leave now, maybe I let her live.'

Then Rodman and Doreen stepped into the room.

Doreen stared at Phillips gripping Genevieve Bower and said, 'That sucks.' She walked toward him. 'I hate guys like you. You think because you've got a dick you get to piss on everyone. Guess what? I've seen a lot of dicks, and I'm not impressed. Guys like you, you mostly piss on yourself.' She kicked him in the leg.

He eyed her like she was crazy, and he tried to move aside. He didn't let go of Genevieve Bower, but he didn't break her neck.

Doreen kicked him again. Harder. In the knee.

He yelled in pain and tightened his arms.

Doreen kicked him.

He let go and went after her. 'Goddamn crazy bitch.'

Rodman moved in and slugged him in the face.

Phillips went down.

Genevieve Bower gasped for air. Rodman and Doreen helped her up. 'Time to go,' Rodman said.

'Uh-huh,' Genevieve Bower said, rocky on her feet. Then she faltered. 'Uh-oh.' She bent and dry heaved. She wiped her mouth on her arm and said, 'Delicate tummy.' She headed for the door.

Rodman and Kelson went out before her.

At the other end of the hall, Harold and Sylvia Crane blocked the way to the reception area. The freckled man Rodman had backfisted stood between them. His hair was almost as red as Doreen's. He wore khakis and a white golf shirt that showed his freckled biceps. Blood spotted his upper lip. He held a short, thick wooden bar of some kind, and he seemed interested in using it as a cudgel.

'You're kidding, right?' Kelson said.

Harold Crane said, 'She stays here.'

Kelson asked Genevieve Bower, 'You want to stay here?'

She shook her head.

'She doesn't want to stay here,' he said.

The freckled man turned the wooden bar in his hands.

'Stupid,' Rodman said, and went for him.

The man smashed the bar against Rodman's shoulder.

Rodman seemed to absorb the pain. He grabbed the man's shirt collar and pulled him toward him. The man tried to hit him with the bar again, but Rodman punched his jaw. The blow drove the man against the hallway wall.

Harold Crane stepped aside.

Sylvia Crane stood in front of Rodman.

'Excuse me,' he said to her.

'Do you realize what you're doing?' she said.

'Yeah, I'm walking out of here with my friends.' His voice calm, gentle.

She pointed a fingernail at Genevieve Bower. 'She's dangerous.'

'Nah, she's a frightened bunny,' he said.

'I can't let you leave with her,' she said.

'I can't see you stopping me.'

She looked like she would lunge at him. He gazed at her with his kind, heavy-lidded eyes. She stepped out of the way.

Kelson, Doreen, Genevieve Bower, and Rodman rode the elevator to the lobby and went outside. Rodman opened the sliding door on the van, and Genevieve Bower climbed in back. 'No reason to advertise you,' he said, then asked Kelson, 'my place?'

'See you there,' Kelson said, and he and Doreen got into the Challenger.

They drove across the parking lot and on to the frontage road, heading toward the Interstate. When they hit Route 176, Kelson collected his thoughts enough to say, 'Huh.'

Doreen put a hand on his thigh. She moved as close to him as the center console allowed. 'I hope this is OK,' she said.

'Yeah, yeah, it's good,' he said.

THIRTY

When Kelson and Doreen reached the Bronzeville neighborhood and parked in front of the Ebenezer Baptist Church, they gazed out of the car for any sign that the Cranes' men guessed where they were going and beat them. When they saw no one, they ran from the car and climbed the two flights of stairs to Rodman's apartment.

Rodman had just helped Genevieve Bower up the stairs and settled her on the couch. When Kelson and Doreen came in, he said, 'She's got a story to tell,' and he went into the kitchen to make coffee.

Genevieve Bower said, 'Next time someone gives me a bottle of strawberry vodka, remind me to knock them over the head with it.'

Kelson pulled over a chair so he could face her. 'Tell me.'

She breathed deep. Her breath stank. 'My uncle takes what he wants,' she said.

'Your – Harold Crane?'

'Uncle Harry,' she said. 'When I was little – nine or ten – he was my favorite. When our family got together, my mom tried to keep me away from him. She called him her psycho brother. Her *dirty* brother. I didn't understand. To me, he seemed so smart. Funny. Rich. He had everything, while my mom and dad were falling apart. He snuck me these amazing presents in little boxes. A little recorder – to sing into and tell my secrets. A tiny spy camera – to take pictures of myself for him. He gave me little toys to play with in bed after my mom and dad went to sleep.' She spoke more to the air in front of her than to Kelson, as if having anyone hear her words would hurt more than containing them in herself. 'When my mom found the camera, she took it away, but I didn't tell her where I got it. My dad hit me when he found the recorder – he thought I stole it. That made me love Harry more. For my tenth birthday, he gave me a necklace with a ruby. I did everything he asked. He had cameras too – good cameras, video cameras. He called what we did "playing". I knew we weren't playing. For a while, I didn't care – or I didn't think I cared. And then I did.'

Rodman brought her a cup of coffee. She took it from him without seeming to see him.

She said, 'The thumb drive that Jeremy Oliver stole had a copy of one of the videos.'

She raised the cup to her face. But instead of drinking, she stared into the brown liquid as if searching for her reflection.

Kelson said, 'You were blackmailing your uncle?'

'Trying to,' she said. 'Trying my damned best.'

He said the obvious. 'He wants the thumb drive.'

'They all do,' she said. 'Family business. If he goes down, they all go down.'

Kelson thought about what she'd told him. 'What was the thing with Jeremy Oliver and the shoes?'

'Sylvia set me up,' she said. 'She knew I'd go to Susan's party. She lined up Jeremy to DJ the party and then to come on to me. Susan knew I was selling counterfeits. I guess Sylvia promised him the crate of shoes to do what he wanted with if he also stole the thumb drive. I guess she didn't tell him what was on the drive. But he looked. If you got back the shoes, I planned to pay you to get the thumb drive. I didn't trust you to try until you showed what you could do. I was afraid. I fell for the whole thing. I'm stupid.'

'Yeah,' he said.

A tear rolled down her cheek.

'I mean, we all are,' he said. 'We're people. That makes us stupid. All of us.'

'Not Uncle Harry.'

Rodman said, 'Tell the rest of it.'

She held the cup to her lips and drank. For a moment, she looked as if the coffee might come back up.

'Tell it,' Rodman said.

'I'm pretty sure no one was supposed to find Jeremy after they killed him,' she said. 'When you went into his apartment and saw his body, he was supposed to be gone. They must've been coming back later to get rid of him. That homeless man shouldn't have found his body in the boatyard either. If he'd come a couple hours later, someone would've sunk Jeremy in the river or taken him out to the lake and sunk him there.'

'How do you know this?' Kelson asked.

She sipped the coffee and seemed to find it bitter. 'When people screw up – even when they don't – they disappear. It's how the Cranes handle problems. When Sylvia was fifteen, she had a crush on a kid who helped his dad clean Harry's pool in the summer. The kid was tall and good-looking *and* Mexican. A teenage crush. Harry saw them together – and so the kid vanished. The kid's dad kept cleaning the pool, and a week or two later, he started driving a new truck. Sylvia asked him where his son was, and he said he sent him to Durango to live with his grandmother. Sylvia didn't believe it. Harry sees threats everywhere. Some are real. Some not so much. He'll tell you that his ability to see them – especially when no one else does – has made him rich. He makes those threats go away.'

She filled her mouth with coffee and forced herself to swallow.

Kelson said, 'It's happened more than once?'

'When G&G distributes funds to its clients,' she said, 'Harry always gets someone new to make the distribution. Someone unnecessary to the company.'

'Which is why he talked to Marty and then hired Neto,' Kelson said.

'Someone disposable,' she said. 'Someone who can vanish – because they do. They all vanish. Some retire or move away – at least Harry says they do. I'm pretty sure the less lucky ones never even pack up their offices – never make it out of the city.'

Kelson stared at Genevieve Bower. 'That's what happened to Neto at the library? They made him vanish?'

'I'm not saying,' she said, 'not necessarily.'

Rodman said, 'You don't need to say.'

Kelson asked, 'Why did you give Marty's name to the Cranes if you knew the danger?'

'I didn't,' Genevieve Bower said. The coffee stayed down, and Rodman went back to the kitchen to make toast. She said, 'I told Susan I went on a couple of dates with Marty. She must've told Sylvia or Harry about him. I wouldn't've mentioned him to Susan if I'd thought she'd do that.'

'Either way, it got Neto killed, if what you're thinking is true,' Kelson said.

'What could I do?' she said.

'You could've told Marty to turn down the job.'

'I didn't know,' she said. 'I didn't know.' Another tear rolled down her cheek. She shook her head. 'But I did bad things.'

'With Harold Crane?' Kelson said. 'That doesn't count. You were a kid. We've got to take this to—'

'You're not listening. I did—'

'The prosecutor will bargain for the blackmail if you testify. They do it all the time. You can cut a deal.'

'You aren't listening.'

'I'll hook you up with my lawyer, Ed Davies. He knows how to do this. He'll make you buy him a steak dinner after he clears you, but that's a good thing – he'll clear you, and then you eat steak.'

'Harry got me pregnant.'

'What?'

'Pregnant. When I was fourteen.'

'See?' Kelson said, but he didn't know what he saw or wanted her to see.

'I ran away,' she said. 'I stayed at a friend's house for a while until her dad tried to screw me too.'

'I'm sorry,' Kelson said.

'I stayed with another friend until I started to show and her mom kicked me out.'

'You don't need to tell me this,' Kelson said.

'You're wrong. I need to tell it – so you understand. The night my friend's mom kicked me out, I got on the El and rode around the city for hours and hours. I couldn't go home. I wouldn't call Harry. Around four in the morning, a couple of girls my age got on my train car – punked up in black and looking scary as hell. When we finished staring each other down, they told me they lived with some other kids in an empty house they'd broken into on Orchard Street. I moved in with them. We spent our days hanging out at a Dunkin' Donuts and our nights riding around the city, sneaking into clubs, and holding parties at the house. Kids came and went. I stayed. I turned fifteen when I was seven months pregnant, and by that time I was like the mother of a family of runaways – some of them gay, some addicted, some just plain crazy, but all of us clinging to each other. The night I had my baby, one of the other kids freaked out and called an ambulance. Everything came down. They let me hold my baby afterward. But then they took her away, and a social worker came, and a woman from the police. I was a kid. I told them my name, and they called my mom and dad. I'd been gone a long time.' She stared at Kelson, her eyes hard now, as if she'd never shed a tear. 'But you know who came to the hospital instead?'

Kelson hated to say it, but he had to and did. 'Harold.'

'Uncle Harry. And you know what he brought me? Another amazing little present in an amazing little box. A gold necklace. He said his mom wore it when he was born. He treated me like I'd done nothing wrong – like *he'd* done nothing. I was confused. I was stupid. I was so tired and I hurt so much. He told me he'd take care of our baby. He said I could go home as if none of this had happened. I could be a girl again – if I let him take care of the baby. I don't know what he promised the hospital. I don't know how much he paid the cop and social worker. I gave my baby to him. He asked, and like every other time he asked, I gave. I don't need to tell you what happened to her.'

Again, Kelson hated to say it. 'She vanished?'

'As if she never existed. I gave my baby to a man who makes people disappear. No one even finds the bones.'

'No way I'll talk to the cops,' she said to Kelson an hour later. Her plate of toast remained on the couch next to her, untouched. 'What would I tell them? Twenty years ago Uncle Harry molested me? I had his baby and I gave the baby to him knowing I'd never see her again – knowing exactly what he would do to her? And no, I don't have any records, though the hospital probably got a big donation from Harry around that time, or maybe a hospital administrator suddenly had a new Mercedes. If the cops could figure out who they assigned to handle this kind of thing back then, maybe I would recognize her, but I was high on pain meds and upset, so maybe not, and even if I could, she can say she doesn't remember me, and who're they going to believe? You don't think I've thought about this? I've ripped myself up over it for twenty years.'

'Tell the cops about Neto,' Kelson said. 'Tell them how Harold Crane makes people disappear. Tell them he's behind the library blast.'

Her mouth twisted as if she would cry, but she laughed a bitter laugh. 'They'd call me a liar.'

'She's right,' Doreen said.

Rodman said, 'They kick people in the ass who have more evidence than she has.'

'What then?' Kelson said.

'We shade it in, man,' Rodman said. 'If we want them to see it, we've got to show it to them. Even if the picture's clear, we can't count on it.'

Kelson considered that. 'Then what are we waiting for?'

So Rodman went into his bedroom and brought back his snub-nose Colt revolver. He gave it to Doreen. 'Stay here and stay safe.'

She turned the gun in her hands and touched the cylinder.

'If anyone you don't know comes through the door, shoot,' Kelson said.

THIRTY-ONE

Rodman and Kelson went out and drove to Emma Almonte's house. By the time they pulled to the curb on Keeler Avenue, a mid-evening gloom hung over the neighborhood. The double security floodlight shined over the yard into the street from under the front gutter, and a porchlight shined on the front steps. Emma Almonte had taken in the American flag from under the floodlight and the rose-embroidered ribbon from between the front door and the burglar bars. Curtains covered the front window except at the edges, where warm yellow light showed.

Kelson and Rodman stepped on to the porch and rang the doorbell.

When no one answered, Rodman moved back into the yard, and Kelson rang again.

No one answered.

Kelson touched the handle on the burglar bars.

Locked.

He reached through the bars and tried the doorknob.

Locked.

He took out his phone and dialed Emma Almonte's number.

It rang twice and she picked up, sounding frightened.

'It's Sam Kelson,' he said. 'I just rang your doorbell.'

'What do you want?'

'I need to talk with you about Victor.'

'I'm done talking,' she said.

'I think I know how your brother died,' he said. 'I think I know who used him.'

She hung up. Then the front door opened, and she peered through the burglar bars into the yard and street. 'Just the two of you?'

'Just us,' Kelson said.

She let them in, closing and locking the door behind them. The front room smelled clean but closed in, as if no one had opened a window or door in days or weeks. The new couch had a dent in it as if Emma Almonte had been sleeping there.

'I don't answer the door after dark anymore,' she said. Last time Kelson saw her, he'd admired her wide olive-brown face and coral lipstick. He'd told her she had great lips. This evening she looked five years older and wore no lipstick.

'What happened to your lips?' he said.

Her expression told him there was something wrong with him, not her. 'Nothing – why?'

'You've had a hard run of it,' he said.

'The FBI locked me up and said I knew things I didn't know.'

'What kind of things?' Kelson asked.

She shook her head. 'You say you've learned how Victor died – how somebody used him.'

Kelson said, 'Did he ever mention a man named Harold Crane or a company called G&G?'

She shook her head again. 'Who are they?'

Before Kelson could explain, Rodman asked her, 'Do you think you could write a list of people he still knew from the army after he got out? Especially anyone who lives in or around the city. Maybe they work private security.'

'The FBI wanted names too,' she said. 'I didn't tell them, the bastards.'

'Are we bastards too?' Kelson said.

She let her eyes rest on Rodman. 'No, you're OK. But it's a short list.' She went into the kitchen and came back with a notepad and pencil. She wrote four names, tore off the sheet, and gave it to Rodman.

Richard Gentian.

Ramsey Garner.

Debbie Turner.

Carlos Rivera.

'Debbie Turner's still in the service,' she said. 'He knew her in Jalalabad. They talked a lot after Victor's friend died from the IED. I don't know where she's stationed now. The other three are out. Richard Gentian's in Indiana with his family. He visited right after Victor came home, and they texted sometimes. I don't know about the other two. When Victor first came back, he talked about getting together with Ramsey Garner, but I don't think he ever did. He mentioned Carlos Rivera a bunch when Rivera was getting out of the army. I guess they served together and didn't get along. I think he lives downstate.'

'Did he ever talk about doing a favor for any of them?' Rodman asked. 'A job?'

'Victor needed help from others. He seemed a long way from doing things for anybody else. Do you think a friend could have killed him?'

'What did the FBI say?' Rodman asked.

'They shut up every time I asked a question. But from the questions they asked me, I got the feeling they thought Victor was everything from a psycho to a Taliban to some kind of Puerto Rican terrorist. I had to tell them, like, three times that we're Dominican, and Dominicans and Puerto Ricans don't even get along.'

Kelson asked, 'Has anyone else talked to you about Victor – other than the FBI, the cops, and us?'

'No, no one,' she said. But she sounded frightened again.

Rodman did his heavy eyelid thing. 'When we came in, you said you don't answer the door after dark anymore.'

She hesitated. 'I'm getting – calls.'

'What kind?'

'The kind you get when your brother blows up people. Hate calls. Threatening calls. Bastards telling me what they want to do to me. People telling me they'll blow up my house. Screaming at me to go back where I came from – which is St Louis, by the way.'

'I'm sorry,' Kelson said. 'Anything else?'

'You want more than that? Yeah, I get real weirdos – the ones that sympathize with Victor and say I'd better keep my mouth shut about him.'

'Do they tell you what they're worried you'll say?' Kelson said. 'Any hints?'

'Yeah, I need to honor the dead. I'd better respect the decisions Victor made. I tell them no one ever respected him more than me—'

The doorbell rang.

Kelson, Rodman, and Emma Almonte looked at each other.

It rang again.

Kelson gestured at the little front hall. 'Want me to answer?'

But Emma Almonte went to the window and peeked outside. 'It's all right,' she said, and she stepped into the hall and opened the door.

Whoever stood on the front porch spoke to her quietly, and she responded quietly. They talked for a minute that way. Then Kelson stepped toward the hall to listen, but Rodman shook his head and said, 'Give her space.'

She talked with the visitor for another minute, then opened the burglar bars and went out to the front porch, pulling the door behind her.

Rodman sat down on the couch. Kelson stared at the white rug with its threadbare middle. He said, 'How do you even wear it out that way?' Three minutes passed. Four. Kelson no longer heard the muffled voices.

He went to the little hall.

'Give her a minute,' Rodman said.

Kelson kept going. He opened the door and stared through the burglar bars. Someone had broken the front porchlight and double security floodlight. He stepped out to the dark porch.

Emma Almonte was gone.

THIRTY-TWO

Kelson and Rodman ran to Kelson's car. They circled the block, then circled the surrounding blocks. They saw no one who looked like Emma Almonte, nothing that indicated where she'd gone.

They drove back to her house and searched it. When she'd gone to the kitchen for a pencil and paper, she'd left her phone on the counter. Kelson pocketed it. Rodman found her purse in her bedroom. Aside from a business card for Ed Davies's law firm, another for FBI Special Agent David Jenkins, and a wallet-sized picture of her and Victor at an amusement park long, long ago, nothing connected her to the Rogers Park Library blast or the evil that seemed to emanate from G&G Private Equity. But Kelson said, 'They made her vanish too.'

'What does she know worth making her disappear?' Rodman said.

'Wrong question. What do they *think* she *might* know?'

'Maybe,' Rodman said.

'What do they think Victor could've told her? How big is the mess they think they need to clean?'

'We need to call this in,' Rodman said.

'What are we going to say? What will anyone do with it?' But Kelson dialed the number on Special Agent Jenkins's card. An answering service picked up, and Kelson recorded a message – 'Emma Almonte's missing.' He left his name and number and hung up.

Then he called Venus Johnson at the Harrison Street Police Station. When she got on the line, he told her, 'Emma Almonte just disappeared.'

'That's OK – the FBI cleared her.'

'You don't understand. She *disappeared*.'

'That's her right.'

'Someone took her.'

'How do you know this?'

'I'm standing in her living room, aren't I?'

'I don't know, are you?' Johnson said.

Kelson tried to explain, but when he told her that Emma Almonte stepped outside of her own house, leaving him and Rodman behind, Johnson said, 'I don't know – after a few days with the FBI, people get screwy.'

'You're ignoring what I'm telling you,' he said.

'Maybe you should take that as a hint,' Johnson said.

When he called Ed Davies, Davies showed more concern but said, 'There's little I can do. You can file a missing person report, but considering all she's gone through with her brother and the ugly news coverage and the crank phone calls, the cops will make this low priority. Good sense for her to go into hiding.'

'They should take it seriously *because* of all she's gone through,' Kelson said.

'You sure she didn't walk away?' Davies said.

'I'm sure, dammit.'

The more worked up Kelson got, the more composed Davies became. 'I'll make a few calls. But keep your expectations low.'

'That's how I live,' Kelson said.

Kelson drove back toward Bronzeville. Beside him, Rodman thumbed through Emma Almonte's phone history.

'Victor called Emma about thirty hours before the library blew up,' Rodman said. 'They talked for eighteen minutes. Last call before that was four and a half hours earlier. They talked for eleven minutes. The day before, six minutes.'

'What's that tell you?' Kelson said.

'Nothing. They talked, is all. Afghanistan might've traumatized him, but he could lean on her.'

'Who else did she talk to?'

'Two calls from David Jenkins at the FBI. Both of them this morning. Each less than a minute. Some other names I don't recognize – one call each. Mostly three to five minutes. A gynecologist yesterday.' He closed call history, checked text messages, and said, 'Nothing here.' He went to voicemail and played a four-second message from Victor, recorded a week before the blast. His voice was thick and sleepy but with an anxious edge. 'Hi, Em – when'll you be home?'

'Ghost voice,' Rodman said.

'A ghost on Xanax,' Kelson said.

Rodman played the next message, which Victor recorded just ten minutes after the first. 'Halogen floods. Ninety watt.' His voice pitched high on the word 'watt'.

Rodman played it again, and said, 'They must've talked between messages. Sounds like he's asking her to pick up bulbs for the security lights.'

'I guess he couldn't see his PTSD hallucinations in the dark,' Kelson said.

Rodman played a recording from two days later. It repeated the earlier message – 'Halogen floods. Ninety watt.' But this time Victor's voice pitched high on both 'floods' and 'watt'.

'That's just weird,' Kelson said.

'Compulsion,' Rodman said. 'Unless he and his sister burned through a lot of bulbs.'

'Or someone kept breaking them – like tonight.'

Rodman played the last voicemail, recorded on the morning of the blast. Now Victor's voice sounded firm and confident. 'I'll get the floods,' he said.

'Ha,' Kelson said. 'Sounds like he got his drugs right.'

'Or found a purpose,' Rodman said.

'Blowing up a library?'

'Hell, I don't know.'

They went up to Rodman's apartment. Doreen, Cindi, and Genevieve Bower sat together on the couch watching *Bill & Ted's Excellent Adventure* on Netflix. Kelson and Rodman stood inside the door and watched them watch. Rodman's snub-nose Colt lay out of reach on the dining table.

'Life confuses me,' Kelson said.

'Escapism,' Doreen said a half hour later, as Kelson drove to her apartment. Rodman and Cindi had made the couch into a bed for Genevieve Bower when the movie ended. 'And anyway, the young Keanu Reeves, right?'

'I guess,' Kelson said, 'but what if you can't escape?'

'There's always alcohol and sex.'

'Alcohol didn't work so well for Genevieve Bower last night.'

'There's always sex. You want to come up?'

He did.

'You're right,' he said at two in the morning, her ass pressed against his naked belly.

'Tell me about it,' she said.

He got up in the dark, went into her bathroom, and showered. When he came back, dressed, she was sleeping. He hung his face over hers until the shape of her lips emerged from the dark. He touched his lips to hers and whispered, 'Good night.'

'Good night . . . Keanu,' she said.

He drove home and parked on the gravel lot behind his building. He went in through the lobby, rode the elevator, and wandered down the hall to his apartment.

As he put the key in the lock, he heard a sound inside. He sighed. 'Just when you think . . .' He removed the key and pulled his KelTec from his belt. He listened at the door. He heard a rustling – a soft voice – and then a long meow. 'Huh,' he said, and he tucked his pistol back in his belt and opened the door.

Sue Ellen, wearing the pajamas she kept at the apartment, was lying on her back on the carpet. She held Payday above her in her left hand. She tossed Painter's Lane a few inches in the air above her right hand. When she turned to see Kelson coming in, the kitten landed on the carpet, rolled, and sprang on to her belly, as if demanding to be tossed again.

'*What* are you doing?' Kelson said.

Sue Ellen smiled up at him. 'I'm teaching them to juggle.'

'It's almost three in the morning—'

'I know,' she said. 'Where have you been?'

'At – *why* are you here?'

'I couldn't sleep, so I came over to play with the kittens.'

'Does your mom know you're here?'

'Of course not.'

THIRTY-THREE

Three hours later, Kelson called Nancy, waking her five minutes before her alarm would go off.

She picked up the phone and mumbled, 'You know I hate when you do this.'

He'd learned in their years together that he couldn't expect a kind word so early in the day. On another morning he might screw with her and say, *Quick, check if Sue Ellen's in bed.* But after so little sleep and a hard day before it, he was wiped out. So he said, 'Sue Ellen snuck out last night. She's sleeping in my bed right now. I'll take her to school.'

Only half awake, Nancy repeated what he told her almost word for word. Then her anger flashed. 'You've got to stop encouraging her to do this.'

'To do *what*?' When Kelson and Nancy were together, he loved that she could kick his ass, but sometimes she perplexed him.

'You treat her like a princess,' she said. 'No wonder she steps on you like—'

'What? I should've kicked her out? And when did she ever step on me?'

'You shouldn't have invited her over.'

'I *didn't.*'

'You shouldn't be so *inviting.*'

'I'll spank her for you when she wakes up.'

'Don't you touch her.'

'I'm going to hang up now,' he said.

She didn't give him the chance. She hung up on him.

Kelson fed the kittens, fed Sue Ellen, fed himself, and drove Sue Ellen to school. 'Your mom says I need to stop being so inviting,' he said, as she got out at Hayt Elementary.

'What does that even mean?' Sue Ellen looked well-rested and well-fed.

'I don't know,' he said. 'I guess it means you shouldn't sneak out at night.'

'I already knew *that.*'

'Tell her, not me.'

He drove to his office, checked his pistols, took out his laptop, and turned it on. As it booted up, he closed his eyes.

Twenty minutes later, his ringing phone woke him – mostly. He was dreaming about the night Nancy did a striptease to Joan Jett's 'I Love Rock 'n' Roll.' He answered the phone, 'Shake it, shake it, baby.'

David Jenkins from the FBI said, '*What?*'

Kelson shook himself awake. 'Do you ever get the sense your life goes in circles?'

'No,' Jenkins said. 'What's this about Emma Almonte?'

'She walked out of her house yesterday when I was talking with her. She disappeared.'

'We released her,' Jenkins said, as if Kelson was accusing him.

'I know you did. Someone else has her. Harold and Sylvia Crane, or their security men.'

'Who?'

'They own an investment firm, and they—'

'Why would they want Emma Almonte?' The FBI man was losing interest fast.

'Let me meet with you for an hour,' Kelson said. 'I'll lay the thing out.'

'You know how busy I am?' Jenkins said. 'You know how many jerks in this city think they've got the lead that'll explain why Victor Almonte did this – because their next-door neighbor's keeping the lights on late, or their cornflakes make a face when they add milk, or their tropical fish squawk them the clue?'

'Fish don't—'

'You know how many jerks think their brother's the next Unabomber?'

'You don't want to meet with me?'

'We determined that Emma Almonte knew nothing about Victor's plans.'

'Somebody else seems to think she knew something.'

'*We* don't,' Jenkins said.

'Why did you—'

'Goodbye, Mr Kelson.'

'You called Emma Almonte twice yesterday,' he said. 'Why? If you're done with her, why call?'

Jenkins went quiet for a moment. Then he said, 'How do you know I called yesterday?'

'I saw the records. I have her phone.'

'She disappeared and then you stole her phone?'

'*No* – well, yes, but no. I took it. DeMarcus Rodman and I did.'

'Goddammit – you've got no business touching any of this. Look, I can't talk to you about it. Do yourself a favor – stay away from it. That's what your friend Venus Johnson told you, right?'

'Venus Johnson wouldn't say I'm a friend. Why did you call Emma Almonte?'

'Goodbye, Mr Kelson,' Jenkins said, and this time he hung up.

Kelson stared at his phone, then turned his chair and looked at the pictures of Sue Ellen and the kittens. He aimed a finger at the one of Payday and Painter's Lane and said, 'Pow.'

He turned back to his desk. 'I don't know why,' he said, then googled one of the names Emma Almonte gave him – Debbie Turner. It was a common name – too common – and he got a hundred sixty thousand hits, including ones for a child actress who played Marta in the film *The Sound of Music*. Kelson started humming 'The Hills Are Alive'. He googled Debbie Turner's name plus the word 'Jalalabad' and got an MSN article titled 'Feds Investigating Deputy's Death in Sperm Bank Mishap'. Kelson told his computer, 'I didn't see that coming.' He read the article. It never mentioned a Debbie Turner. It never mentioned Jalalabad.

He scrolled through the other links. The only promising one showed a picture of a Debbie Turner in the online alumni magazine of the Georgia Military College, which also included a profile of a man who'd served as an advisor in Jalalabad. Kelson spent five minutes with the magazine before saying, 'Nah.'

Emma Almonte had said Richard Gentian lived in Indiana with his family. That combination gave Kelson a twenty-seven-year-old in Indianapolis. Gentian's Instagram pictures showed a tall, straw-haired man playing basketball with friends and goofing around with a German Shepherd. 'Looks like corn bread,' Kelson said. Another site seemed to show that Gentian worked as a maintenance technician for a company called Camp Insulation. Kelson saw nothing that eliminated him absolutely from setting up Victor Almonte with a backpack bomb but nothing that made him a likely player either.

According to Emma Almonte, Victor had planned to get together with Ramsey Garner but wanted to stay away from Carlos Rivera, who'd just gotten out of the service and might live downstate. Kelson googled Ramsey Garner. The name got over a thousand hits, so he added the word 'Chicago', clicked on the first link – for a Facebook page – and said, 'Oh shit.' The red-haired, freckled man Rodman backfisted and then punched into a wall at the G&G offices stared back at him.

Kelson spent the next half hour making a list of everything he could find out about Garner. It added up to little. The man was twenty-six years old. He'd served one tour in Iraq and three in Afghanistan, the last two as an ordnance disposal specialist. Now he lived in a house on West Peterson in the northwest corner of the city, two blocks from the Interstate. He worked by contract for a firm called KVC Security Services, Inc. Facebook pictures showed him driving a black Jeep Wrangler with a bumper sticker that said *Póg mo thóin* – Irish for 'Kiss my ass', Kelson learned when he googled it. Kelson found no mention of a girlfriend – or boyfriend – or family. Garner seemed to like guns. His pictures showed him at a gun range, at an outdoor training exercise, and shirtless at a kitchen table with an assault rifle. Kelson told the picture at the kitchen table, 'Hate to say it, Ramsey, but you look like a dick.'

Kelson found Garner's home phone number and dialed it. When the call went to voicemail, he said to the recorder, 'What did Victor do to deserve this?' He left his name and number and added, 'Call me.'

Then he looked up KVC Security. They had Chicago, Los Angeles, and London offices, the Chicago location in Northbrook, halfway between the city and G&G. 'Why not?' Kelson said. He wrote down the Northbrook address, turned off the computer, slid his KelTec back into his belt, then took it out and said, 'Stupid – walking into a beefcake security company asking to get shot.' He strapped the pistol under the desktop and started toward his office door. 'Stupid,' he said again, and returned to his desk. He turned on his laptop and googled the name Carlos Rivera. 'Because – if . . .' he said.

Google gave him over four hundred thousand hits for the name. A narrowed search that added 'Jalalabad' and 'ordnance' produced just two – one of them with a picture of a Puerto Rican soldier from Marion, Illinois. The picture looked like no one Kelson had seen at G&G or anywhere else. 'Better to know than not,' he said, and turned off the computer again.

But as he stood to leave, someone knocked on his office door.

He felt a momentary, baseless fear, and froze at his desk. Then he said, 'Stupid,' and went to the door.

Two men and a woman stared at him. They probably were in their fifties but had the kind of clear, smooth, childish skin that never seems to age until a last illness, if then. The men were thin and wore neatly tailored navy blue suits. One had on a white Oxford shirt and patterned tie, the other a pale blue Oxford and a steel blue tie. The one in the blue shirt had a white pocket square and a silver tie clip the shape of a golf club. 'Natty,' Kelson said to him. The woman wore a red skirt and jacket, with white hems and lapels. She had tiny but very fancy red shoes. 'Petite,' he said to her.

That brought neither a smile nor a frown to her face.

The man in the white Oxford said, 'Mr Kelson?'

'Yes?'

'We're the Winsins.' As if the name should mean something. 'May we talk?'

'Your voice sounds like money,' Kelson said, 'or like you're trying to sound like it.'

'Which means?' the other man asked.

'Come in.'

THIRTY-FOUR

'Are those Jimmy Choos?' Kelson asked the woman when they were sitting. She set her feet side by side, neat enough to ski.

'Never,' she said, as though he should know better.

'What's wrong with Jimmy Choos?'

'Nothing – if you *wear* Jimmy Choos.'

'Which you don't?' Kelson said.

'I would hope not.'

'I have no idea what that means. Am I supposed to call you "Winsin", or do you have a first name to go with the last?'

'People who work for us usually call me Ms Winsin.'

'First, I'm not working for you. Second, I have almost zero control over how I speak.'

'We prefer that you try,' the white Oxford said.

'See, a couple years ago, I got shot in the—'

'We've looked into your background,' the blue Oxford said.

'My name is Christine,' the woman said. 'Chris, if you prefer.'

'Bob,' said the white Oxford.

'David,' said the blue Oxford.

'Well, David, Bob, and Christine, I'm buried to my ears in a couple of jobs right now. What do you think I can do for you?'

'We hope to bury you a little deeper in one of them,' the woman said. 'We would like you to locate a gentleman named Marty LeCoeur.'

'What do you want with him?' Kelson said.

Bob Winsin folded his fingers over his belly. 'We've invested money through G&G Private Equity – money that G&G seems to have misplaced. We understand that Marty LeCoeur represents our best chance of getting our money back.'

'How much money?'

'Will you help find him?' he said.

Kelson said, 'Did you get Marty's name from the Cranes?'

'We did,' he said.

Kelson said, 'The Cranes couldn't get Marty to find your money, and they're vicious. What makes you think you can do it?'

Christine Winsin tapped the toes of her tiny shoes on the carpet as if they were windup toys. 'Harry and Sylvia Crane are tightlipped about everything they do at their firm. They put buffers throughout their investment and distribution processes. That's the main reason we've used their services. But they gave us Marty LeCoeur's name – and yours – with hardly a protest.'

Kelson grinned at her. 'You little fellows twisted their arms?'

She stopped tapping her shoes. 'Don't make the same mistake others have made, Mr Kelson. Our research says that despite appearances, you're smart.'

'You use the word "research" like a knife.'

Bob Winsin said, 'We pay well for the services we value, Mr Kelson.' He reached into the inside pocket of his suit jacket and pulled out a checkbook.

'No,' Kelson said.

'Excuse me?' As if Kelson had spoken in a strange language.

'I could get Marty for you easy enough, but I won't do it. He's a friend. Crooked as hell, but he's a good guy, you know. And I don't like you. At all. I don't know where you get your money or what you do with it, and I don't care. Now, if you'll leave, I'll walk out with you – I have somewhere to go that I do care about.'

The Winsins stayed in their chairs, as if they'd bought the office out from under Kelson. Christine Winsin said, 'Do you know where real power lies? A long time ago, it was with men like you – men who muscled through the world. Then, for many years, it was with governments and churches, with their collective muscle. Then with money.' When Kelson smiled at that, she said,

'Yes, it still lies with money. But do you know what the backbone of power is? The nerve center?'

'I know you're boring me,' Kelson said.

Christine Winsin pressed her tiny feet together. 'The backbone – the nerve center – is personal information. Everyone values it, but few aside from big corporations have the resources to access it. For example, your daughter Sue Ellen – eleven years old – goes to Hayt Elementary School. You should talk with her about the C she's earning in math. She likes to draw. She has a stuffed animal – a monkey – she keeps on her pillow. You should also probably talk with her about posting personal pictures on the internet. Less easily discoverable, she has a habit of sneaking out of her mother's house at night. Some might call that a cry for attention.'

Kelson tried to speak – tried to tell her what he would do if she or her brothers ever hurt Sue Ellen or even thought of hurting her – but his words tangled in his mouth. So he reached under the desktop, pulled out his KelTec, and aimed at her.

She and her brothers showed no fear.

'Now who's the little fellow?' she said.

But David Winsin said, 'Good, we're getting down to business,' as if all they'd talked about up until this moment was a tedious preliminary to what mattered.

Bob Winsin said, 'You should understand, we have no interest in harming anyone. Why would we want to hurt a little girl? Why would we want to hurt her mother? Think of all those kids with unfilled cavities. Why would we want to hurt your friend DeMarcus Rodman? When someone dies in his neighborhood, the police turn their backs and the nightly news does a story on Girl Scout cookie sales.'

Kelson shifted his pistol so it pointed at the middle of his white Oxford shirt.

'The point is,' Christine Winsin said, 'we wish to meet with Marty LeCoeur. We wish to discuss positive outcomes with him. Everyone might benefit – Mr LeCoeur included. Why don't you contact him – through whatever means you wish to use? Ask him whether he would like to enter a mutually beneficial arrangement with us. If he agrees, we will write you a second check. In the meantime . . .'

She didn't need to glance at her brother. Bob Winsin pulled out a pen, wrote a check, and laid it on the desk in front of Kelson.

Kelson picked it up. It was for ten thousand dollars. He made to rip it.

'Don't make the same mistake others have made,' Christine Winsin said again.

Kelson eyed her tiny red shoes. He eyed the silver tie clip on David Winsin's tie. He eyed Bob Winsin's ageless face. Then he put the check in his top desk drawer.

He said, 'I'll talk with Marty. I'll see if he'll meet you.'

'That's all we ever wanted,' Bob Winsin said.

The Winsins got up together as if responding to a silent signal. Bob Winsin set a business card with a phone number on the desk. 'Soonest would be best,' he said. He, his brother, and his sister left Kelson's office. When they shut the door behind them, it made no sound.

THIRTY-FIVE

K elson drove north toward KVC Security Services, talking on the phone with Rodman.

'Yeah, I can get a message to Marty,' Rodman said. 'He's holed up at—'

'Don't,' Kelson said. 'These people tapped into Sue Ellen's school and social media. For all I know they're listening right now.'

'If they touch Sue Ellen, I'll break their necks,' Rodman said.

'Only after I do,' Kelson said. 'Problem is, they're snakes. I don't know they have necks to break. I do know they aren't worried about me breaking them.'

'I'll get the message to Marty.'

'How's Genevieve Bower?' Kelson asked.

'Cindi says when I snore I crack the ceiling paint. But that woman kept me up all night.'

'She's very physical,' Kelson said.

'She's a beast.'

'The Cranes are looking for her. Can you put her with Marty?'

'Yeah, I could do that. But she dated him, and Janet might have a problem. Marty's a lover – can't say what'll happen if we get them together in a hideaway.'

Kelson laughed. 'Marty's a lover?'

'For a guy people underestimate, you're a bad judge of character. Marty's got moves. I heard Janet telling Cindi what he does with that hand of his.'

'You're screwing with me now.'

'God's truth.'

KVC Security operated out of a large brown single-story building with tinted windows in an industrial park east of the highway. American-made pickups and German sports cars filled the narrow parking lot.

Kelson turned off his engine in a visitor spot, glanced at himself in the rearview mirror, and, as usual, was surprised by the face that stared back. 'Here goes,' he told his reflection. 'Watch my back.'

The bald man at the lobby reception desk had wide, unblinking blue eyes and a voice so tremulous Kelson had to lean in to make sense of his words.

Kelson introduced himself and said, 'I'd like to talk with somebody about one of the KVC security men.'

'That would be Mrs Ricks in HR.'

'Excuse me?'

'Mrs Ricks. HR,' the man said. He sat in his desk chair with the rigid posture of a back injury victim.

Kelson waited for him to do something. When he didn't, Kelson said, 'Could you let her know I want to talk with her?'

The man picked up his phone, tapped an extension number, and mumbled.

Then he looked up at Kelson and said something to him.

Kelson leaned in. 'Excuse me?'

'Which security officer?'

'Ramsey Garner – works at G&G Private Equity.'

The man mumbled the name into the phone, then told Kelson, 'Mrs Ricks will be right out.'

Kelson said, 'Did something terrible happen to you?'

'No, why?'

'The way you look – and talk.'

'No one shot *me* in the head,' the man said. 'I'd duck if a drug dealer pulled a gun on me.'

'You scare me,' Kelson said.

'We make inquiries.'

Then a woman in her late forties came from a door at the far end of the lobby, her heels loud on the tile floor. She wore a beige pantsuit. Her blond hair fell to her shoulders, and she had a single strand of pearls around her neck.

She held a hand to shake Kelson's before she neared him. 'I'm Jennifer Ricks. Let's go to my office.'

She never acknowledged the man at the reception desk, and they left him staring unblinkingly at the building entrance.

'What's his problem?' Kelson asked as she led him into a bright hallway.

'Does he have one?' She opened an office door.

The room had no windows, no art or photographs on the walls. Except for a pad of yellow legal paper and a pen, the desktop was bare. The woman rounded the desk and gestured at a chair across from her. 'Please.' She sat and picked up the pen. When Kelson sat too, she gave him a cold smile. 'How can I help you?'

'Do all of your security workers hire out as goons?'

'"Goons"? Really?'

'What's the industry term? Strong-arm thugs? Gorillas?'

'KVC has been in business for thirty years,' she said. 'We've always remained above reproach.'

'Because you beat up or kill anyone who reproaches you?'

'Because we maintain high standards.'

'Stop reading from the handbook,' Kelson said.

'Then stop being rude.' Her voice and expression were placid.

'Tell me about Ramsey Garner.'

'Who's asking?'

'You know who I am. Even zombie-boy at the front desk knows.'

She tipped her head, as if to acknowledge the truth of what he said. 'What's to tell? Mr Garner has worked for us for the past eight months. He has a military background, as I guess you know. He trained for the SEALs but dropped out before completing the program. We don't hold that against him. He's received high evaluations in the jobs he's worked for us.'

'How long has he been at G&G?'

'We don't discuss clients.'

'Then what do you know about the blast at the Rogers Park Library last week?'

'Nothing, except what the news has said. What *should* I know?' Placid.

'Do you know Ramsey Garner used to pal around with the man the FBI and cops are accusing – Victor Almonte? They served together in Afghanistan.'

For the first time, she hesitated. But her face showed no surprise or concern. 'I didn't know that.'

'Do you know that one of the men who died from the blast was cooking the accounting for G&G?'

'We don't discuss clients.'

'Does KVC send you to special school to do that?'

'Do what?'

'You and zombie-boy tell me nothing with your faces. With zombie-boy, it's just strange. With you, it's dishonest. I could tell you that G&G farts poisoned gas, and you'd give me the same flat-faced *We don't talk about clients.*'

'I've read about you,' she said. 'Mr Garner asked for a profile after encountering you and a colleague yesterday. As part of company protocol, our team circulates summaries of potentially troubling figures to all regional employees. When I read yours, I admit that I dismissed you. But now that you're here, you fascinate me. What exactly do you want?'

'The man who died while doing the G&G books – he was the nephew of a friend of mine. A woman named Genevieve Bower who Ramsey Garner and some other G&G security men have been hunting – she's my client. I'm pretty sure Garner or his friends killed a guy she was dating. And I'm pretty sure Garner set up Victor Almonte. So I want you to tell me how much you and your bosses know about this. How much of it you've let happen. Or made happen.'

As he spoke she fingered her strand of pearls like rosary beads. But when she saw that he noticed, she laid her hands flat on the desk.

'I can assure you—' she said, but stopped and assured him nothing because two men entered the office behind Kelson. One of them, about the age of the HR woman, wore a tight black T-shirt over his muscled chest and biceps. The other was Ramsey Garner, who wore khakis and a green golf shirt. He had a bruise on his freckled jaw where Rodman had punched him and a scabbing split over his lip where Rodman had backfisted him. He looked like he wanted to hit someone the way Rodman had hit him. He looked like that someone was Kelson.

THIRTY-SIX

'Stand up,' said Ramsey Garner, aiming a black pistol at Kelson.

Kelson stood, put his hands in the air, and said, 'I left mine in my office.' The man in the black T-shirt frisked him. 'I say dumb stuff, but I'm not stupid. Ask Mrs Ricks. She's got the research – a word I'm starting to hate, by the way.'

'Shut up,' Garner said.

'Good one,' Kelson said. 'You *know* I can't, right? I'm constitutionally – cognitively – unable to—'

Garner hit Kelson's head with his gun butt – hard enough to silence most men.

'Ouch,' Kelson said.

'Another word, and I hit you again.'

'Please don't. My therapist says a concussion—'

Garner hit him harder.

'Jesus, don't do that.' Kelson spun and tried to punch him.

Garner aimed the pistol at Kelson's chest. 'Are you crazy?'

Kelson yelled at him, 'In spite of appearances, no.'

'Sit down,' Garner said.

'Gladly.' Kelson sat.

Garner nodded at Mrs Ricks. 'Out.'

'Yes, sir,' she said, and left the office, closing the door behind her.

'*Who's* in charge?' Kelson said.

'I guess it's the man with the gun,' Garner said. He went behind the desk and sat in Mrs Ricks's chair.

The man in the black T-shirt stood behind Kelson, his arms crossed over his chest.

Kelson glanced at him and said, 'Stop flexing your muscles, Squirt.'

'You really can't shut up,' Garner said.

'I really can't. Especially when I'm nervous.' His eye twitched.

'Let's keep you nervous, then. Where's Genevieve Bower?'

Kelson made a face, struggling to keep his mouth shut. It was no use. 'She spent the night at my friend DeMarcus Rodman's apartment – he's the one who clobbered you in your freckled face yesterday – but now she's gone.'

'Gone where?'

'*Got* you,' Kelson said. 'I don't know. DeMarcus is taking her to stay with someone else who interests you – Marty LeCoeur. I don't know where Marty's hiding. I swear. But something else might interest you. Marty's a lady's man. You'd never guess it – or I wouldn't. He's like Squirt.'

Garner fingered his pistol.

'Does Squirt have a name?' Kelson asked.

Garner scratched his face by the bruise. 'He won't tell it to you. He won't tell you a damn thing. But he'll make you tell me anything I want to know. If necessary, he'll make your friends talk too. The sounds grown men make once he starts on them are terrifying.'

'I get it,' said Kelson. 'Squirt's a mean little bastard. He spits acid. He pokes holes in human hearts with his pointy fingers. But I have a question for you. Why did you set up Victor Almonte?'

'Jesus Christ, I should just shoot you.'

'If you do, neither of us will get what we want.'

'Yeah, but I'll save myself the aggravation.'

'Why did you set up Almonte?'

Garner stared at him square, and Kelson tried not to swallow hard. Garner said, 'Do you know how Jeff Finch died?'

Kelson said, 'I don't even know who Jeff Finch is.'

'He served with me and Almonte in Afghanistan,' Garner said. 'Drunk or sober, he was the best bomb disposal guy in the unit.

Until Almonte fucked up. All Almonte had to do was carry a bag from the truck. Every goddamned job, you carry the bag. He didn't carry the bag. When he went back to the truck for it, the IED exploded. No more Jeff Finch.'

'Ahh,' Kelson said.

'Ahh what?'

'You blame Almonte for your pal's death.'

Garner gave him a gaze as if from far above. 'I don't blame anyone. Sooner or later we all fuck up. When we do, someone dies. It was Finch's turn, is all. But Almonte blamed himself. Finch's death tore him apart. I did him a favor at the library. He went out with purpose – on a mission – the way he meant to die.'

'Bullshit,' Kelson said. 'He died to make the Cranes more millions.'

'He didn't know that. He thought – no, he *knew* he served a greater cause. I told him so, and that's all he needed to know. He died like a good soldier.' Garner tapped the pistol with a forefinger as if he was sending code. 'Now, where is Genevieve Bower?'

'Don't know,' Kelson said. 'How did you do it?'

'What? Convince Almonte to set off the bomb?' Garner glanced at the man in the black T-shirt. Kelson sensed that if Garner twitched or bared his teeth or wiggled his nose, the man would make him churn out terrifying sounds. But Garner said, 'A variation on a cell phone trigger. Anybody who's done the first week of disposal training can take one apart and put it together again. I threw in a couple of neat tricks to satisfy certain requirements, but nothing fancy. Simple is best.'

'A simple death.'

'All death is simple,' Garner said. 'You're living, then you're dead. A light switch.'

'Except when someone else's death tears you apart, like Victor Almonte.'

'Maybe he didn't understand how simple it could be. He thought too much. Where's Genevieve Bower?'

'I told you, I don't know.'

Garner didn't twitch. Or bare his teeth. Or wiggle his nose. But the man in the black T-shirt was suddenly choking Kelson.

As the man gripped him around the throat, Kelson felt himself lose breath – felt a fast-approaching loss of consciousness, felt what seemed like a cascade of blood from his brain into a cavity he'd never known existed. He reached to grab the man, to gouge his eyes or rip off his nostrils – anything at all – but his hands found empty air. So he signaled submission, total surrender.

Then he could breathe again – a rasping breath that scraped his throat. He tried to talk. No words came out. He ripped more breath into his lungs.

'Take your time,' Garner said.

Kelson breathed – tried to breathe – for a minute, then another, and his breath felt like he was bleeding inside. Garner tapped his pistol and watched. The man in the black T-shirt stood behind Kelson again, his arms crossed over his chest.

When Kelson spoke, his words cracked, as if the man in the T-shirt had bent his windpipe. 'I'll take you – to DeMarcus. You can – ask him – where.'

Garner looked disappointed. 'Coward,' he said. 'You lasted like seven seconds. Even the weakest soldier lasts ten or eleven before giving up his friends.'

'Not' – the word creaked – 'not – giving – up. Playing you – for time.' When Garner started to grin, Kelson added, 'DeMarcus – will break you – in half. I'll break – Squirt.'

Garner laughed at him. 'You're a real trip, Mr Kelson.'

THIRTY-SEVEN

As Garner drove to the city, Kelson's voice came back, and he could breathe without feeling like he was tearing holes in his throat. They rode in a green four-door Ram 1500 pickup, the man in the black T-shirt sitting next to Kelson in the backseat.

'That's a cool move,' Kelson said. 'You ever accidentally kill someone with it?'

'Don't bother,' Garner said.

'Ironic, huh?' Kelson said. 'Me talking too much, him talking too little.'

'I wish you'd follow his example,' Garner said.

'Wish away.' He directed Garner south into the city and told him about Payday and Painter's Lane. He pointed him through the streets toward Rodman's Bronzeville apartment building and had him park by the Ebenezer Baptist Church. 'In this neighborhood, you might want Squirt to stay in the truck if you like your wheels and stereo.'

'We'll take the risk,' Garner said.

They climbed the stairs and knocked on Rodman's door. When Cindi answered, she eyed Kelson, then Garner, then the man in the T-shirt. 'DeMarcus went out,' she said. She wore a brown blouse, a long brown skirt, and sandals.

'We'll come back later,' Kelson said.

But Garner pushed past him into the front room. The man in the T-shirt shoved Kelson inside and closed the door.

'Sorry,' Kelson said.

Cindi gave him a cold look but said, 'No worries.'

Garner had his pistol out. He went from room to room, making sure they were alone. When he came back he pointed the gun at the couch and told Kelson and Cindi to sit down.

Cindi said, 'Coffee?'

'What?' Garner looked at her hard for the first time.

'Do you want coffee?' she said. 'DeMarcus went out for a couple hours. Sometimes he doesn't come back when he says he will. Sometimes not for days.'

Garner gazed at the portraits of Malcolm X, Cindi, and Martin Luther King, Jr, over the couch, and he smiled. 'Aren't *you* the princess? Cute too. I'll bet DeMarcus has a lot of fun with you. What a shame if that all ended.'

'Does that mean you don't want coffee?' she said.

The smile fell. 'It means I want you to call DeMarcus and tell him to get back here because some men are threatening to do very bad things to you.'

Kelson said, 'If you try anything, DeMarcus and I will destroy you.'

But Cindi surprised him. 'This gentleman knows what he wants. Let's give it to him.'

Garner looked suspicious but said, 'You're the passive one in the couple, aren't you – the Martin Luther King? And your boy DeMarcus, he's the fighter – the Malcolm? You like a man who takes charge?'

'I like a strong man,' Cindi said.

'I'll bet you do,' he said. 'Call DeMarcus.' He wiggled the gun at Kelson. 'And *you* sit down.'

Kelson sat on the couch, and Cindi called Rodman. As the line rang, she watched Garner and said, 'He isn't picking up.'

Garner held his hand for her phone. 'Give it to me.'

But she kept it and left a message. 'Hey, baby, there's a couple of men here. They say they need to see you right away. Or bad things will happen. That's what they seem to think.' She hung up and offered Garner the phone. He waved it away and gestured at Kelson. 'Sit down with him.'

'You sure you don't want coffee?'

'Just sit.'

'Anything at all, baby,' she said, like she meant it.

Garner eyed her. 'And stop that shit.'

An hour later, the man in the black T-shirt still looked as cool as when they walked in, but Garner was sweating.

'Call again,' he told Cindi.

She dialed, waited, and left another message, asking Rodman to call back.

A half hour after that, Garner demanded her phone. He dialed the last number Cindi had called and left a third message. 'Listen, you asshole, I'm here with your girl. You really, *really* want to be here too, because what's a girl going to do when a man leaves his home?'

Another hour passed. The man in the black T-shirt went to Garner and whispered.

Garner nodded and said to Cindi, 'Coffee. And food.'

'Anything, baby,' she said.

'Keep fucking with me and I'll fuck with you for real,' he said.

She went into the kitchen, and for a while the man in the black T-shirt stood in the doorway and watched her cook. Then he went to Garner and whispered again.

'Guess so,' Garner said, and looked at Kelson. 'He thinks we don't need you anymore. You're extra baggage. What do you think of that?'

'I think you scare the hell out of me,' Kelson said. 'But I also think until DeMarcus comes back, I'm all you've got – and maybe DeMarcus isn't coming back for a long time.'

Garner nodded and said to the man, 'He right?'

The man seemed to think. As he did, his right eyelid hung lower than his left. He went to the couch and sat next to Kelson.

Kelson said, 'Why do I figure he could kill me before I even saw him move?'

Garner said, 'Because you're smarter than you look?'

Five minutes later, Cindi brought two plates of scrambled eggs and toast from the kitchen. She gave one to the man on the couch and set the other on a table for Garner. She went back into the kitchen and returned with two cups of coffee.

When the men started to eat, Kelson said, 'How about me?'

Garner laughed at him. 'She's a good little house bitch. She knows who's boss.'

Kelson rose from the couch – but the man in the black T-shirt rose with him, and Garner swept his pistol into his hand.

Cindi told Kelson, 'It's all right.' Soothing.

Garner said to him, 'Listen to the girl – everything's cool. You want it to stay that way, don't you?'

Cindi asked Garner, 'You mind if I make some food for him and me?'

Garner smiled. 'I like you, sweetheart. You go ahead – and if you spit in his eggs, I won't tell.'

'Yes, sir,' she said, and disappeared into the kitchen.

Kelson and the man in the black T-shirt sat on the couch again. Garner sat at the table and ate, threatening to shoot Kelson if he didn't shut up. The second time he threatened him, a lump of scrambled egg fell from his mouth on to the table. He looked at it, perplexed, picked it up, and put it in his mouth again.

Then the man in the black T-shirt went to sleep. His fork dropped from his hand. His plate tilted on his lap.

Garner didn't seem to notice. He was concentrating on steering his own fork to his lips.

'Huh,' Kelson said. He poked the man next to him in the ribs. The man grunted – the most sound Kelson had heard him make.

Garner picked up his toast, brought it halfway to his face, then seemed to find it too heavy. His arm lowered to the table, the toast still in his fingers, and he left it there. He half stared at his pistol on the table. He tried to speak. The words seemed too heavy. He reached for the pistol, missed, and the momentum tipped him off the chair. The impact when he hit the floor woke him, and he pushed to his hands and knees. Then he sagged, and his body sank facedown.

Cindi came from the kitchen with two more plates of eggs and toast. She stopped when she saw Garner and the other man. 'Demerol,' she told Kelson. 'I used the max dosage for when we want them to sleep at Rush Medical. End-of-life care.'

She set the plates on the table across from where Garner had sat and studied the unconscious men. 'No,' she told Garner, 'it's *not* all right.' She kicked him in the ribs. 'It's wrong.' She kicked him again.

Ten minutes later, when Rodman burst through the apartment door, fire in his eyes, Kelson and Cindi were eating eggs and toast, and Garner and the other man, their arms and legs bound with electrical cords, were sleeping on the floor by the couch.

THIRTY-EIGHT

'You know I love you, Sam,' Cindi said to Kelson, 'but defending my honor? It's insulting.'

They sat at the table in the apartment while Rodman ate an omelet he made after calming down. Bound and gagged, Ramsey Garner and the man in the black T-shirt lay on the floor.

'I didn't mean to insult you,' Kelson said.

'And it's embarrassing to *you*. You boys want to fight each other, all I need to do is stand back and let you knock each other down.'

'Or crumble some Demerol in our scrambled eggs?'

'Mama's little helper.'

'I was trying to help.'

Rodman swallowed a piece of toast. 'Cindi takes care of herself.'

Kelson smiled at the big man. 'That's why you crashed through the door?'

Rodman picked up his cup of coffee, considered it, downed half of it. 'Maybe it's a boy thing. Wanting to save the girl when we can't even save ourselves.'

Cindi smiled at him too. 'You didn't want to save anything when you came in. You wanted to stomp on it.'

Rodman narrowed his already narrow eyes. 'Speaking of.' He stood and picked up Ramsey Garner the way another man might heft a sand bag. He carried him toward the back of the apartment.

'What are you doing?' Cindi said.

'Throwing him off the fire escape.' But a few moments later, the sound of the shower came from the bathroom.

Cindi used Rodman's fork to spear a bite of omelet. 'Going to take more than cold water to make that hophead talk sense.'

But when Rodman dragged Garner, still bound and gagged, back into the room by his shirt collar, leaving a trail of bath water on the floor, the freckled man looked awake and angry.

Rodman released his collar and Garner flopped to the floor. 'Look what I found,' Rodman said, then stepped over Garner, straddling him. He stared down at him. 'My girlfriend thinks I'm the kind of man who'd piss on you,' he said with perfect calm. 'Do I look like that kind of man?'

Garner's eyes shined with anger.

'I need an answer,' Rodman said, 'because I'm trying to figure out who I am right now. Call it an identity crisis.'

Garner made a sound like he was spitting into his gag.

'Option two,' Rodman said. 'My friend Sam and I go out for an hour and leave you with Cindi. I've got this testosterone thing, but she's hardcore.'

Garner made more sounds.

So Rodman pinched the gag in his big fingers and pulled it from Garner's mouth. 'You trying to say something?'

'Fuck you.'

Rodman put the gag back over his mouth. He hovered over him, and, when he spoke, his voice was calm and quiet. 'I'll tell you a little story. Fifteen years ago, Sam and I went to police academy together. I always wanted to be a cop – since I was a kid, right? Then my little brother stepped into the middle of a drug bust and a cop shot him. The cop said my brother had a pocketknife, but if he did, no one else saw it. The review board ruled the killing justifiable. I dropped out of the academy the next day. Everyone said I was distraught. I suppose I was. But the real reason I dropped out was I knew if I ever bumped into the cop who shot my brother, I would tear his lungs out. I don't know why I thought about his lungs. They just seemed right for big hands like mine. You got anything to say to that?'

Garner nodded.

Rodman pulled the gag off.

Garner said, 'Fuck you.'

Rodman said, 'Some guys never learn.'

He grabbed Garner's collar and lifted him to his feet. Garner's ankles were bound tight, and Rodman held him, wobbling, as if he might let him fall to the floor again. But he pulled him to the table and pushed him down in a chair. A pool of shower water stood on the floor where Garner had been lying. Another pool formed around his feet.

'You're a mess,' Rodman said.

Garner eyed his partner on the floor by the couch. 'Is he dead?'

'Sleeping,' Cindi said.

'You did this?' the freckled man said.

'You're an easy trick,' she said.

'Cunt.'

She got up. Calm. Like maybe she would clear the table. But she slapped his face. She sat back down on her chair. 'I get so tired of men like you,' she said.

A welt rose on his cheek. 'Bitch.'

Kelson said, 'Explain what happened. How the library bomb worked. How the Cranes got you to set it up. Exactly what you told Victor Almonte to convince him to do a suicide job.'

Garner spat at him.

'Does the army train you to do that? Insult your captors? Rock them back on their heels?'

Garner called him a motherfucker. A cocksucker. A half dozen other names.

Kelson laughed at him and said, 'You're betraying the fear you won't admit to.'

Rodman said, 'You can talk to us, or we'll let Cindi loose on you.'

Garner forced a grin. 'I like it when a nigger girl hits me.'

'You like it when I knock out all your teeth?' Cindi said.

Garner licked his lips. 'You let me lick you afterward, that'll be fine.'

'How'd you get this way?' she said. 'Did your daddy spank you too hard when you were three? Did your mommy tickle your tinkle in the tub?'

Rodman said, 'Answer our questions, we'll let you go.'

For the first time, Garner cut the psycho act. 'Why would you let me go?'

'Why would I want you here stinking up my apartment?' Rodman said.

'And what about him?' Garner nodded at the unconscious man in the black T-shirt.

'We keep him here until he wakes up,' Rodman said. 'Feed him coffee. Get his heartbeat where it belongs. Chat with him. If he behaves, we let him go too.'

'He won't talk to you,' Garner said.

'Then I'll throw him off the fire escape.'

'He doesn't talk,' Garner said.

Rodman looked at Kelson.

Kelson said, 'It's true. I don't know if he can. He whispers some, though.'

Rodman told Garner, 'Then if you want to lug him out of here asleep, be my guest.'

Garner thought some more. 'What do you want to know?'

Rodman pointed a thumb at Kelson. 'What he said. How did the whole thing work?'

'I told him before,' Garner said. 'I did a variation on a cell phone trigger.'

'What was the variation?' Kelson asked.

Garner stared at the man in the black T-shirt, as if willing him to get up and help. He said, 'The accountant – your friend Neto – needed to finish the transactions. I gave him a number to text when he was done. The text set off the backpack.'

'How's that a variation?' Kelson said.

'You usually use a cell phone trigger to keep from getting blown up,' Garner said. 'I used it to contain and destroy the evidence, including Neto and the phone. Good plan if Neto'd sent the money where he should've.'

'But a blast gets attention,' Rodman said. 'Why do it?'

'Talk to Chip Voudreaux. His idea.'

'Not the Cranes'?' Kelson said.

'Voudreaux handled the details. He asked me to help, and I know explosives. I guess you use the tools you've got.'

'Stupid way to do it,' Rodman said.

'How did you convince Victor Almonte?' Kelson said.

'Like I said, I told him this was part of the bigger effort. Almonte came back from Jalalabad broken. I fed him a story about a computer whiz kid who was using the library to send funds to the insurgents. Neto played his part like he was born to it. Those last days, Almonte got healthy. That bomb didn't rip him apart. It put him together again.'

Cindi said, 'Keep telling yourself that.'

He gave her a superior smile. 'Unless you were there, you don't know.'

'You've got a sick head,' she said.

Rodman said, 'How does Genevieve Bower tie in?'

'Does she need to?' Garner started to look smug again. 'She was Harry Crane's hobby twenty years ago. He should've cleaned up when he got tired of her. Now he's got me and the others to do the job.'

Cindi said, 'You take any job no matter how nasty?'

'I don't judge,' Garner said. 'You know how many fifty-year-old Afghans I saw with fourteen-year-old wives? Send Harry Crane over there, he'd be a warlord, and all the fathers would give him their daughters. Not so long ago, he could've stayed in the good old USA. He could've floated down the Mississippi and plucked *you* off a plantation when you were fourteen, and afterward the other men would pour him a glass of whiskey and congratulate him on his good taste. No, I don't judge.'

'Well, I do,' she said, 'and I think you're filthy.'

'Each to his own.'

'Not in my home,' she said, and she got up and hit him again.

THIRTY-NINE

M arty rented two rooms a mile from his house, in the basement of a South Wabash office building. In one room he had a bed, a refrigerator, a hotplate, and a microwave oven. In the other he kept four computers, seven decks of cards, a green plastic bowl with three disposable phones in it, and the necessary furniture. Above his computer desk, a monitor showed images of the corridor outside the rooms and the street upstairs. Marty got in trouble often enough that he kept this hiding place to disappear into until he could worm his head out without getting it blown off. Sometimes he woke at his house in the middle of the night with a gut sense that someone was coming for him, and he'd grab his bag and *go, go, go* – but only the one mile to his basement rooms. He knew that most fugitives got caught by running to unfamiliar ground, where they revealed themselves by using credit cards and ATMs or just by looking lost. He kept the basement refrigerator stuffed with microwave dinners. On top of the refrigerator, he stacked cans of pork 'n' beans and SpaghettiOs, which he'd loved since he was a kid. He could stay for a month or more pigging out on comfort food, watching internet porn, and playing solitaire.

When Kelson, Rodman, and Cindi came, Genevieve Bower and Doreen were sitting on a brown leatherette sofa playing blackjack. Marty, in a sleeveless white T-shirt that exposed the mushroom-like stump of his missing arm, worked at one of the functioning computers. The room smelled of sweat and SpaghettiOs.

Genevieve Bower said to Doreen, 'If you can't find a job in Chicago, you could clean up at the blackjack tables in Reno.'

'More likely we'll all be living here with Marty for the next year,' Kelson said. 'You've got some vicious guys coming after you. You know someone named Ramsey Garner?'

'Shh,' Marty said, and tapped the keys on his keyboard.

Genevieve Bower put down the deck of cards. 'Is he one of Uncle Harry's people?'

'He does it all for Harold – builds a backpack bomb, hunts for missing relatives like you, takes a punch without complaining too much.'

'Shh,' Marty said again.

'And he has a funny friend who doesn't talk,' Kelson said.

Marty tapped more keys, hit enter, stared at the computer screen, and shouted, 'Fuuuck.' Then he looked at Rodman, Cindi, and Kelson with tired, red eyes. 'I'm getting real close, but this is a bastard.'

Genevieve Bower said, 'He works day and night – he doesn't sleep.'

'This one's for Neto,' Marty said.

'You're close?' Rodman asked.

'Three, four times, I think I'm in,' Marty said. 'But I'm a fucking rat in a fucking maze. I see the cheese, but when I go to grab it, it isn't fucking there. I'd hate Neto for it if I didn't love the little fucker so much.'

'If you get the money, you'll give it back to G&G?' Kelson said.

'You're joking, right? After what they did to Neto? I've got places to hide it so deep, they'll need a fucking submarine.'

'One of the families that put their money with G&G – the Winsins – came to see me. They want to talk to you.'

'Yeah, DeMarcus told me. Screw that.'

'They want to make their case,' Kelson said. 'They threatened to hurt you if you don't talk.'

Marty blinked his red eyes. 'I'm snug in this little hole. I can stay here for fucking ever. You can tell these people this rat would rather chew off a leg than deal with pricks like them.'

'I'll quote you,' Kelson said.

'I appreciate that.'

Kelson said, 'You know, for this kind of money, others will come after you.'

Marty gave him a tired smile. 'It's a hard fucking world.' He offered to heat pork 'n' beans for everyone, though he had only two bowls and they'd need to share. Rodman said they'd just eaten, and, after convincing Marty to call if anyone tried to break in, he, Cindi, Kelson, and Doreen went up through the stairwell and out to the street.

Late that afternoon, after dropping off Rodman and Cindi at their apartment and Doreen at hers, Kelson sat alone in his office. He slipped his shoes off under his desk and rested his feet on the desktop. His KelTec lay in his lap, warm and reassuring.

He called Emma Almonte's number and, when the recording prompted him, said, 'Where did you go?' He left his name and number and asked her to call.

Then he called his lawyer Ed Davies and filled him in on all he'd learned since they last talked.

'This goes from bad to worse,' Davies said. 'What am I supposed to do with it?'

'The Cranes have money and power,' Kelson said. 'The Winsins too. Enough to make life rotten for the people they don't like. How they get away with it, I don't know. I figure they have connections at the police. How many or how deep, I don't know either. If I vanish or turn up dead the way people around the Cranes do, you'll at least have what I've told you.'

'Sounds like the smart thing for me to do would be to forget it.'

'You could do that. I wouldn't be around to stop you.'

'Be careful,' Davies said. 'I don't want to have to face that decision.'

Next, Kelson dialed Nancy at the Healthy Smiles Dental Clinic. The receptionist said his ex was filling a cavity. Kelson said he would hold.

Five minutes later, Nancy picked up the line. 'What?'

'You know how sometimes the professional bleeds over into the personal?' Kelson said.

'I know I've got a nine-year-old with gauze packed in his cheeks and he keeps making pukey noises. So unless you want to help with the Lysol, make it quick.'

'I'm working a job with some people who might have threatened you,' Kelson said.

'Me?'

'And Sue Ellen.'

'Jesus, Sam – why did you tell these people about Sue Ellen?'

'I didn't,' he said. 'I *wouldn't.*'

'Of course you would. You can't help yourself.'

'OK, I would, but I didn't. She never came up until these people mentioned her. It's what they do. They intimidate.'

'What did they threaten to do?' She'd forgotten the nine-year-old with the gauze.

'They kept their options open.'

'Jesus, Sam.'

'I know. Watch her close right now.'

'I always watch her close.' As if he'd insulted her.

'Don't let her sneak out at night.'

Now he'd gone too far. 'Look, she does that because of *you.* What am I supposed to do? Lock her in her room?'

'If that's what it takes.'

'You're a lousy dad, Sam.'

'I try as hard as I can.'

'Try harder.'

'Watch out for yourself too,' he said. 'These people scare me.'

She hung up on him.

'I try,' he told the dead phone.

Then he dialed Venus Johnson at the Harrison Street Police Station.

'You won't like this,' he said, when she picked up.

'Then don't bother me with it,' she said.

'What can you tell me about Victor Almonte's backpack bomb?'

'That's police and FBI business,' she said, 'which means it isn't yours.'

'You'll want to look close at the cell phone that triggered it.'

She sounded angry. 'How do you know it had a phone trigger?'

He said, 'When the FBI does the forensics, they'll find the number that called to set it off. Don't waste your time running around looking for the other phone. It's in the debris you bagged from the library.'

'What the hell are you talking about?'

'I know – you wonder why Victor Almonte called his own phone when he could just set off the bomb with a switch or button. The answer is, he didn't. You won't find his prints on the second phone – or, if you do, they'll be there because someone made sure they were there in the days before the blast. But you'll find other prints if enough remains of the phone to lift them. They'll match one of the victims – Neto LeCoeur.'

'What you're saying makes no sense.'

'I'm telling you what I've heard.'

'Who's your source?'

'One of Victor Almonte's army pals – a guy named Ramsey Garner.'

She seemed to catch her breath. 'Hold on a second,' she said, and when she came back, 'Does this Ramsey Garner have red hair? Freckles? Maybe dress in a green golf shirt?'

'See? I've always thought highly of you,' Kelson said.

'His name popped up on my screen fifteen minutes ago,' she said. 'Seems forty minutes before that, a pickup truck pulled to the side by the I-94 exit at Randolph and shoved Garner's body on to the pavement.'

'He's dead?'

'Sure, if a broken neck is dead.'

'Huh. Anything else in the report?'

'Yeah, we caught a guy we think did it, though the witnesses could only identify the truck – and only with a partial description. This guy sent a patrolman to the ER. We have him in lockup on charges of fleeing and resisting.'

'Got a name?'

'The report says he isn't talking.'

'How about a description?'

'Medium height, Caucasian. Blue jeans and a—'

'Black T-shirt.'

'Now how the hell did you know that?'

'I spent the morning with him and Ramsey Garner,' Kelson said.

'Why would he kill Garner?'

'Maybe Garner talked too much.'

'You need to come to the station,' she said. 'Now.'

'Thought you'd never ask.'

FORTY

Kelson sat with Venus Johnson at a metal table in a homicide unit interview room. After a while, FBI Special Agent David Jenkins joined them. His partner Cynthia Poole came in a minute later.

'Tell them,' Johnson said.

'First,' Kelson said, 'Harold Crane and his daughter Sylvia – who run an investment company called G&G – are tied to the Rogers Park Library blast.'

Cynthia Poole looked skeptical. 'An investment company blew up a library?'

David Jenkins sounded like he knew he was wasting time but was used to it. 'Mr Kelson called and threw that at me before. He has this theory—'

Kelson said, 'They make people disappear.'

'Disappear?' Poole exchanged a look with Jenkins. 'Like who?'

Kelson was prepared for that one. 'Emma Almonte.'

The FBI agents exchanged another look. Poole nodded at Jenkins. He said, '*We* have Emma Almonte.'

'You have her? How so?'

'We took her into custody again,' Jenkins said. 'For further questioning.'

'But when I called you – after she walked out of her house – you said—'

'We don't reveal everything to private citizens,' Jenkins said. 'That would defeat the purpose.'

'But—'

'But nothing,' Poole said. 'We asked you before to stop interfering. Every minute we spend with you takes a minute away from the work we need to do.'

Venus Johnson said, 'He knew about the cell phone trigger.'

Jenkins pressed his lips together. 'Backpack bombs come with detonators of three kinds. Timer, manual trigger, or cell phone. Suicide backpacks almost always use manual triggers or cell phones, because why bother with a timer? So, now you're fifty-fifty. It takes more than a coin flip to impress us.'

'Who do you think called the cell phone?' Kelson said.

Poole said, 'We have Emma Almonte in custody.'

Kelson laughed. 'You think she—'

'We think she can help us determine who did call,' Poole said.

'Neto LeCoeur,' Kelson said.

'The kid playing Grand Theft Auto on the computer two seats from Victor Almonte?' she said.

'The twenty-three-year-old man who dug into the G&G books and transferred its funds – and who has a hacking background.'

'Our digital forensics people—'

'Your digital forensics people suck. Tell them to look closer at the library rubble. They'll find the phone that set off the trigger. Neto texted from it.'

Jenkins suppressed a smile. 'Unless Neto LeCoeur was a computer genius, he couldn't do this.'

'I don't know about a genius,' Kelson said, 'but he was damn good.'

Cynthia Poole smiled outright. 'So this was – what, a double suicide bombing?'

'It was a robbery,' Kelson said. 'Neto transferred the G&G money into his own account. G&G wanted him to text them when he finished their job – which he finished, but by ripping off their money. He set them up. But they set him up too. The text went to the phone in Victor Almonte's backpack. *Boom.*'

'That's it?' Jenkins said.

'That's a big part of it,' Kelson said.

'Keep the rest to yourself, OK?' Jenkins pushed his chair from the table and stood. 'You lost me the moment you opened your mouth.'

Kelson spoke to Poole. 'G&G hired one of Victor Almonte's army friends to work security. A guy named Ramsey Garner. Strong-arm stuff. He told me this.'

'All of it?' Poole said.

'Enough of it.'

She still smiled. 'Where is he now? If he's talking to you, why isn't he talking to us?'

Venus Johnson said, 'He's dead.'

Poole pushed her chair from the table too. She said to Johnson, 'You called us based on a dead witness and the word of a brain-damaged ex-cop?'

Johnson said, 'I called based on information I thought you should have.'

Kelson said, 'She's got a mute guy in lockup too.'

When the FBI agents left the room, Johnson gave Kelson a look as if she would tear him apart. But she said, 'Jagoffs.'

'They're looking at Emma Almonte?'

Johnson shook her head. 'They're looking at Tom Runeski.'

'The other victim's husband? A guy who cuddles his baby girl on the news? That's harder to fit than Neto.'

'Runeski does web design. He did a site for a business Emma Almonte's company worked with, like, three years ago – before Emma Almonte even took her job at the company, but still.'

'These FBI people are as bad as the Cranes. Do they have Runeski in custody too?'

'That's what I hear.'

'They're wrong,' Kelson said.

'But they're the FBI. They get to be.'

'You can fix this,' Kelson said. 'Are you going to talk to the man who threw Ramsey Garner out of the car?'

'Right after you called, two lawyers showed up for him. Then a third lawyer.'

'Sent by the Cranes?'

'No one's saying – at least the lawyers aren't. I don't know how they learned we had their man here.'

'Money talks,' Kelson said. 'Any chance I can see him?'

'Why do you ask dumb questions?' she said. 'It gives people a bad impression of you. What would you even ask him?'

'I'd *tell* him,' Kelson said. 'I'd say he's next on the Cranes' list. They can't risk having him reveal their secrets. He's got to disappear. And in jail there's only one way to disappear – unless they can get him out on bail, and then there's still only one way, though maybe then his body's never found. I figure he knows all this already, but I want to tell him anyway. Maybe then he'll mumble his story to someone with good enough ears to hear it before he gets a shank or a bedsheet around his neck.'

'I *knew* you could think a thought or two,' she said. 'I'll get him moved where he's safe.'

'Make sure you know the guards who bring him dinner.'

'You've got a bad attitude about cops,' she said.

'I used to be one,' he said.

'You must've hated yourself.'

FORTY-ONE

Instead of leaving the station through the main entrance, Kelson went down to the prisoner intake room. A handcuffed man with eyes that looked drugged into another universe swayed by a large wooden desk as a tall cop talked to the desk officer. At one end of a row of wall-mounted plastic seats, a man in a charcoal-gray suit sat talking quietly but heatedly with Sylvia Crane. At the other end of the row, standing by the wall, another man, older but dressed like the first, talked with Christine Winsin. A woman in a blue skirt and matching jacket, with a black briefcase, stood in the middle of the room reading her phone.

Kelson went to her and said, 'Door number three?'

'Pardon me?' She had straight blond hair with strands of gray.

'Who sent you?' he said.

'I'm sorry – who are *you*?'

'Sam Kelson.' He took a business card from his wallet and gave it to her. 'And you're here for the mute man? I call him Squirt.'

She blinked. 'You'll have to excuse me – you seem to have mistaken me for—'

'Ms Crane has her lawyer, and Ms Winsin has hers,' Kelson said. 'Whose are you? Are other G&G clients sticking their fingers in? Is Squirt looking out for himself?'

'Excuse me,' the woman said again, and she moved away, looking down at her phone.

So Kelson went to Sylvia Crane and her lawyer. 'Don't worry about him telling your secrets,' he said to her. 'He doesn't talk awake *or* asleep.'

'Oh, hello, Mr Kelson,' she said, as if they ran into each other at police stations all the time. 'This is one of our G&G lawyers, Jim Edwards.'

Kelson shook hands with the man and said, 'She didn't trust you enough to send you alone, huh?' Then, to Sylvia Crane, 'You're really worried about Squirt, aren't you? You want him in your own hands. Are you going to try to cut a deal with him, or just make him go away?'

She gave him an almost convincing look of bafflement. 'I have no idea what you're talking about.'

He said to the lawyer, 'How does it work? When they announce bail, do you and Christine Winsin's lawyer count down from three and then race to see who can pay it? My money's on the blue skirt. She's got the legs to win anything up to a half mile.'

Sylvia Crane gave him a wry look. 'You know Christine Winsin?'

'And her brothers. They visited me in my office. They seem to share your interest in Marty LeCoeur – but maybe with a different result in mind.'

'Marty who?' she said.

He started to answer, then realized what she was doing. 'You're pretty good. The problem is, I think you need to be better than pretty good to survive in the game you're playing.'

He went over to Christine Winsin and her lawyer. 'Hello, Ms Winsin. Ready for the auction?'

The lady looked at him, irritated at the interruption. 'Excuse me?'

'You going to buy yourself a mute? Cut a deal with him before Sylvia Crane can?'

'I'm sorry?' As if she didn't know him.

Kelson grinned at her. 'You aren't even pretty good. You come here with your thousand-dollar shoes and your million-dollar lawyer, and you don't belong. You should call it in, or have your assistant's assistant do it. Next time, stay home with the show dogs. But I guess you're afraid to leave Squirt alone even with your lawyer – like Sylvia Crane.'

Christine Winsin asked the lawyer, 'Do you have any idea what he's talking about?'

The lawyer gave her the tiniest shake of his head.

So Kelson went back to the woman in the blue skirt and said, 'My bets are on you. If they can't pin more than a traffic violation and throwing a couple of punches at a cop on him, you'll have him out in a few hours.' Then he left the intake room and walked outside into the early evening.

FORTY-TWO

Kelson ate dinner with Sue Ellen at Taquería Uptown.

As he downed his *pollo en mole*, his mind buzzed with the threats and craziness of the day. He knew he should keep his stories to himself, but as always when his brain spun and lurched, he spilled them.

When he finished, breathless, Sue Ellen looked at him wide-eyed and said, through a mouthful of *carnitas*, 'Holy shit, Dad.'

'Eleven-year-olds shouldn't talk that way.'

'Dads shouldn't tell eleven-year-olds these things.'

'Fair enough. You want another taco?'

She wanted two.

'How's math?' he asked, while they waited for them.

'We're doing proportions,' she said. 'I like proportions.'

'I was never very good at them,' he said. 'Even before I got shot in the head – your mom can tell you.'

'And unit rates. For example, if I drive a car seventy miles an hour for two hours, where will I go?'

'I don't know. Peoria?'

'Jail. I'm too young to drive.'

'Is that a sixth-grader joke?'

'No. Are you going to marry Doreen?'

'Hell, no.'

'Mom isn't going to marry Jason either.'

'Who's Jason?'

'Mom's boyfriend I'm not supposed to tell you about.'

'Is he nice?'

'Old.'

'How old?'

'Older than you.'

'Grandpa old?'

'No. He's a dentist – like Mom.'

'Scary. Two dentists. What do they talk about? Molars?'

'Sex.'

'Huh?'

'When they think I'm sleeping.'

'I didn't want to know that.'

'You tell me things I don't want to know all the time.'

'But you ask them,' he said.

'Did you or didn't you ask what they talk about?'

'Right. Want dessert after all this?'

She wanted the flan and the *tres leches*.

The next morning, Kelson had an appointment with Dr P at the Rehabilitation Institute. When she asked how he'd been doing since their last appointment, he started to tell her the same stories he'd told Sue Ellen over dinner.

Dr P held up a thin hand. 'We have only a half hour, Sam.'

'Right,' he said. 'You remind me of my daughter, but she listens better.'

'Sorry,' she said.

'No you aren't.'

'No,' she said, 'I'm not.'

He said, 'What does it mean if no matter how hard I try to help others I feel like I'm hurting them?'

Dr P sipped tea from a thermos mug she kept on a table by her chair. During their appointments, she drank from it whenever he said something that demanded thought. Once she drank so much she had to excuse herself to pee. Now she said, 'It might just mean you're human. We all do it sometimes. Who did you hurt?'

'It's a feeling, is all. I dreamed last night that everyone I know was tangled in balls of string. I picked at the loose ends but that tightened the knots around them.'

'A strange metaphor, but OK.'

'They rolled around on a giant floor and got more and more tangled.'

'Stranger.'

'Then the balls of string rolled under my bed and made growling sounds.'

'Ah, a kitten metaphor. How are Payday and Painter's Lane?'

'Cute. I think a lot about kittens.'

'You could have worse fixations. They're a bright spot.'

'Why are they tangling everyone I know in string?'

She sipped from her mug. 'How are the headaches?'

'I haven't had a bad one in three days.'

She scribbled a note on a pad she kept in her lap. 'I want to start weaning you from Percocet.'

'I like Percocet.'

'What's not to like? Except for the constipation, blurred vision, and dry mouth.'

'I don't have any of that. You ever work with adults who were abused as kids?'

She laid the pen on the pad. 'Only if they also suffer from a physical brain injury. I've had a couple of patients like that. Why?'

'What do you make of a woman in her thirties who keeps pictures and videos of her uncle abusing her when she was a kid?'

'This is someone you know?'

'A client. One of the people I worry I'm doing more harm than good.'

'I'd need to talk to her to know. Does she tie her sense of self to the abuse? Did her uncle damage her so badly that she needs these images for sexual pleasure? Is she using the images to gain power over her uncle? All three? Something else? A lot of possibilities.'

'In my experience, people keep pictures and videos like these because they're worth money,' he said. 'Blackmail. Extortion.'

'That's more your professional expertise than mine. Whatever she's doing, she sounds like she's in pain. Now, I have a question for you. Why did you change the subject from Percocet?'

'I like Percocet,' he said.

'Yeah, that worries me.'

Kelson drove to his office with a new prescription in his pocket – for half the dosage he'd gotten used to taking. 'You can pace yourself,' Dr P had said, as she wrote the order, 'or you can pop them the way you're used to and suffer through the rest of the week cold turkey.'

'Or I can go to a park I know on the westside and buy more off a guy I busted once when I was a narcotics cop,' Kelson said.

'Or you can hold a gun to your head and pull the trigger.'

'One bullet in the head's enough.'

'Stay safe,' she said. 'Stay clean.'

Now he left his car in the parking garage, rode the elevator to his office, and let himself in.

He sat at his desk, checked his KelTec and Springfield, and returned them to their places. He turned on his laptop and watched the screen as it booted up. Then someone knocked on his door. The knock sounded urgent, and Kelson got the KelTec from the desktop rig and slipped it into the back of his belt.

But when he opened the door, the third lawyer he'd seen in the police station intake room – the woman in the blue skirt – stood in the corridor. She clutched her black briefcase like she might need it as a shield. She looked scared.

He let her in, closed the door, locked it, hesitated – and unlocked it again.

She sat down on one of the client chairs and watched him take his KelTec from his belt and return it to the hidden rig.

'I need to hire you,' she said.

'You and everyone else lately,' he said. 'What's up?'

'They're trying to kill him.' Her blond hair looked grayer in the office light than at the station. 'The police won't protect him.'

'Who is he?'

'He'll pay whatever you charge. He needs to stay safe until he can make arrangements.' She set the briefcase on the desk and opened it. Kelson let his hand dangle by the underside of his desk, close to the KelTec. But she removed an envelope, took a number of bills topped with a hundred from it, and laid the money on the desk.

'Who?' Kelson said. 'Squirt?'

She looked at him like he was missing the obvious. 'His name is Stanley Javinsky.'

'Let's stick with Squirt.'

FORTY-THREE

'No,' Kelson said. 'No way.'

The lawyer said her name was Jane Richardson. She'd worked for Stanley Javinsky's family since Javinsky was fourteen and got picked up for shoplifting a plastic bag of bite-sized Kit Kats. Javinsky went downhill from there, landing in jail for auto theft at nineteen. Before that case went to trial, his cellmate tried to kill him. 'The man almost choked Stanley to death,' Jane Richardson said. 'The attack damaged his vocal chords. It put him in the hospital for three months, and, after that, he couldn't talk right. When he got out of jail, he taught himself that one trick – how to choke a man the way he got choked, the way that changed his life.'

'He perfected it,' Kelson said. 'When we met, he almost turned me into a whisperer. Is that what he used on Ramsey Garner before throwing him out on the highway?'

She sat across from Kelson, nervous, holding her back away from the chair. 'Stanley says Garner threatened to kill him. Something about him falling down on the job when you had them at your friend's apartment.'

'DeMarcus Rodman's.'

'Whatever. Stanley says you're the first man who's gotten the better of him in the past ten years.'

'That was DeMarcus's girlfriend Cindi. DeMarcus and I just swept up the pieces.'

'Stanley knows you must be angry at him.'

'Angry? That's what he said? He almost killed me. He threatened Cindi – my best friend's girlfriend. He threatened Genevieve Bower – my client. Maybe I'm a little irritated.'

'I bailed him out seven hours ago. The Cranes already sent a man to try to put him down.'

'How'd that work out?' Kelson said.

'Stanley says he "did" him.'

'"Did" him?'

'That's what he says. When his cellmate choked him, he suffered minor brain damage. It affects his ability to control violent impulses. He says something like that happened to you. He says you'll understand.'

'He wants me to sympathize with him? He wants to be pals?'

'He wants you to look out for him until he can cut a deal with the prosecutors – or can figure out a place far away from here to hide.'

'No,' Kelson said. 'That's stupid. Why would he come to me?'

'I told you—'

'Yeah, we both got conked on the head. Big deal. Still stupid.'

'Where else does he go? When he got out after stealing the car, he had nothing. Who'd want to be friends with a guy likely to choke them over an argument? Who'd hire an ex-con they couldn't even put on a phone to do telemarketing? Turns out Harold and Sylvia Crane had a place for him. Now, the Cranes want him dead. You're all he's got left.'

'He's got *you*,' Kelson said. 'Why worry so much about him?'

She looked embarrassed. 'I married his brother. My husband's eleven years older than Stanley. It was one of those second-father situations – until Stanley tried to kill him too. But yeah, he's got me. I bailed him out, though I can't keep him safe.'

'You really feel bad for him?'

'Bad? Sure. Am I also afraid of him? Absolutely. Do I hate him for making my life harder than it needs to be? Yes. He's done a lot of terrible things, and he'll do more in the future. But right now he needs help.'

'No,' Kelson said again. 'No, no, no.'

She stared at him.

'*No*,' he said.

'I'm sorry you feel this way,' she said, and she stood up.

'Would he even talk to the cops if they would listen?' Kelson said.

She narrowed her eyes. 'Honestly, I don't know. He trusts no one.'

'What would keep him from turning against me if I helped?'

'Just don't make him mad,' she said. 'He's loyal to people who treat him well.'

'Like a pit bull?'

'Pit bulls are gentler – but less loyal.'

Kelson thought about pit bulls. He thought about Payday and Painter's Lane in a room with pit bulls. He said, 'I can't do it.'

'I understand,' she said, though she looked like she didn't.

'You're one of those good people, aren't you?' he said.

'I don't know what I am. Sometimes I think I'm a fool.' She went to the door.

Kelson asked, 'Does he have somewhere to hide for now?'

'He's in the men's room.'

'The—'

'Down the hall.'

Kelson shouted at her. 'You brought him with you?'

'Where else would I put him?'

'Anywhere. The sewer. A hole in the ground. You could buy him a bus ticket. Jesus, get him in here before he kills one of the computer school students.'

She gave him a long, uncertain look. 'Yeah, the two of you should get along.' She left the office.

A minute later, she tapped on the door and came in again with Stanley Javinsky, who wore jeans and a fresh black T-shirt.

Kelson's KelTec lay on his lap under the desktop. As Javinsky came to the desk, Kelson said, 'Keep your hands to yourself. My neck still hurts.'

'Sorry.' Javinsky's voice – the little there was of it – sounded like someone had raked a metal comb down the inside of his throat.

Kelson pointed at a client chair. 'Sit.'

Javinsky did. Jane Richardson sat in the chair next to his.

'Why me?' Kelson asked him.

'Who else?' Javinsky said.

'Sandpaper,' Kelson said. 'You sound like you swallowed sandpaper.'

Javinsky's right hand worked the denim on his right pant leg, and his left biceps twitched.

'I say too much,' Kelson said. 'If you can't handle that without strangling me, get out now.'

'I'll try.'

'And I'll try to call you Stanley or, if you prefer, Mr Javinsky, but I'll probably end up calling you Squirt.'

Javinsky's left biceps twitched.

'Cut that out,' Kelson said.

'Sorry.' Grittier than a rasp. 'I can't help it.'

'Me either,' Kelson said. 'To tell the truth – and I always tell the truth – I don't know what I can do for you.'

'You hid Marty LeCoeur.' Speaking seemed to cause him pain. 'And Genevieve Bower. Why not me too? Put me where you put them.'

'You want me to hide you *with them*?'

'If that works.'

Kelson laughed at him. 'Listen, Squirt, you can sneak from bathroom to bathroom and fool your sister-in-law – if that's who she really is – but don't treat me like an idiot. Yesterday you were gunning for Genevieve Bower and Marty LeCoeur, and today you want me to put you with them? Maybe you want me to tie them up for you first and stick an apple in their mouths. Why would I ever believe you? For all I know, you're still pals with the rest of the G&G security guys.'

Anger fell over Javinsky's face, and he stood.

Kelson snatched his pistol off his lap and showed it. 'Easy, Squirt.'

Javinsky pulled up his T-shirt. He'd taped a bandage over the right side of his ribcage. A bloody spot the size of a half dollar had soaked through the gauze. 'They tried to kill me this morning.' He had other scars, old and new, and a tattoo of a tiny tiger above his belly.

'OK, Tiger, sit down,' Kelson said.

Javinsky eased his shirt over his stomach and sat.

'Tell me everything,' Kelson said, 'and if I like what you tell me, I'll *think* about helping. No promises.'

Javinsky told him very little. Maybe the Cranes kept their family secrets tight. Maybe they considered Javinsky too deranged and undependable to trust with inner-circle information. Maybe he knew more than he let on. He admitted he knew about Genevieve Bower's thumb drive – the Cranes said he could do what he wanted to her as long as he got the computer files. But he denied knowing what those files were. When Kelson, unable to stop himself, told him what Genevieve had said – that the drive held videos of Harold Crane abusing her – Javinsky dug at his pant leg and his biceps twitched again. He admitted that

G&G worked with dirty money. He'd made two previous accountants disappear – he'd bought a plane ticket to Costa Rica for one
and shipped the other back to his family in Latvia. His voice
sounded sandier and sandier as he went on, every word ripping
at the damaged tissue in his throat. Harold Crane called most of
the important shots, he said, though the orders often passed
through Sylvia or Chip Voudreaux.

When Javinsky finished, Jane Richardson looked at Kelson
hopefully.

'*What?*' he said to her.

'Can you?' she said. 'For a few days? Until we work something
out?'

Kelson had one more question for Javinsky. 'Tell me about
the little tiger tattoo on your belly.'

'I got it after they let me out of jail that first time,' Javinsky
said. 'It's a tiger kitten.'

'Damn,' Kelson said. 'It had to be a kitten.'

With his KelTec in his lap, he dialed Marty at his hideaway
and said, 'I've got an idea, and I want you to tell me it's insane.'

FORTY-FOUR

'A re you fucking crazy?' Marty said when Kelson told
him Stanley Javinsky's request. 'No fucking way.'

'That's what I told him,' Kelson said, but then he
mentioned that Javinsky killed Ramsey Garner – who'd set up
Victor Almonte with the bomb that ripped Neto apart – and then
chucked Garner out of his car like an empty beer can. 'So he
kind of got revenge for you – kind of.'

'Ah, fuck,' Marty said.

'Which means?'

'Fuck, fuck, fuck.'

'I thought you might feel this way,' Kelson said.

'If he tries anything, I swear I'll kill him,' Marty said.

'If he doesn't kill you first.'

*   *   *

When Kelson knocked on the basement apartment door a half hour later, Marty opened it looking angry, but he softened at the sight of Javinsky the way twins separated at birth sometimes feel an immediate affinity when reunited as adults. Within five minutes, Marty offered to heat a can of pork 'n' beans for the man.

Kelson told Marty, 'You know he almost choked *me* to death.'

Marty gazed at Kelson as if he might have more to object to than that and, when he didn't, said, 'Which one of us is perfect?'

Genevieve Bower stared at Marty and Javinsky warily and retreated to the far end of the leatherette sofa. Kelson sat down with her and asked, 'What's wrong?'

'I made mistakes,' she said. 'Big ones. And now I'm holed up with a couple of psychopaths.'

'You dated Marty. You know he's a good guy, in his way.'

'For a psychopath. I want this to stop. It's gone too far. I'm done.'

'What do you mean? What are you done with?'

'Can you arrange a meeting with Harry and Sylvia? I don't want anything from them. I just want my life back. I don't have the thumb drive. They can look for it and keep it – I can't do this anymore.'

Javinsky had started listening. Now his sandpaper voice said, 'It's too late. When I found you, I was supposed to do you.'

'*Do* me?' She looked ready for another bottle of strawberry vodka.

'No one's *doing* anyone,' Kelson said.

'I won't do you,' Javinsky said to her. 'But they'll send others. For you. And me. Harold makes up his mind.'

Genevieve Bower looked at Kelson. 'Arrange a meeting. Tell them I want to come in.'

'I'm with Squirt on this one,' he said. 'It's a bad idea.'

'But I get to decide,' she said.

'Not really,' he said. 'You hired me to do a job, and along with any job I protect a client. So I can't turn you over to the Cranes, even if you think it would work out.'

'But I could fire you,' she said.

'You could. Another bad idea.'

Marty told her, 'You don't want to fire Sam. He comes off dumb but he knows his fucking shit.'

'Thank you, Marty,' Kelson said and, to Genevieve Bower, 'Give me more time.'

'How much? A day? A week?' She frowned. 'More?'

'I don't know,' he said.

'Give him a day,' Marty said.

'What happens in a day?' she said.

'Yeah,' Kelson said, 'what's a day?'

'Hell if I know,' Marty said. 'But what kind of detective are you if you can't make something happen by then?'

Genevieve Bower agreed to a day but only after Marty said she could sleep in his bedroom with the door locked, while he and Javinsky slept on the front room floor.

Back at his office an hour later, Kelson worried about Marty's promise that he would make something happen. 'Truth is,' he told his KelTec, 'I'm tired – as if truth gives a damn. About me.' He ran his finger the length of the pistol barrel. 'As if it should shiver. As if it should burst with pleasure.'

He set the pistol on his desk, pulled out his phone, and dialed Venus Johnson's number at the Harrison Street Police Station. Her phone rang three times and went to voicemail. He hung up.

He checked the KelTec magazine. Then he held the gun between his flattened hands as if he was praying with it. He held it so the barrel faced him. He closed one eye and stared with the other into the tiny tunnel with its enormous darkness. He felt a shiver of fear and pleasure.

Then his phone rang.

He jumped. 'Holy shit.' He set the pistol on his desk, the barrel pointing at the door.

His phone rang again. Caller ID said *Nancy*.

He breathed hard – in and out – and answered. 'Hiya.'

'Two questions,' she said.

'Uh-huh?'

'Why did you buy Sue Ellen fancy sneakers, and why did you send them to her at my clinic?'

'Fancy sneakers?'

'Pink high-tops studded with stars. Jimmy Choos. Do you really think she'll wear them?'

Kelson's mind raced, and he yelled, 'Don't touch them.'

'Why?'

'They might . . .' He didn't know what.

'I tried them on. They fit. Did you realize Sue Ellen and I have the same size feet? Our little girl is growing up.'

'Dammit – take them off. Wash your feet.'

Nancy had perfected her exasperated tone years ago. 'And floss between my toes? You know you're sounding more than a little crazy again. The shoes were a nice thought. Misguided for an eleven-year-old, but nice.'

'I didn't send them.'

'The packing slip says you did.'

'They're a threat,' he said.

'Sneakers are a threat? Who sends sneakers as a threat?'

'The Winsins,' he said, 'probably the Winsins. It's a double threat – sending *you* the shoes for *Sue Ellen*.'

'Do you mind if I keep them?'

Kelson explained the situation as well as he could. When he finished, she still sounded calm. She almost always did. Her fearlessness had drawn him to her when they first met – he found it sexy. Now he found it maddening, and told her so.

'I won't throw out perfectly good shoes,' she said.

'It's not the shoes,' Kelson said. 'It's what they *mean* – what the Winsins mean them to mean.'

'Shoes can't *mean* anything,' she said. 'If the Winsins show up at the house, I'll kick them in the head with them.'

When they hung up, Kelson stared at the pistol on his desk as if it threatened him as much as Jimmy Choo sneakers. So he strapped it back under the desktop and said, 'Better, I guess.'

Then, for the first time in days, a piercing headache started in the bone above his left eye and needled backward. He swore at it, as if he could chase it out of his head. His left eye started to twitch. He took his vial of Percocet from the middle drawer, unscrewed the cap, and swallowed a little blue tablet. 'Take *that*, Dr P,' he said.

He closed his eyes, caressed his forehead, breathed in deep, and breathed out. He imagined clouds scudding across the sky over the skyscrapers in the city. 'Nice clouds,' he said. Then, as the medicine did its thing, his phone rang again. He returned the

vial to the drawer and checked who was calling. This time caller
ID said *Zoe Simmons* – JollyOllie's high school friend who lived
next door to his gay cousin Rick.

Kelson answered, 'Hiya,' again.

'Right. Do you still want the thumb drive?'

Kelson felt the same kind of jolt as when he'd stared into the
KelTec pistol barrel. 'You've got it?'

'Rick's boyfriend had it. I took it from him.'

'You at home?'

'Yeah.'

'Don't let anyone else in. Don't even answer the phone. I'll
be right there.'

FORTY-FIVE

'Oh *no*,' Kelson said. He sat with Zoe Simmons in her
living room and watched a video from the red thumb
drive on her laptop.

'I've never seen anyone do that before,' Zoe Simmons said,
'and I watch a lot of porn.'

'That's Harold's daughter, Sylvia – the son of a bitch.'

'At least she's old enough.'

'Maybe.' Then he shouted at the screen, 'No, don't do that.
Oh, *man*.'

Zoe Simmons blushed. 'I'm open-minded, but—'

'Where does someone even get one of those?'

'Home Depot?'

'Go to the next video, OK?' he said.

She opened a new one.

She'd found the thumb drive after Jeremy Oliver's cousin got
in a fight with his boyfriend. She said Rick came home from a
lacrosse game early and found his boyfriend with another
boyfriend – and this and that and so on – and Rick threw all of
his boyfriend's belongings out on to the sidewalk. As the
boyfriend loaded the stuff into the trunk of an Uber, Zoe Simmons
came from her apartment to see what the deal was, and she

plucked an envelope – addressed to Rick Oliver – from the pile.
Along with screwing other men on the side, the boyfriend soothed
his insecurities by neglecting to tell Rick when friends and relatives called, and by stealing Rick's mail if it looked important.

The second video showed two men, one of them Harold Crane.

'Ah, shit,' Kelson said, twenty seconds in.

'The old guy has interesting tastes, I'll give that to him. What
happened to his nipples?'

'Do we really want to know?'

'Who's the other guy?'

'His name's Chip Voudreaux,' Kelson said. 'One of the execu-
tives at G&G.'

'The old guy keeps it all in the family, doesn't he?' Zoe
Simmons said. 'At least all in the business.'

'Everyone but the receptionist.'

'There's still one more video.'

'Let's see it,' Kelson said.

She played the third.

It was the one Kelson dreaded, with Genevieve Bower. Harold
Crane enjoyed inflicting pain, and here that pain bloomed into
real evil as he experimented on a twelve-year-old girl.

A sound came from Kelson's throat – a sound that seemed
like it should stop time – but it couldn't undo all Harold Crane
did to Genevieve Bower. Kelson tried to tell Zoe Simmons to
turn off the video, but another sound like the first came from his
throat, and when he looked at her, she was crying.

He gasped, and the words finally came. 'Turn it off.'

She wouldn't. She insisted on watching the video through, as
if witnessing it would offer Genevieve Bower a salve or at least
acknowledge an injury that would never heal.

The video lasted two minutes fifty-eight seconds, and it seemed
like forever. When it finally ended, Kelson said, 'You don't put
that back together.'

'Damn,' Zoe Simmons said, and she wiped tears from her face
with trembling fingers.

Kelson stared at his hands and wondered what they might do
to Harold Crane. Might they grip the man's neck and deprive his
brain of the oxygen he needed to stay conscious and alive? Might
they grip pistols – the KelTec on the right, the Springfield on

the left – and fire a dozen bullets into Crane's body? Might they grip Crane's ankles and drag him – down stairs, across pavement – and dump him at the Harrison Street Police Station?

He realized he'd asked these questions out loud only when Zoe Simmons asked if he wanted to see the other files on the thumb drive.

'Huh?' he said.

'Documents,' she said. 'Do you want to see them?'

'Yeah, right,' he said. 'I guess.'

She opened the first of five – a spreadsheet with numbers but no words explaining what the numbers meant. The other four documents included detailed information about the past four distribution cycles at G&G, leading up to but excluding the one that ended with the library blast. The information revealed much of what the Cranes supposedly tried to make disappear with their vanishing accountants. Names of banks in the Bahamas, Hong Kong, and the Caymans. A multi-step route through Panama. Names of investors, including the Winsins. One investor's trans-actions were each for under a million dollars. Four were for over five million. The rest were in between.

Zoe Simmons opened the first document again and scrolled to the bottom – her tears dry, her face pale again under her black hair – and said, 'Numbers and numbers,' as if nothing disgusted her more than numbers.

Kelson said, 'This is the dirt – the real pain. The Cranes will kill to hide Harold's sex life, but this money pays for him to exist. Without it, he would shrivel. The investors must know he's the devil. They pay him to play the part, and I'll bet having a devil of their own allows them to throw a couple extra nickels in the offering plate on Sunday. But the devil only gets away with being the devil if he stays underground.'

Zoe Simmons closed the document, ejected the thumb drive, and gave it to him. 'What will you do?'

'Good question,' he said, as he drove south into the Loop. 'With only one answer.' He parked at a meter by Marty's basement hideout. A city bus, gray with grime, blew past. He went through the building lobby, down through the stairwell, and into the base-ment corridor lined with insulated pipes.

When he knocked on Marty's door, no one answered.

He knocked again and waved at the ceiling-mounted security camera.

The door opened, and Marty looked up at him. 'What?'

Kelson stepped into the room and peered around. Stanley Javinsky sat on the leatherette sofa eating a microwave pizza pocket from a paper plate. On the table, Marty's computer showed line after line of code. Kelson went to the bedroom door and looked in. Empty.

'Where is she?'

'Genevieve? She busted out an hour ago,' Marty said. 'She kept talking about making peace with Uncle Harry. I've got a high tolerance for crazy, but that chick is fucking loony. Can you believe I dated her? Can you believe *she* broke it off with me because *I* was too much work?'

'She went to G&G?'

'Nah. She said she was heading to Uncle Harry's house – to see the old man himself.'

Javinsky raised a finger, swallowed a bite, and looked as if swallowing hurt. He croaked his words. 'What's the matter?'

Kelson fished the thumb drive from his pocket. 'This.'

Javinsky's hard eyes lit up.

'Don't even . . .' Kelson said to him. 'I need to ask her some questions.'

'You'll go after her?' Marty asked.

'Got to.'

Javinsky rasped. 'You want a hand?'

Kelson stared at him. 'I'm sure that's a generous offer. But no. Really, *no*.'

Javinsky gave him a funny little smile. 'Harry'll tear you apart.'

FORTY-SIX

Outside of Marty's building, Kelson called Rodman. Because Javinsky was right. Kelson had already hit the Cranes too hard and too often to expect anything but an ugly welcome. Also, if Harold Crane asked where the thumb drive was, he would tell him. And if Harold asked where Marty had holed up, Kelson would give up the street address and directions to the basement door. Kelson needed Rodman to stick a fist in his mouth or do something – *anything* – to keep him from talking too much.

'Meet me at my office?' he said when Rodman answered his phone.

'What's up?' Rodman said.

'I'll tell you on the way,' Kelson said.

'The way where?'

'Bring a weapon,' Kelson said. 'Or two.'

'Yeah?'

'Or three.' He went to his car, opened the trunk, dug under the mat covering the spare tire, and tucked the thumb drive by a bolt that kept the tire from sliding around.

Next, he called G&G and asked the receptionist for Harold Crane's address. 'An acquaintance of mine is with him there,' he said.

'I'm afraid I'm not at liberty to give out that information,' the receptionist said.

'What if you call and tell him Sam Kelson knows about his nipples?'

'I'm sorry?'

'Tell him I've seen more of him than I wanted to – more than anyone should be forced to see, though he seems willing enough to bare it all.'

'I'm sorry, I don't know what you're talking about, and we don't disturb Mr Crane at home except in emergencies.'

'What does an emergency sound like to you?' Kelson said. 'Do you need sirens? If I can't talk to Harold, I can send some his way.'

'Hold on.' She sounded exasperated.

When she came back several minutes later, she said she'd talked with her boss. She gave Kelson an address and said Harold Crane would expect him.

Twenty minutes later, Kelson and Rodman stood in Kelson's office. Kelson strapped on an over-the-shoulder rig and holstered

his Springfield. He tucked the KelTec into his belt, then put on
a blue windbreaker that mostly hid the guns.

Rodman wore a big Beretta 92 in a hip holster. He cupped his
little snub-nose Colt revolver in his hand like a baby bird. 'Harold
and his own daughter?' he said. 'I didn't see that coming.' He
dropped the little gun into his jacket pocket.

'And Chip Voudreaux,' Kelson said.

'Swings left, swings right.'

'And Genevieve Bower.'

'Who now forgives all?'

'More likely Harold scared her into giving up.'

'Busy old pecker. When does he have time to earn those millions?'

They drove north through early-afternoon traffic. The sky was the
deep blue of coming summer, but when Rodman cracked open
the passenger-side window, a cool wind whipped through the car.

The gate in front of Harold Crane's house was open. It was
tall and wrought iron, with a stamped-metal image of a wading
bird – probably a crane – in the middle. The driveway that
extended from it was the smooth gray-black of a bicycle inner
tube, and it curved around a large oak tree with the bright, tender
green leaves of late May. As Kelson and Rodman pulled past the
tree, Rodman said, 'Why don't you stay in the car?'

'And miss the excitement?'

A giant brick house with gas lamps on either side of a big
wooden front door and a gabled porch roof supported by two-
story columns rose at the far end of a circle where the driveway
looped back on itself. White drapes were drawn across tall first-
floor windows. The second-floor windows had no drapes but,
reflecting the afternoon sun, were opaque and offered no clues
about the life behind them.

'Sometimes you bring too much excitement,' Rodman said.
'Maybe I go in and find out the deal. If I need you, I yell.'

'*You* yell? You never use more than a church voice.'

Rodman patted his pocket. 'Or maybe I shoot someone. If you
hear a gunshot, you can come in.'

'Or maybe I go in with you and we don't worry about it.'

'Until you give up the thumb drive and draw a map to Marty's
apartment.'

'I'm ready for any questions,' Kelson said.

'Did that ever work for you before?'

'Sometimes,' he said. 'A little.'

So Kelson parked at the bottom of the broad front steps, and they climbed to the broad front porch, where Rodman rang a little doorbell.

A short man in khakis opened – Greg Cushman, the G&G security officer Kelson had already rescued Genevieve Bower from once after he and his partner, Stevie Phillips, kidnapped her and Doreen from Kelson's apartment.

'Pipsqueak,' Kelson said.

'Watch it,' Rodman said.

But Cushman knew when to grin. 'Welcome,' he said. 'Mr Crane's in the sunroom.'

The wide hallway behind him was dim and cool, and as Kelson and Rodman stepped inside, Phillips – a good foot and a half taller than Cushman – emerged. He held a handgun, which he pointed first at Rodman's chest and then at Kelson's.

'My man, Stretch,' Kelson said.

'We've got to do this, you understand,' Cushman said, and he frisked Kelson, taking his two pistols. He hesitated in front of Rodman, but Rodman said, 'Go ahead – one in a hip holster, one in my pocket,' and Cushman took his guns too.

Phillips lowered his gun then, and Cushman told Kelson and Rodman, 'You get them back when you leave.' He set the four guns side by side on a large entry table under a gilt mirror.

'*If,*' Phillips said.

'Shut up, Stevie,' Cushman said.

'We understand,' Rodman said, so calm and smooth that Phillips raised his gun again.

As Cushman led them through the wide hall toward the back of the house, he said, 'The call from the office surprised Mr Crane. He didn't expect you to come running – at least not so soon. He thought you'd be grateful to have Genevieve off your hands. The day has been full of surprises.'

'For all of us,' Kelson said. 'You'd never guess—'

Rodman touched the back of Kelson's neck with a big hand.

'Nope, I never would,' Cushman said. He seemed strangely cheerful.

'What's the joke?' Kelson said.

'No joke, nothing funny at all,' the short man said, and led them into a high-ceilinged living room with double French doors that opened into a long sunroom. Through a plate-glass window on the outside wall, Kelson saw a swimming pool, full and sparkling in the cool weather.

Cushman stopped before the French doors and let Kelson and Rodman go in before him. Then he and Phillips stepped in behind them, as if to block the way out.

Harold Crane sat on a high-backed, plush-cushioned wicker chair, as large as a throne. He wore a bathrobe the rich blues and greens of peacock feathers. It fell to his knees, and, though he'd belted it snug around his waist, a tuft of chest hair poked from the top. His hair was wet, as if he'd come down from a shower or in from a swim. In one hand, he held an icy glass of something that included tomato juice.

Genevieve Bower sat on a wicker sofa across from him, deep in the plush cushion. She'd squeezed into a black bikini. She splayed her legs like a man taking two seats on a train. She held a highball glass of ice and a clear liquid and a fat slice of lime. She looked as drunk as when Kelson had tried to talk to her as she vomited in his office. She raised the glass to him and Rodman, nearly tipping over from the effort, and said, 'Cheers, boys.'

FORTY-SEVEN

'What the hell did you do to her?' Kelson said.

Harold Crane smiled at him. 'Offered her a drink. Would you like one?'

'And what's *this*?' Kelson gestured at the black bikini. 'Other than a pretty great idea.'

'Have you swum this time of year? Before the heat? It's bracing.'

'It would shrink my testicles.'

Crane looked at Kelson's crotch, as if judging what kind of testicles he had to shrink. 'Why did you call my office? What do you need to talk to me about?'

Rodman spoke over Kelson. 'What would you say if we told you we have evidence that you abused this woman when she was a child?'

'I'd call you a liar.'

'I never lie,' Kelson said.

'I'd still call you a liar – and the people who matter would take my word.'

Rodman said, 'Until the videos run on the nightly news. Even edited down for family-friendly TV, they'll tell everyone what you did.'

'If you had this video – any video – why would you come here? Why not take it to the police?'

Kelson said, 'I have the—'

Rodman swatted the back of his head.

But Kelson tried again. 'I've got the—'

Rodman swatted him harder.

Crane stared at Kelson with his sharp blue eyes. 'The thumb drive? I assure you that you don't. When Genevieve arrived a couple of hours ago, she told me what she did with it. It's gone – destroyed. Do you think I would have let her in – and poured her several drinks – if I doubted her?'

Kelson said, 'It's in—'

'Goddammit, shut up, Sam,' Rodman said.

'Let the man talk,' Crane said. 'What's it in?'

'It's incredible how stupid you are,' Kelson said. 'I've seen what you did to her. And to Sylvia and Voudreaux.'

Crane's smile seemed to disintegrate. Genevieve Bower looked at Kelson with vague interest. Crane said, 'Let's imagine for a moment that you have something. Do you know the law?'

'I was a cop for fourteen years.'

'Then you must know the statute of limitations in this state for what you say happened. I'll recite it for you, because I've learned it well. Prosecution may be commenced within twenty years after a child victim attains eighteen years of age. Do you know Genevieve's age?'

She brightened up. 'Thirty-nine,' she said, as if that would win her a free drink. Then she drank from the highball.

Crane said, 'So if what you say happened really did happen, you'd still have to say, *Oops, too late*. Unless you were a civil attorney. But you're not, are you? You've got no training that way at all. So even if what you say happened were true, there wouldn't be a damn thing you could do about it.'

'We could kill you,' Rodman said. Calm. Smooth.

Phillips aimed his gun at the big man.

'Not saying we would,' Rodman said. 'Just correcting an inaccuracy.'

'Thank you for doing so,' Crane said, 'though, as Stevie's reaction should tell you, killing me might be harder than you think. No, the only person who can hurt me is Genevieve, but why would she? She's back with the family. We're gold. So who are you to threaten me?'

'Then why did you fight so hard to get the thumb drive?' Kelson said.

Crane fingered the belt on his robe. 'If what you say happened really did happen – and if Genevieve really had evidence of it *and* we still had a disagreement – she could file a very messy, very damaging civil suit. As you might imagine, I would greatly prefer that a video such as the one you describe never be seen, for obvious reasons.'

Rodman said, 'I expect your clients would get pissy if their banker showed up on the nightly news diddling a little girl.'

'My clients have thicker skin than you think. As long as their names stay out of the story and they make money, they're happy.'

'I know their names,' Kelson said.

Crane's laugh sounded like tin. 'The Winsins? You're a bad judge of character, son. The Winsins take heat like they were born to it. You name them, and they'll figure out how to turn a profit. They'll start by taking you to court and stripping you naked.'

'How about the others?' Kelson said.

'What others?' Crane directed the question to Genevieve Bower, whose face and neck were tinging red.

Kelson thought of the names from the thumb drive files. 'David Vance? He's the biggest in your over-five-million club, right? Or Joshua and Denise Seiden, or Siddhartha Chowdhury? They're sneaking up on Vance. The Winsins barely make it into the club.'

Crane glared at Genevieve Bower. 'You goddamned bitch.'

So she threw up – mostly clear liquid, which ran over her chin and down her front.

Crane turned his eyes to Kelson, as if he could make anyone he looked at go belly up. 'What do you want?'

'I thought you'd never ask,' Kelson said.

Crane said, 'You should understand, I'm asking only once. After that I take without asking.'

'Let's make it simple, then,' Kelson said. 'I want you to go with us to the cops and admit what you did to Neto LeCoeur – and Jeremy Oliver – and' – he gestured at Genevieve Bower, who was wiping her neck with a bare hand – 'her. We can work out the rest later.' As he spoke, Rodman drifted toward Cushman and Phillips.

Crane said, 'I've navigated this world for a long time, and I've come through storms you can't imagine. If you think a brain-damaged ex-cop, his big black boyfriend, and my lying twat of a niece worry me, you underestimate me.'

'But this time you might've sailed out too far,' Kelson said. 'I've got the videos and the names and numbers.'

Crane glanced at Phillips, who held his pistol at his side. Phillips gave him an almost imperceptible nod.

'I'll ask once,' Crane said to Kelson. 'Where is the thumb drive?'

'Well, if you put it like that,' Kelson said, 'it's right outside in my car.'

Crane glanced at Cushman, who smirked and shook his head.

'A smartass,' Crane said. 'Even at a time like this – when you might save your life.' Phillips raised his pistol and aimed at Kelson.

But Rodman smashed the tall man's shoulder with his fist, and the pistol clattered to the tile floor. Phillips ducked as Rodman tried to hit him in the head. Cushman scooped Phillips's gun from the floor, and aimed it at Kelson again. Turning, Rodman punched Cushman in the face, and the short man and the pistol hit the tile together. Phillips reached for the gun, and Rodman shouted at Kelson, '*Go.*' They ran through the French doors into the living room as Phillips squeezed off a single shot, the bullet shattering a glass pane in one of the doors. Then Phillips went after them.

'Wait,' Crane shouted at him. 'Shoot *her.*'

Phillips stepped into the sunroom again. His gun rang twice. Kelson tried to turn back.

Rodman grabbed his arm and yanked him toward the hallway, but Kelson pulled free and moved back through the living room.

Framed by one of the sets of French doors, Phillips stood over Genevieve Bower, his pistol shaky in his hand. She had a spot of blood on her forehead and another in the valley between her breasts.

'Let's go,' Rodman said, beside Kelson.

But Kelson tried to go to the sunroom. He wanted to breathe life into Genevieve Bower's lips. He wanted to save her though he knew she was beyond saving.

Rodman gripped his elbow and pulled him into the hall.

When they came to the front foyer, they swept their guns up from the entry table, and Kelson turned toward the hall again.

'What're you doing?' Rodman was breathing hard.

'We need to get her.'

'She's dead,' Rodman said. 'It's done.'

'Then I'll get Crane – and Phillips and Cushman.'

'Listen to yourself. You're—'

At that moment, Phillips came up the hall, his pistol aiming at Kelson, his finger on the trigger.

Rodman lifted his big Beretta 92 and squeezed a single shot. The sound exploded through the hall, and Phillips's chin disintegrated into blood and bone.

Rodman looked into Kelson's eyes and said, 'Let's get out of here *now*.' His voice was quiet, but Kelson heard nothing smooth or calm.

FORTY-EIGHT

They raced down the driveway toward the street in Kelson's Dodge Challenger.

'Call nine-one-one,' Kelson said.

Rodman drew his phone from his pocket. 'You know they'll clean up fast.'

'Not *that* fast,' Kelson said, 'and if they do, I want them talking to the cops instead of following us.'

But as they turned from the driveway on to the street, a blue pickup truck emerged from beside the house and charged after them. Kelson drove through the stop sign at the first intersection without slowing, and the pickup rounded from the driveway a second later, barely holding the pavement.

Kelson's Dodge Challenger had six cylinders, enough to leave most cars behind, but the pickup grew in the rearview mirror.

At the next intersection, a brown station wagon crossed as Kelson and Rodman approached. Kelson eased the gas.

'Go, go, go,' Rodman said.

'I'm sick of this prick,' Kelson said. He hit the brakes, and the car slid to a stop.

'Goddammit,' Rodman said.

'Yep.' Kelson grabbed his KelTec and Springfield and got out.

Rodman got out too, with his Beretta and Colt revolver.

The blue pickup charged to within three car lengths and stopped. Cushman stared at them over the dashboard. If he punched the gas he would crush them or, if they leaped aside, destroy Kelson's Challenger.

Kelson and Rodman raised their guns and aimed at the pickup windshield. For a long moment, Cushman sat in the truck and Kelson and Rodman stood on the suburban street.

Then Cushman shifted into reverse and backed the truck a half block, turned it around, and drove toward Harold Crane's house. Kelson and Rodman waited until it turned into the driveway, and then they got into the car and headed toward the Interstate.

When Rodman called the cops, the local dispatcher seemed to doubt anything bad could happen at Harold Crane's mansion – the kind of doubt Crane must've either paid for with cash or earned through generous civic deeds. The dispatcher agreed to send a cruiser to check things out only after making Rodman tell his story three times.

'Crane's got them in his pocket,' Rodman said after hanging up. 'He won't even need to let them in the front door.'

As they headed toward the city, Kelson swore at the windshield, swore at the other drivers, and most of all swore at himself. When he ran out of breath, he drove for a mile, panting, then swore some more. When he ran out of breath again, he said, 'I got her killed.'

Rodman, who'd said nothing for the past five minutes, said, 'Next time, stay in the car.'

The words hit Kelson hard. 'You mean it?'

Rodman was silent again, then said, 'No. I'm just pissed off. You didn't shoot her. Phillips did. Or Harold Crane did – more or less. One thing led to another.'

'So you're pissed at me.'

'Just stay in the car next time.'

'I can't,' Kelson said. When Rodman said nothing, Kelson added, 'You know that.'

'Yeah, I do.'

'You wouldn't really want me to.'

'*Yeah*, I would.'

They kept the windows up now, as if the cool May wind would turn their blood to ice.

'She had a lot of life in her,' Kelson said. 'You wouldn't think they could punch it out with a couple of bullets.'

They drove toward Marty's basement apartment, cut through city streets jammed with rush-hour traffic, and pulled into the self-park garage at Wabash and Adams. Kelson turned off the engine, popped the trunk, and pulled the thumb drive from under the spare. 'You treacherous little bastard,' he said to it, and put it in his pocket.

They went out to the street and then in through the lobby of the building where Marty had his hideout. When Marty let them in, Stanley Javinsky was sitting on the leatherette sofa where they'd left him a couple hours earlier.

Javinsky's throat rasped. 'Harry didn't tear you apart.'

'He tried,' Kelson said. He dug the thumb drive from his pocket and gave it to Marty. 'Will you copy the files? We need a backup.'

Javinsky's eyes lit up again at the sight of the thumb drive, and he stood to see what was on it.

Rodman said, '*Stay.*'

Javinsky stared at the big man, as if measuring his neck for a squeeze, then eyed the Beretta in Rodman's hip holster. He sat down.

Marty copied the files, then ejected the thumb drive and gave it back to Kelson. Kelson considered it, considered Javinsky – who watched as if he was thinking of a way to snatch it – and said, 'Nah. Be right back.' He left the basement apartment.

He meant to take the thumb drive back to his car and put it in the trunk, out of reach unless he told Javinsky or anyone else where he'd hidden it – which he might, though he hoped not. But kitty-corner to the parking garage, there was a FedEx store. He crossed the street and ducked inside. He confused the clerk by asking for the slowest mail option, then addressed a mailing tube to himself at his office, stuffed one end with bubble wrap, dropped in the thumb drive, and stuffed the other end.

He went back to the basement apartment and said to Javinsky, 'Outsmarted you.'

'Doubt it,' Javinsky said.

'Unless you want to strangle a FedEx clerk,' Kelson said.

Then Marty, who sat at his computer, said, 'Jesus Christ, Kelson, why didn't you give me this before?'

Kelson looked at the screen. Marty was staring at the file that had only numbers, no names. 'I didn't have it before – or I had it, but only before we went after Genevieve Bower. I—'

'Jesus Christ,' Marty said again.

Kelson stared at the numbers. They looked like numbers. 'What?'

Marty ran his cursor across a block of them and highlighted it. 'See that?'

'Nope,' Kelson said.

'That's Chip Voudreaux.'

'In what possible sense?'

Marty gave him the kind of glance he might give a worm he'd stepped on. 'Shut up a minute will you?' He scrolled down the screen.

'How is that Chip Voudreaux?'

Marty spoke distractedly as he read blocks of other numbers. 'It's the string that always goes with his name. I've seen it while trying to crack through Neto's work.' He highlighted another block. 'But I don't know who *this* one is.'

'What's the big deal?' Kelson said.

'If I'm right,' Marty said, glancing up at Kelson, 'and I'm *always* right, Neto didn't really redirect money that was heading to the G&G customers. He redirected money that was heading to Voudreaux and' – he tapped the highlighted block on his screen with a little index finger – 'whoever this guy is.' Marty sat back in his chair. 'Which explains a fuckload of my confusion.'

'I don't get it,' Kelson said.

'That's because you're a dumbass,' Marty said. 'And I'm a dumbass too, because I didn't see it – but not as dumb as you, because I see it now.'

A windy noise came from Javinsky's throat. Kelson stared at him and realized the man was laughing.

Marty said to Kelson, 'Don't you see it? The funds were never going to the customers. They were going to Voudreaux and whoever his partner was. Voudreaux and the other guy were ripping off G&G.'

Kelson tried to work through what Marty was telling him. 'Voudreaux tried to hire you – and then he hired Neto—'

'And he lined up Victor Almonte to light up the fucking library,' Marty said.

Javinsky sounded as if he was gasping, but a horrible grin was pasted on his lips.

Kelson put it together. 'Voudreaux was stealing the G&G money, and he blew up Neto to cloud over what happened – or at least to slow down the Cranes or anyone else who might figure out what he did. But then Neto stole it from Voudreaux.'

'Neto fucked him over good,' Marty said. 'Him and whoever *this* is.' He tapped the screen again.

As Kelson and Rodman watched over his shoulders, Marty ran through the numbers, showing them the places where the unidentified string appeared. In every case, it appeared next to the numbers he connected with Chip Voudreaux. He highlighted a longer set of numbers near the bottom of the screen. 'And this is where Neto must've emptied the G&G accounts.'

'How do you know?' Rodman said.

Marty tapped the screen as if he could feel the power in the numbers. 'Simple math,' he said. 'Intro to hacking.'

At some point, as Marty highlighted blocks of numbers and explained what they meant, Javinsky's wheezing laugh stopped. No one noticed until Marty glanced from his computer to the security monitor over his desk.

'Fuck,' he said.

As he, Kelson, and Rodman watched, Javinsky sprinted down the basement corridor toward the stairwell.

'No, no, no,' Kelson said, and he ran after him – out through the door, down the corridor, and up the stairwell steps. He burst from the stairwell into the building lobby as Javinsky disappeared out to the sidewalk. Kelson ran through the lobby and outside after him. He looked up and down the street. He stared at the other building entryways. He stared at the second floors of the buildings, the third and fourth floors, and up and up, as if Javinsky might have scaled the walls.

But Javinsky was gone.

'Dammit,' Kelson said.

A woman passing with a Macy's bag shook her head at him. 'There's no need for that.'

FORTY-NINE

Two hours later, as Marty's fingers danced across the computer keyboard, Rodman went out and brought in dinner from Panda Express. After her shift at Rush Medical, Cindi met them for the meal in the basement. Marty refused to stop to eat. He crammed an eggroll between his lips like a fat cigar, and he worked and worked, sucking in bite by bite.

'We aren't safe here anymore,' Kelson said.

Marty's response got lost in his mouthful of eggroll.

After they cleaned up, they ate their fortune cookies. Kelson's fortune said, 'You have a deep interest in all that is artistic'. 'I don't know what that even means,' he said.

Marty ignored his cookie and said, 'I'm close, man, I'm fucking close.'

So Kelson called Doreen. 'Lock your door tonight,' he said.

'I lock my door every night.'

'It's a metaphor.'

'What's metaphorical about locking my door?'

'I pissed off Harold Crane. And I screwed up bad with one of his security guys. He'll send his men after me, and if they can't find me, they might go after the people I love.'

'You love me?'

'You know what I mean.'

'No, but I'd like to talk about it.'

'Lock your door,' he said.

'You interested in joining me?'

'I'm interested in all things artistic. I'll come by, but then I've got to check on Sue Ellen and Nancy.'

'I'll leave the door open,' she said.

'Ha.'

Marty said Rodman and Cindi could sleep in his bed while he worked. 'The more of us the better,' he said. 'We stay together.'

Rodman looked at Kelson. 'You're coming back here afterward, right?' – more a command than a question.

'I need to feed Payday and Painter's Lane.'

'How long's that take?' Cindi said.

'I'll come back in the morning,' Kelson said.

'Be smart,' Rodman said.

'Always,' Kelson said.

'No, I mean, don't be stupid – come back tonight.'

'I know what you mean.'

Kelson drove to Doreen's apartment. He glanced at the rearview mirror. 'Be smart,' he said to the face that stared at him. 'As if that's possible.' He thought about the videos of Harold Crane with Genevieve Bower, Chip Voudreaux, and Sylvia. 'Jesus,' he said. He thought about Genevieve Bower at Harold's house, sitting on the wicker sofa with bullet holes in her head and chest. 'Jesus,' he said again. He thought about Stanley Javinsky bolting from Marty's hideaway. 'Dammit,' he said. He thought about Sue Ellen and – 'No, no, no,' he said, trying not to go *there*. Then he thought about the red thumb drive floating through the FedEx system. 'Like an unscratchable itch,' he said.

Doreen let him into her apartment, wearing an unbuttoned silk shirt, her ankle monitor, and nothing else. He stayed for an hour, and they didn't talk about love. But for that hour, Kelson's mind left the events of the day and of the days before it. The sounds that came from his mouth weren't even words.

When he left, he drove to Nancy's house, parked at the curb, and stared up at Sue Ellen's window – dark now – and at the window in the room he once shared with Nancy, a light on behind the shade.

Sitting in his car, he checked the rounds in the magazine of his Springfield pistol and sighed. Nancy always took his concern for her as an insult, as if he questioned her ability to care for herself and Sue Ellen.

He got out, climbed the porch steps, and knocked on her door – softly, to keep from waking Sue Ellen. He practiced his words for when Nancy opened the door. But she didn't open the door. He knocked harder and practiced some more.

Then Nancy opened and said, 'What?' She wore a shirt that looked too much like the one Doreen had worn.

'Wow,' Kelson said.

'It's eleven at night,' she said. 'You knock, looking like a frightened animal. And the best you can do is "Wow"?'

'No,' he said, '*no*.' He offered her the Springfield pistol, grip-first. 'I want you to have this.'

She didn't touch it. 'Why?'

He tried to remember the words he'd prepared. 'In case you – if . . .'

She looked at him as if he'd lost his mind. 'You know I have my old service pistol.'

'Loaded?' he said. 'By your bed?'

She squinted at him. 'In the gun safe – where I always keep it.'

'Maybe you should take it out.'

'What's wrong with you?' she said. 'You look like you did something you shouldn't've.' She stepped out of the house, as if she would poke him in the chest. Then she stopped. 'You smell like sex. If this is a weird guilt trip, I don't want it.'

'It's not. I didn't. Well, I did, but—'

'Don't,' she said. 'Don't bother – don't say anything.' She went into the house and slammed the door.

Kelson stood on the front porch, then yelled, 'Lock it.'

He drove to the Harrison Street Police Station and tucked his Springfield and KelTec under his seat. 'Be smart,' he told himself, and got out. He wouldn't mention Rodman or Marty LeCoeur if he could help it. He wouldn't dip them deeper into the mess than they dipped themselves. Not that he could necessarily help it. But he could try. Not that trying necessarily worked – sometimes it made things worse. But he could try to try. 'That's smart,' he said, and he pushed through the revolving door into the station. 'At least it's something,' he said, too loud.

The uniformed woman working at the metal detector said, 'Sorry?'

'Keeping them out of it,' Kelson said. 'It's something. They've got enough troubles already.'

'Whatever,' the woman said. 'Empty your pockets. Keys in the dish.'

'I used to be a cop,' he said, as he put his things in a basket for the X-ray machine.

She looked at him like he was just another kook. 'You must be very proud.'

The man at the reception desk seemed to recognize him, or else treated everyone who came into the station that way. Kelson asked to see Venus Johnson or Dan Peters, and the man said, 'Yeah, Peters walked out a couple hours ago, but I'll see about Johnson.'

When Johnson came into the lobby, her forehead was oily with sweat. She carried two thick black binders, as if to show Kelson how busy she was. 'I'll give you ten minutes before I kick you out on your ass,' she said, and she led him down a corridor to a little conference room that smelled of old coffee and rotten food.

Then she gave him forty minutes and – after leaving to call the Mundelein police about Kelson's story and then returning with a digital recorder – another half hour. He told her about going to Harold Crane's house to get Genevieve Bower. He told her about Stevie Phillips shooting Genevieve Bower in the head and chest. Though he tried not to, he told her about Rodman shooting Stevie Phillips. He told her about the thumb drive and the videos on it, and he started to explain the strings of numbers, but Venus Johnson was hung up on the videos.

'Harold Crane is fucking his own daughter?'

'Or she's fucking him. They both seemed into it. Unlike Genevieve Bower, which was straight-out abuse. Harder to tell with Chip Voudreaux. Genevieve Bower included him on the highlight reel, whether because it was gay sex or because it was forced, I don't know.'

Johnson said, 'The lady I talked to in Mundelein said they recorded the nine-one-one from Rodman, but, as you guessed, the reporting officer said Harold Crane told him nothing had happened at his house, and the officer saw no reason to investigate.'

'Crane's people would've cleaned the place by the time he came anyway,' Kelson said. 'At least cleaned it enough to ease the minds of the local PD.'

'If I want to move this at all, I need the thumb drive,' Johnson said. 'The captain will laugh at me without it. The DA won't even waste breath laughing.'

'Because *I'm* the source?'

Johnson looked at him square. 'Yes.'

Instead of arguing, Kelson said, 'The thumb drive comes to my office in two days, but I can get copies of the files.'

'Do it.'

So, as she watched, Kelson called Rodman, gave him Johnson's email address, and asked him to have Marty send the copied files from his computer.

Rodman sounded angry. 'You're talking with the cops?'

'Just with Venus Johnson.'

'I thought I told you to be smart.'

'Send the files, OK?'

'You know how they'll twist this?' Rodman said. 'I *shot* a man, dammit.'

'I don't know how they could twist it more than it already is.'

'They'll find a way.'

'Send the files.'

'I don't think so. I'll see what Marty says. In the meantime, shut up with Johnson before you talk yourself – and your friends – into more trouble.'

'Lock the door,' Kelson said.

Twenty minutes later, with no email from Marty, Kelson left the station and drove home. He parked in an alley a half block away, got his guns out from under his seat, and snuck into the building through the service entrance. He hit the call button for the freight elevator and then listened to the sounds of the building – the clicking and running pipes, a cooling unit, a quiet rushing of air from somewhere he couldn't identify. The elevator came, he hit the button for his floor, and, as the doors closed, he told the sounds to shut the hell up.

When the doors opened again at his floor, he gripped his KelTec, listening again. He heard only the muffled voices of late-night TV playing in a nearby apartment. He stepped into the hallway, and no strange shadows shifted in his neighbors' doorways.

He went down the hall to his door. No worrying sounds came from inside.

He shoved the door open a crack, slipped into the crack, and closed it behind him – all in an instant. He left the lights off and stood listening, his fingers sweating on his KelTec, ready to shoot anything that moved.

Something hand-like touched his ankle. He yelled and kicked at it.

Then something touched his other ankle.

It made a mewling sound.

Kelson reached down and petted Payday. 'I could've killed you,' he whispered. '*You* could've killed *me*.'

He jiggled the lock mechanism on the door and felt the reassuring clack of the deadbolt against the strike plate.

Then he fed the kittens in the dark, showered and brushed his teeth in the dark, laid his KelTec on the carpet next to his bed and his Springfield pistol next to the KelTec, and climbed into bed in the dark. He talked to the kittens about the deeper darkness he'd traveled through in the bright light of day. Images of Genevieve Bower overtopping her black bikini, two spots of blood cratering her skin – and images of Stevie Phillips falling down in Harold Crane's dim hallway when Rodman shot him in the face – and images of the shattered pane of glass from the French doors leading to the sunroom – and images of Greg Cushman's face staring through the pickup truck windshield as Kelson and Rodman aimed guns at him on the street outside Harold Crane's house – images and images flashed and flashed through his brain. 'You'll never, never understand,' Kelson told the kittens, and that thought reassured him as much as jiggling the lock did. When Painter's Lane tried to lie on his face, he told her to *be smart*. When she tried again, he rolled over and fell asleep facedown.

In his dream, he'd failed to come home, and the kittens, raging with hunger, shredded his apartment, tearing his bedspread, the mattress, and bedframe, grinding holes in the kitchen cabinets with their little claws. He couldn't blame them. He fought obstacle after obstacle to get to them but never got closer. They ate the torn-up furniture – the tattered bedspread, the clothes from his closet, strips of torn carpet, wooden drawers, and a broken lamp. They gnawed on the bathroom door. They grew to the size of adult housecats, then larger – the size of German Shepherds – and larger, until they prowled the apartment like cougars.

Kelson startled awake – or seemed to.

His room was dark, darker than when he climbed into bed, though he sensed the shape of his bed around him, and sensed the dresser and table across the room – whole, uneaten – which reassured him again. But he sensed an absence too. Payday and Painter's Lane were gone. He made a *ntching* sound, but the kittens were hiding. He mumbled for them. They didn't come.

He waited for them. Waited. Then he closed his eyes and seemed to sleep without dreaming – for moments or minutes – before startling awake again.

He sensed with dread that something new had come into the room. Three objects. Standing by his bed.

He made himself close his eyes. He thought he must be dreaming again.

Then his bedside lamp went on.

Kelson opened his eyes.

Christine Winsin and her brothers Bob and David gazed at him. She wore a neatly tailored dress the beige color of a safari jacket. It had button-down epaulettes. Bob wore a white Oxford shirt and black slacks, David a pink golf shirt and khakis. A black satchel hung from David's shoulder.

'Wake up, sunshine,' Bob said.

Kelson asked him, 'Are you a dream?'

The man shook his head. 'A goddamned nightmare.'

FIFTY

'Be smart,' Christine Winsin said, when Kelson shouted. 'With our kind of money we can get in anywhere. Building superintendents, landlords, everyone is happy to help when we show our generosity.'

Kelson grabbed for the guns he'd left beside his bed. They were gone. 'Be smart, be smart,' he said. 'Everyone wants me to be smart. What if I want to be stupid?' Still he groped for his guns – until Payday swatted his hand from under the bed.

'Get up,' David Winsin said.

Kelson held his bedsheet. 'No.'

'Are you a child? Get up.'

'What do you want with me?'

Christine Winsin said, 'When Neto LeCoeur played hide-and-seek with our money, we lost five million dollars – five million, eighty-three thousand, eight hundred and seventy-seven, to be exact. We want it back.'

'Give me a moment, I'll check my wallet,' Kelson said.

'You're too easy,' she said. 'The only surprise is you didn't get shot in the head long before you did. Or were you sharper before your accident?'

'I hate when people call it an accident,' Kelson said.

'Get up,' Bob Winsin said.

'How's it work with you?' Kelson said. 'Do you all live together in a big castle – with a tower for each of you?' He gripped the sheet. 'You know, it's strange for you to lurk in a guy's apartment in the middle of the night.'

Christine Winsin said, 'We would much rather be home in our beds. But certain times call for wakefulness.'

'Five million bucks of wide awake?' Kelson said. He looked at her feet. She wore plain brown shoes.

'Enough to keep us pacing at midnight,' she said.

He sat up in bed, still holding his sheet around him. 'What do you want?'

'Take us to see Marty LeCoeur,' David Winsin said. 'Convince him to use the information from the files to get our money.'

'How do you know Marty has the—' Then he realized. 'Squirt ratted?'

'Excuse me?' Christine Winsin said.

'Stanley Javinsky told you?'

'We had a brief conversation with him,' Christine Winsin said. 'If you must know, Harold and Sylvia Crane outbid us for him.'

'What do you mean?'

'The information Mr Javinsky could sell – about where to find Marty LeCoeur and the account information he has – is even more valuable to the Cranes than it is to us. That doesn't mean we want what's ours any less. It just means the Cranes have more to lose in this instance.'

'Squirt sold out Marty?' Kelson got up from bed and started to put on a shirt.

'At a very attractive price.'

Kelson pulled on his pants. 'Give me my guns.'

Bob Winsin said, 'Are you really this stupid?'

'I'm not going anywhere without them.'

Bob Winsin said, 'We have Sue Ellen.'

Kelson took a single step and slugged him in the face. The man fell hard on the carpet.

Christine Winsin said, 'Bob's lying.' Then, to her other brother, 'Give him his guns. He'll use them wisely.'

David Winsin pulled the KelTec and Springfield from his satchel and gave them to Kelson.

Kelson pointed the guns at him and his sister. 'Get the hell out.' He nodded at the man on the carpet. 'And drag him with you.'

'Or not so wisely,' Christine Winsin said – then to David again, 'give him his ammunition.'

'Really?' Kelson said. He released the magazine from the Springfield. Empty. 'Shit.' He checked the KelTec magazine. The same.

'This all works better if we trust each other,' Christine Winsin said.

'You break into my apartment in the middle of the night. You threaten me. You threaten my daughter. And you ask me to trust you?'

David Winsin said, 'We used a key.'

'That's still breaking in,' Kelson said.

'I'm sorry Bob threatened your daughter,' Christine Winsin said.

'Give me the ammunition,' Kelson said.

David Winsin scooped the bullets from the bottom of the satchel and poured them into Kelson's hand. Kelson sat on his bed, sorting the bullets for the KelTec from the ones for the Springfield, reloading the magazines, and sliding the magazines into the guns. Christine and David Winsin watched. Bob Winsin stirred on the carpet, sat up, and looked bewildered, a red welt rising on his left cheek, his left eye swelling shut.

When Kelson finished with the guns, he aimed them at Christine and David Winsin again. David Winsin shook his head as if Kelson would never learn.

Kelson said, 'Where did you see Squirt?'

Christine Winsin pressed her lips together. 'We arranged a meeting with the Cranes at Sylvia's house. They've put Chip Voudreaux in a room and have Stanley Javinsky guarding him. As I said, it was a short conversation.'

'The Cranes have Voudreaux?'

David Winsin still shook his head, disappointed in Kelson.

'Stop that,' Kelson told him.

'We thought you knew,' Christine Winsin said.

Kelson lowered the Springfield, though he held the KelTec steady. 'They figured out he was trying to steal the money?'

'The two of them were trying, yes,' she said. 'But now he wants to go to the police.'

Bob Winsin pushed himself to his knees, then stood up, wobbly.

'The *two* of them?' Kelson said.

Christine Winsin's eyes showed mild surprise. 'Chip Voudreaux and Genevieve Bower, yes.'

Kelson almost dropped his guns. '*She* was in it with him?'

'Jesus help us,' David Winsin said.

His sister stepped back. 'Stop waving your guns around, Mr Kelson.'

Kelson went to the dining table where he'd left his shoulder holster hours earlier. He strapped it on over his shirt. 'The other numbers,' he said.

'I'm sorry?' Christine Winsin said.

'When Marty looked at the files on the thumb drive, he saw a string of numbers he couldn't identify. It was her. Genevieve Bower. She and Voudreaux must've figured they had the money coming to them after what Harold Crane did to them.'

'I have no idea,' Christine Winsin said.

'It's why she wouldn't go to the police even after the Cranes' men beat her up – or even after they broke into her motel room and then kidnapped her from my apartment. It's why she tried to stage JollyOllie as a suicide when she found him dead in his apartment. It was all or nothing.'

'It's time to go,' Christine Winsin said. 'We've let the Cranes know our relationship with them is over. If they go wherever Stanley Javinsky tells them to before we get there, we won't see our money again.'

Her brothers moved toward the door.

But Kelson froze. 'My phone.'

'Nonsense,' Christine Winsin said.

Kelson aimed both of his guns at David Winsin and gestured at his satchel. 'I won't take you there without warning them we're coming.'

'Wouldn't that make them leave before we get there?' David Winsin asked.

'It might. They get to decide.'

David Winsin reached into his satchel again. But he pulled out a large black pistol and aimed it at Kelson.

'Trust works both ways,' Christine Winsin said. 'When we reach Marty LeCoeur's place, you can call him. Not a moment sooner.'

Kelson lowered his guns. 'You're tough,' he said.

'Yes,' she said, and she turned toward the door. 'No one tougher.'

FIFTY-ONE

Something in the building on Wabash was burning. Smoke snaked from the shattered lobby doors, crossed the sidewalk, and slid into the street. Four firetrucks, six police cruisers, and an ambulance lined the curb. As Kelson and the Winsins ducked under the police tape and walked up the opposite sidewalk, a half dozen firefighters in oxygen masks, helmets, and flame-retardant overalls and jackets stepped through the smoke into the building as if shouldering past an invisible monster. They carried axes and picks, fire extinguishers, and pry bars. Bright lights mounted on the sides of two of the trucks shined on the dark face of the building. A man without a helmet shouted into a handheld radio, and the truck engines rumbled.

For all that, no one seemed in a rush. There was smoke but no visible blaze.

'A little thing,' Kelson said.

Christine Winsin stepped into the street, her heels clicking on the pavement, and went to the man with the handheld radio. She looked up at him and spoke, and he looked down at her – as if an odd little bird had landed on the street beside him in the smoky night – and answered. When she came back to Kelson and her brothers, she said, 'The fire started in some basement rooms. But no one's there.'

'Which means the Cranes have them – or they got out before the Cranes came in,' Kelson said.

David Winsin reached into the satchel and gave him his phone.

'Right.' Kelson dialed Rodman's cell number.

The phone rang once and Rodman answered, saying, 'Don't go to Marty's place.'

'I'm there right now,' Kelson said, 'along with about fifty firefighters – and the Winsins. Are you OK?'

'The Cranes sent some of their biggest and baddest. But I'm bigger and badder than they are, or at least we were quicker. Marty saw them coming on his security monitor, so we hid in the stairwell while the jerks rode the elevator to the basement. What are you doing with the Winsins?'

'They got this funny idea that I like people coming into my apartment without knocking. Now they want their missing money. Joke's on them.'

'How did they get you to take them to Marty's?'

Christine Winsin moved close to Kelson. 'Ask where they are.'

'Shut up,' Kelson told her.

David Winsin reached into the satchel again and left his hand there, as if to show Kelson he was aiming his pistol at him.

Kelson turned his back on him. 'A lot of gun and a little logic,' he told Rodman. 'They say they only want *their* money, and they gave me information that'll help us get the Cranes.'

'Dirty money,' Rodman said, 'and they see an opportunity because we've hurt the Cranes. What did they tell you?'

'First, Genevieve Bower and Chip Voudreaux tried to steal the G&G money together.'

'Well, shit.'

'Second, the Cranes have locked up Voudreaux at Sylvia's house. Third, Voudreaux wants to go to the cops.'

Christine Winsin inched around Kelson and faced him again. 'Where are they?'

'Shh,' he said, then, to Rodman, 'did you take Marty's computer with you?'

'Hell, yeah – and he's through to Neto's account.'

'It's up to you whether I bring the Winsins to you,' Kelson said. 'If you think it's a stupid idea, I'll cross the street and talk with the cops.'

David Winsin stepped around him. He let the pistol barrel peek at Kelson from the top of the satchel.

'Even your money wouldn't buy you out of that kind of trouble,' Kelson told him.

'Let me talk to Marty and Cindi,' Rodman said.

Kelson looked at Christine Winsin. 'Hold on.'

When Rodman came back, he said, 'What the hell, let's make it a party. If we don't like their company, we'll kick them down the back stairs.' He told Kelson where they were hiding.

'In plain sight, as it turns out,' Kelson said to the Winsins as they drove toward the Bronzeville neighborhood where Rodman and Cindi lived.

Five minutes after they swung into the alley by the Ebenezer Baptist Church and climbed the steps to Rodman's apartment, the Winsins were haggling with Marty under the gaze of the paintings of Malcolm X, Cindi, and Martin Luther King.

'You only want what's yours?' Marty asked.

Christine Winsin said, 'Five million, eighty-three thousand, eight hundred and seventy-seven dollars.'

'What about my commission?' Marty said.

'We let you live. Is that enough?' Christine Winsin said.

'That and thirty percent,' he said.

She smiled as if she appreciated the tough little man. 'Let's make it an even five million. You keep the eighty-three thousand.'

'What about the rest of the money?' he asked.

'Do what you want with it,' she said. 'We want only what's ours. We're honest people.'

'There's nothing honest about you, honey,' Marty said.

'Honorable, then,' she said.

'I can work with that,' he said.

'How much is the rest?' Kelson asked.

'After the five million?' Marty wiggled his outstretched hand. 'Another thirty-one or thirty-two – in the neighborhood.'

'Fancy neighborhood,' Kelson said.

So Marty plugged in his computer, tapped into Rodman's Wi-Fi, and thirty minutes later routed five million dollars from Neto's account – which he'd started calling 'my account' – into three separate offshore banks where the Winsins kept money. While Marty worked, the Winsins sipped coffee that Rodman brought from the kitchen. Even Bob Winsin, despite the welt on his face and his swollen eye, looked at ease with his place in the world.

When Marty showed Christine Winsin the adjusted accounts, she sighed and said, 'All this trouble. Was it necessary?'

'Shit happens,' Marty said.

'Yes,' she said, 'Shit happens. But it mustn't happen again. I worry that with your abilities and your knowledge of us, you could go into our accounts again and empty them – not only of the money you've returned. That mustn't be the case.'

David Winsin had left his gun in the satchel on the floor by his ankles, but everyone in the room understood the woman's threat. Marty said, 'Ma'am, if I wanted to get into your panties, I could. But I believe in honor too.'

She considered him. 'I guess we'll have to be satisfied with that.'

Two hours before dawn, she thanked Rodman for the coffee and led her brothers out and down to the street. Rodman stared at the door as if he expected her to burst back through. Then he went to it and locked it. Marty watched the door and said, 'If she was thirty years younger, I could fall in love, Janet or no Janet.'

Then he turned to his computer and, in twenty minutes, he buried access to the remaining thirty-one or thirty-two million dollars under lines and lines of encryption code. 'I'm like a fucking dog,' he said, as he typed. 'Like a fucking dog burying a fucking bone.'

FIFTY-TWO

K elson found Sylvia Crane's address by searching online property records for the town of Mundelein and then the surrounding towns of Libertyville, Vernon Hills, Hawthorn Woods, and Long Grove. He expanded the rings until he found a two-acre plot with an enormous house on Cambridge Lane in Lake Forest, twenty-five minutes from the G&G headquarters.

As the sun rose, Kelson and Rodman laid their weapons on one end of the couch, under Malcolm X's gaze – Kelson's two pistols, Rodman's snub-nose Colt, his big Beretta, and a Walther semiautomatic rifle with a twenty-inch barrel, which he pulled from the cabinet under the kitchen sink.

'Dibs,' Marty said, and picked up the Walther.

Rodman let his eyelids hang low. '*Dibs*?'

'Fuck, yeah,' Marty said.

At nine, Kelson, Rodman, and Marty rode in Rodman's van to a South Halsted store called The Cop Shop, which sold everything from pink T-shirts that said *Sleep tight, Chicago, we got this* to Blackhawk duty holsters, knee-high combat boots, and Damascus riot gear. The clerk spent twenty minutes finding a Kevlar vest that fitted Rodman. Marty settled for a bright yellow petite vest, which he refused to take off once he got the Velcro straps right, instead grabbing a pair of mirrored tactical sunglasses off a display and marching around the store in them.

'Give the man a little money, and see what he turns into,' Rodman said.

Rodman and Kelson laid their vests on the counter and picked three folding combat knives from a glass case.

Along with the yellow vest, glasses, and knife, Marty wanted a black leather glove with integrated steel knuckles.

'Why?' Rodman said.

'For later,' Marty said.

'I don't want to know,' Rodman said.

'I do,' Kelson said.

Marty said, 'It's a thing I do. Janet's cool with it, so why shouldn't I?'

After putting their purchases in the van with the guns they ate a second breakfast up the block at a diner called George's, because, as Rodman said, 'We're skipping lunch today. Either we're sitting with cops as they pound us for our stupidity, or we're bleeding in a hospital.'

'Or worse,' Kelson said.

'I don't see it,' Marty said. 'I see us doing the fucking job and driving away. Maybe *you* need a shower afterward. Me, I'm going in and out clean.'

They filled their bellies with eggs, pancakes, and bacon anyway.

Then they drove north to Lake Forest in mid-morning traffic. It was the last day of May, and the air was warm, the sky clear, so they rode with the windows open. Kelson called the main number at G&G and asked the receptionist to put him through to Sylvia Crane.

'She's not in today,' the receptionist said.

'I didn't think so,' Kelson said. 'Harold Crane?'

'I can take a message,' the receptionist said.

'I'll deliver it myself.' Kelson hung up.

Downtown Lake Forest had shops for the kinds of people who had Lake Forest needs – luxury foods, Italian housewares, and designer clothing, with a UPS store in case the residents wanted to send friends and relatives luxury foods, Italian housewares, and designer clothing.

'Just like the hood,' Rodman said.

'Just like the westside warehouse district where I grew up,' Marty said.

'Just like the inside of my head,' Kelson said.

'What the fuck are you talking about?' Marty said, and, when Kelson started to explain, said, '*Please* don't tell me.'

Sylvia Crane lived on a thickly wooded lot at the top of a gently rising slope. Rodman, Kelson, and Marty pulled into the end of the long driveway, and Rodman turned the van sideways across the pavement so it would block cars from coming in or leaving. As they readied their guns, they glanced at the house. It was all white, with a veranda that extended across half of the long front, and big windows, rounded at the top, where the veranda ended. The house rose two stories, plus a high dormered roof where hired help could live.

'A damn hotel,' Rodman said. He pinched little bullets and dropped them into the little revolver cylinder.

'An *inn*,' Kelson said. 'Like the ones you see in old movies – with Bing Crosby and Fred Astaire. The kind of place that should always be surrounded by snow.'

'Like *Holiday Inn*,' Marty said, 'where they sing "White Christmas".'

'Exactly,' Kelson said. He popped the magazine from the KelTec, checked that he'd loaded it tight, and popped it back in. 'I didn't see you as a movie guy,' he said to Marty.

'I love that fucking movie,' the little man said. 'Always makes me cry.'

'It's a musical comedy.' Kelson popped the magazine from the Springfield, checked it.

'To each his own,' Marty said, and he jacked a round into the chamber of the Walther.

'Looks more like that lodge in *The Shining*,' Rodman said, and climbed out of the van.

Standing at the end of the driveway, Kelson called Venus Johnson, got voicemail, and said, 'If you hear this message anytime soon, you'll want to scoot up to Cambridge Lane in Lake Forest. Three of us are about to visit Sylvia Crane.'

Then he called the Lake Forest police.

'I want to report shots fired,' he told the dispatcher, and gave her the address.

The dispatcher tried to keep him on the line. 'How many shots?' she asked. 'Is anyone shooting now?'

'They're about to start,' Kelson said, and hung up.

*　　*　　*

The men marched up the driveway toward the house.

'Lightheaded with fear,' Kelson said to Rodman and Marty, or to himself – he wasn't sure.

'No,' Marty said, strutting in his little yellow vest.

Rodman glanced at Kelson with concern. 'You OK?'

'Sure. I'm always lightheaded.'

'Don't be a pussy,' Marty said.

'Listen, Tweety—' Kelson said.

'Guys,' Rodman said, smooth and calm.

Then the thick boom of a shotgun sounded from one of the second-story windows.

'Fuck,' Marty yelled. He stared at his vest. Buckshot had dented the yellow Kevlar.

'Your ear's bleeding,' Kelson said.

Gripping the semiautomatic, Marty wiped a dot of blood with the back of his hand. 'A nip,' he said.

The shotgun fired again, the sound booming over the yard.

Kelson, Rodman, and Marty ran for a stand of trees.

Kelson peered out and saw two men arguing at an open second-story window.

'Someone got overexcited,' Rodman said. 'Why would they want to scare the neighbors?' He stepped out from the trees and raised his hands over his head, his Beretta tucked into the back of his pants, his little revolver in his side pocket. 'They should want us inside where they can try to get their money and the thumb drive without so much noise.'

No one shot at him.

'You're a smart guy, DeMarcus,' Marty said.

'I hope you can still say that later,' Rodman said. He walked – slow, calm, staying near the trees – through the yard and toward the house.

Kelson and Marty followed him, Kelson's hands high, his guns in his belt, Marty cradling his semiautomatic.

The men in the window – Kelson recognized one of them as Stanley Javinsky – watched them come. Another man appeared behind a closed window a couple of rooms from the first, his face obscured by the glaring glass.

As Rodman, Kelson, and Marty approached the veranda,

Javinsky aimed the shotgun down at them from the open window but didn't pull the trigger.

Rodman, Kelson, and Marty went up the front steps and under the shelter of the veranda roof. Rodman and Kelson each got out a gun – Rodman his Beretta, Kelson his KelTec. Marty slipped to the side, crouched, aimed his gun at the front door, and readied it to shoot.

Kelson slipped to the other side. Then Rodman kicked the door in.

FIFTY-THREE

Javinsky, now at the base of the stairway, fired the shotgun out the doorway and across the veranda, the noise thundering.

Rodman was suddenly by Kelson, out of the blast pattern. The two of them and Marty waited a moment, then fired back into the house, shattering wallboard, glass lamps, a large mirror.

Then they stopped shooting.

Silence rang in their ears.

Footsteps came up the hall toward the door – hard little heels.

Marty glanced at Rodman for a signal. Rodman shook his head.

The footsteps stopped, then started again.

The three men aimed their guns at the doorway.

Sylvia Crane stuck her head outside and eyed Marty and then Rodman, before holding her gaze on Kelson. 'You goddamned fool,' she said. She ducked back inside, and the footsteps retreated down the hall.

'What?' Kelson said, then called into the house. '*What?*'

Marty moved from the side of the doorway toward the middle. When no one shot at him, he disappeared into the house.

'Hard-ass canary,' Kelson said, and followed him.

Rodman went in behind Kelson, but when Marty and Kelson went down the hall toward the back of the house, he peeled off into a big living room decorated all in white.

The hardwood floor at the front end of the hallway was covered with dust and broken glass, but as Marty and Kelson went back they entered a gleaming dining room with a dark-wood table set for twelve with glistening china and glassware. The high-backed chairs were tucked against the table, the creased white linen napkins bedding a selection of three forks.

'Huh,' Kelson said.

'Shh,' said Marty, and he went through another door into a kitchen.

Harold Crane stood by the marble counter wearing a white shirt, white pants, and white Adidas tennis shoes. When Marty and Kelson pointed their guns at him, he raised his hands with a wry smile.

'What's the joke, old man?' Marty said.

Harold Crane nodded toward an open door at the far end of the kitchen. It led to a book-lined room, where Sylvia Crane and three men, including Stanley Javinsky and Greg Cushman, surrounded another man, who was tied to a chair. The tied-up man was Chip Voudreaux, and the third man held a pistol to his neck. Bruises covered Voudreaux's face and arms. His mouth hung open, bloody and missing teeth. Stanley Javinsky, seeing Kelson and Marty, came to the doorway. He pointed the shotgun at Kelson.

'Huh,' Kelson said again.

Marty shoved the barrel of the semiautomatic into Harold Crane's ribs. 'I'll shoot him.'

Javinsky rasped, 'Why does anyone need to get shot?'

Kelson aimed his KelTec at him. 'Listen, Squirt . . .'

Javinsky raised his gun a few degrees, aiming at the ceiling over Kelson. 'Come in,' he said, the words sounding like pain.

Kelson followed Javinsky into the book-lined room. Marty came in after them, prodding Harold Crane along with the gun barrel.

Sylvia Crane looked like she wanted to spit on Kelson. She wore a blue pantsuit with the jacket buttoned once above her belly. Kelson pointed his KelTec at that button. 'Where's your other friend?' she said.

Before Kelson could tell her where Rodman went, Marty said, 'He's a pussy. Ran for the woods. Big black dude like that, you'd never guess it.'

She told the man who held the pistol against Voudreaux's neck, 'Go after him.' The man slipped out of the room, leaving only Javinsky and Cushman with guns to face Kelson and Marty.

'That's better,' Kelson said. 'Evens the odds.'

So Sylvia Crane reached into her jacket pocket, drew out a small silver pistol, and, without seeming to need to aim, shot a bullet into Voudreaux's left foot.

Voudreaux screeched – the hoarse screech of a man who'd been screeching a lot.

Kelson yelled, 'Why'd you do that?'

'With me, you'll never have even odds,' she said, and she pointed the gun at him. 'The thumb drive.' Cold and controlled.

He looked at her from her head to her toes, which she'd tucked into blue stilettos that matched her pantsuit. 'Nice shoes.'

She stared at Marty. 'And our money. All of it. Now.'

Marty aimed the semiautomatic at her. 'You're making two mistakes,' he said. 'First, you think the money's yours. Second, you think shooting this asshole in the foot changes anything. It doesn't scare us. Sooner or later, it doesn't even scare him.' He wiggled the stump of his missing arm at her. 'Proof positive. Shoot a man in the foot, he'll hop after you and kill you.'

So she shot Voudreaux in the other foot.

Voudreaux howled high and long. Before he stopped, Marty shouted at her, 'He'll fucking crawl. If you shoot him in the chest, *I'll* drag his fucking corpse after you to show you what a man can do.'

'You're a vicious little bastard,' Sylvia Crane said.

Voudreaux made a whining moan.

Standing next to Marty, Harold Crane laughed – a strange high-pitched laugh that harmonized with Voudreaux's moan.

Kelson moved toward Voudreaux but stopped when Sylvia Crane turned her pistol toward the injured man. 'What did he do to deserve this?' Kelson said.

'Besides trying to steal our money?' she said. 'Besides trying to blackmail and extort my father? Besides threatening to bring our whole lives down on us?'

Harold Crane said, 'Besides betraying all *I* did for him?'

'You fucked him,' Kelson said. 'I saw the video.'

'I did nothing he was unwilling to do,' Harold Crane said.

'And I made him a rich man.' He smiled. 'I made him *into* a man.'

Voudreaux tried to speak, but his pain and brutalized mouth got in the way.

Harold Crane looked down at him with smug satisfaction. 'Now I'm taking back his manhood. A piece at a time.'

'You' – Voudreaux forced the word out – 'wrecked – me.'

'Yes,' Harold Crane said. 'Yes, I did. I made you and destroyed you. That was my prerogative.'

Then, a sound from outside the room interrupted them. Out on the street – a block away, maybe two blocks – sirens approached.

A flash of fear crossed Sylvia Crane's face. She seemed to calculate. 'We finish this now,' she told Stanley Javinsky and Cushman. 'Then we clean up.'

Kelson laughed at her. 'No way you can buy your way out of this now.'

'Don't underestimate me,' she said. She stepped close to Voudreaux, pressed her pistol against his forehead, and shot him dead.

Marty opened his mouth as if he would say something to her. Instead, he fired the semiautomatic five times into her body.

Javinsky and Cushman stared at Kelson and Marty. Then everyone was shooting. Everyone but Harold Crane, who'd hit the floor when Marty shot Sylvia. In the small room, a shooter could hardly miss. But Marty hit Javinsky first, in the shoulder, and Kelson hit Cushman, in the neck. The two wounded men fired wild and wide, ten or more shots crashing into bookshelves, lamps, a settee, and a framed painting of a girl with an umbrella. Kelson and Marty pumped round after round into the men until the men fell.

Harold Crane stayed down until the shooting stopped. When Stanley Javinsky's pistol clattered across the floor and came to a rest against his thigh, he didn't dare touch it. But with the shooting over, he fingered it – as if it might be hot – and picked it up.

Kelson and Marty stood in the hazy light, stunned by the noise and the blood. They let Harold Crane get up with Javinsky's gun in his hand. They did nothing as he stared at the gun. They seemed to come to themselves only when he lifted it and pressed the barrel against his jaw.

'Huh,' Kelson said.

'Uh-uh,' Marty said, and pointed the semiautomatic at Harold Crane, as if he could stop him from shooting himself by shooting him first.

'Uh-huh,' Harold Crane said, and he smiled a childish smile.

Then Rodman stepped into the room behind Crane. Quiet. He stuck his big pistol into his belt. Then he grabbed Crane's gun arm and yanked it up and away. Crane squeezed a single shot into the ceiling before Rodman broke his wrist.

Crane crumpled to the floor as if Rodman had broken bones throughout his body. Rodman stared down at him and said, 'Letting you die would be easy. You don't get easy.'

FIFTY-FOUR

The Lake Forest police arrested everyone still alive at Sylvia Crane's house, including Kelson, Rodman, Marty, and a cook and a maid who'd holed up in the garage when the shooting started. The cops put them in handcuffs, all except Harold Crane, who marched out of the house cradling his broken wrist with his other hand, looking indignant and righteous.

But eighteen hours later, when Ed Davies led Kelson, Rodman, and Marty out of the station into the warming air of the first June morning, no charges filed against them, Harold Crane sat alone in a jail cell, accused of multiple murders, embezzlement, and money laundering. That afternoon, the police arrested Susan Centlivre. The evening news showed the FBI raiding the G&G office.

Two days later, White Dove Cremations incinerated Neto's remains, and afterward, as Neto's little circle of friends drank to his memory at Fuller's Pub, Kelson asked Marty where he would scatter the ashes. Marty looked hurt. 'Now on, that boy stays with me. Get a nice fucking jar and put him on a shelf where I can keep an eye on him.'

Janet, whose mascara streaked her big cheeks from all the tears, squeezed him hard.

'Careful with the goods,' he said.

They sat at three tables they'd pushed together near a stage where rock 'n' roll bands played live on Fridays and Saturdays.

'You've got money now, Marty,' Rodman said.

'Yeah,' the little man said, staring into his beer, 'a fuckload.'

'What're you going to do with it?' Rodman asked.

'That's what I've been thinking about,' Marty said. 'You know how much I got? Almost thirty-two mil. Seems like after one or two million, it's cheating. I worked for it. I risked my life. But a little prick like me, who am I kidding? I'm discount basement. But *you* guys, you're the best. Gold fucking standard. So, what I'm saying is, we share it. We did this together, right?' When no one said anything, he looked from face to face. 'Right?'

Kelson turned down the money. 'I worked a job,' he said. 'Anyway, if you gave me the money and anyone asked, I couldn't help telling them where I got it.'

Rodman and Cindi turned it down too. 'I've got what I need,' Rodman said. 'The hustle's good. With money in the bank, I'd get fat and lazy.'

'No you wouldn't,' Cindi said, 'because if you took a penny of it, I'd kick your ass so hard you'd never sit down.'

Janet said she'd take a piece – but no more than a million or two, or at most three.

'Three for you, two for me,' Marty said. 'That's twenty-seven for a place.'

'For a *place*?' Rodman said.

'That's what I'm thinking,' Marty said. 'A place to help kids like Neto. Smart kids who get in trouble and need a way out. Teach them good fucking manners. Teach them skills.'

'Wasn't Neto's problem that he had *too many* skills?' Kelson said.

'Teach them the *right* skills,' Marty said.

'Aww,' Janet and Cindi said together.

'Neto would be proud,' Rodman said.

The little man blushed and puffed up, and Janet squeezed him again.

'Careful with the goods,' he said again, and squeezed her too.

Doreen didn't join them at the gathering. The previous afternoon, a judge had revoked her bond after the news included her name in reports on the bloody collapse of G&G Private Equity and the wealthy family who ran it.

'But she did nothing wrong,' Kelson said to Ed Davies.

Davies sighed and said, 'Getting close to you is wrong enough.'

'They can jail a woman for that?'

'Apparently.'

Late in the evening at Fuller's, when Kelson found himself alone with Rodman by the bar, he dug a folded envelope from a pocket. He opened it and took out the red thumb drive.

'What are you going to do with it?' Rodman asked.

Kelson held it in front of his eyes the way he might a large pill he was thinking about swallowing. 'Some things shouldn't be,' he said.

'Does the DA have enough on Harold Crane without it?' Rodman signaled the bartender for a shot of Wild Turkey.

'Venus Johnson says Crane's talking. He thinks he'll cut a deal. She thinks he's already talked himself into life in max.'

Rodman watched the bartender pour the shot. Then he raised the glass to his lips and drank it like medicine. 'Some things shouldn't be,' he said to Kelson.

'What good would it do?' Kelson said.

'Genevieve Bower hired you to take it out of circulation. She didn't want anyone to see it.'

'But if anyone asks, I'll tell them what I did with it. I won't be able to stop myself.'

'True. It would be destruction of evidence,' Rodman said.

'Yeah, that's what it would be.' He dropped the thumb drive on the floor.

It was just a little thing.

He stomped on it.

'Obstruction of justice,' Rodman said.

'Some things' – Kelson stomped again – 'shouldn't be.'

ACKNOWLEDGEMENTS

Many, many thanks to Julia for her first readings, to Lukas, Philip, and Anne-Lise for always advocating, to Kate and the great people at Severn House for making me better, and to Michael for putting a good face on me. I'm grateful to Dr K for our conversations about disinhibition and autotopagnosia and to books and articles by Angélique Stéfan, Jean François Mathé, Andrea Kocka, Jean Gagnon, and Oliver Sacks for filling in many of my remaining gaps. My love to Julie, Isaac, Maya, and Elias, who bring me laughter and the noise of life.